For Rae and Ben, who pushed my little boat back out to sea whenever it veered towards the rocks

I   Acceptance   1

II Denial   91

III Bargaining   275

It is a sorry thing to spend your days and nights in vain, thinking about things that might be, planning for tomorrow's livelihood, and hesitating to forsake what should be forsaken, and to practise what should be practised.

Eihei Dōgen, *Shōbōgenzō Zuimonki*

I

ACCEPTANCE

1

I dreamt of falling. Every night, and before long, every day. Suspended in mid-air, then the release. Not gently, not gracefully, but hard and fast – gravity and a white-knuckled fist. The sensation of not knowing quite where your body is in relation to the walls or ceiling, intent only on placing your limbs in the correct alignment for when you meet the floor again.

It wouldn't leave me alone, kept forcing its way back into my head, so often that I thought it might make me ill. Trapped in an air-conditioned office, my daily targets pushed to one side, I lived a fantasy that others could only guess at.

As co-workers busied themselves, slyly murmuring trick questions into the phones or leaning back in padded chairs to plan a new entrapment – strategising, they called it – I would close my eyes and remember the joyous thud as my back hit the mat, the air exploding from my lungs, my brain struggling to readjust to its surroundings. Then I would see myself on my feet again, ready for more, desperate for another hit. Grabbing the cloth of my practice partner's white *judogi*, then letting him throw me again, and again, and again. And then some more. Over and over until I knew I was edging close to arcane knowledge, one of the essential elements of the art: learning how to fall.

There's no shame in it – being thrown, I mean. In Japan, where judo was conceived, they're not bothered at all. There's no stigma attached, it's simply a vital part of training. And kind of Zen, I suppose, like learning to dampen the ego, empty the self of the self. Falling off body and mind.

Of course, each time I lost myself to it I would be forced to open my eyes again and look around the office, recoiling from its strip-lighting indifference. Then I'd experience a different kind of impact, a different kind of pain. And each day it was getting harder to pick myself up.

Publishing sales – how did it come to that? I tried to tell myself it could be worse; after all, I wasn't slogging up and down the M1 every day trying to flog vacuum-cleaner parts. But still, twenty-four years old, my whole life stretching into the distance, and they go and make me sales manager for their little magazine. Sand to Arabs, Steve, fridges to Eskimos. Trying to bend me, to make me pliable, same as I did to all their clients. And eventually, like most of them, I relented. Accepted the deal, pretended it meant something, just to make the voices stop. I was the golden child, able to sell ad space in my sleep. Which was just as well, because I was sleepwalking through most of it. Sleepwalking and dreaming.

'Hey Steve, you coming to see Digby's band play tonight? We're all going.'

I didn't fit in. They knew it, I knew it. Which is probably why, on the night in question, they'd left it until five o'clock to invite me to a gig everyone had probably been talking about for weeks. The chasm between us was immense; I felt like a tightrope walker, the whole act put on for the benefit of the cameras. And yet I felt sorry for them, in a way, fresh from red-brick universities and excited beyond belief to be part of another gang. And with their very own desk space too, a little chunk of territory. Free pens with the company name down the side, Post-It notes in all the colours.

I couldn't force myself to have that same pack mentality, which I think puzzled and irritated them. I was always turning down invites, preferring to see non-work friends rather than go out for what was always an extension of office life, and, in effect, my job. Borderline rude, I suppose, but I don't imagine they were getting too hung up on it.

And what was there for me to be thrilled about anyway? Phone apps? Two-for-one happy hour? Regimented enthusiasm for the next hot band, the uniformity of tastes – take your marching orders.

'Sorry, can't, watching a competition tonight. Thanks though.'

'Ah,' said Lewis, bearer of the belated invite. 'Kung Po chicken, if you prease.'

He put his hands up, karate-style, and made a couple of swift chopping movements, lips pouted like a drag artiste. At the very least I wanted to point out that he was imitating the wrong sport, but he was working with limited resources so I let it slide. I tried to smile, to be calm, wondering if I could have him disciplined for racist behaviour.

'You got it,' I said. 'Have a great time though. Say good luck to Digby from me.'

As Lewis put his palms together and bowed solemnly, I had an overwhelming urge to pull him to the floor and place him in an elbow lock. Ignore his screams, apply pressure to his forearm until I heard the bone crack. So what if this wasn't a sporting situation – screw the social niceties. This was the modern sales environment, teams pitted against each other, where tension is the driving force and very much encouraged. If you start to go under, there's the door.

I watched Lewis strut back to his seat, grinning, ready to embellish his exploits to an eager congregation. On the column next to his desk was a poster with that tired old cliché, *The only thing you have to fear is fear itself*. For months I had wanted to put a line through the first 'fear' and write 'sell' above it, but I knew any subtlety would be lost on them. They'd think I'd come over to their side. So I just sat there, my chest a little tighter every day.

They were obviously trying to disguise looks of relief as word spread about my non-attendance at The Fox and Hell Hole. No doubt the little comments wouldn't be too far behind: Steve, the single guy, didn't make it through university like the rest of us, into all that weird Eastern stuff. They probably assumed I sat at home every evening watching Jackie Chan movies. The thought of trying to explain everything to them just made me weary.

And who on earth was Digby anyway? I'd never heard of him. Some other mag maybe, somewhere else. A different floor.

I checked my desk, made sure everything was spotless. No bits of scrap paper, nothing left out where it shouldn't be; my Portsmouth FC mug cleaned ready for the morning, notebook and pen aligned next to the keyboard.

I knew they were watching me, ready to burst out laughing when I left, preparing more gestures. Pretend to clean a sheet of paper perhaps, maybe get a ruler out.

'See you tomorrow,' I said.

Lewis raised his hand, repeated the chopping motion. I ignored him and headed for the door.

The place was starting to get busy when I arrived, although the competitors outnumbered the spectators, which isn't unusual. Like most judo competitions, this one was taking place in a hall pretty much devoid of atmosphere, a comprehensive school in Deptford that encouraged inner-city youngsters to resist other temptations and get involved with activities like martial arts. Quite a big ask, I reckon, but at least some were making the effort.

Tonight was different though, because we'd be watching a senior-level competition, which was a blessing considering the mood I was in. I wanted to see people suffer, albeit willingly.

In the centre of the hall the large judo mat, the *tatami*, lay empty and expectant. The few officials present were busying themselves, one holding a clipboard, while half a dozen *judoka* wandered around or went through elaborate stretching routines. I sat down on one of the plastic chairs and waited, sipping machine tea from a polystyrene cup. I absent-mindedly started biting the lip of it, enjoying the sensation of the spongy material giving way beneath my teeth, until it looked like a rat had been gnawing at it.

Deptford. Not what you'd call exotic, but that didn't matter. It was in these kinds of places, these parts of the city, that I felt at home, a rare commodity. And excited. A different kind of anticipation than you'd get from going to a football match; something less tribal, a little more personal. I don't know, maybe I'm over-analysing. I'm good at that.

The tea tasted horrible.

'Mind if I sit down here?'

I turned to my right to see a bloke, mid to late 50s maybe, pointing at the seat next to me. He looked friendly enough, if a little stern. Short but stocky, ex-military perhaps, dressed smartly. Looked like he could handle himself. Almost bald but shaved his head anyway, and muscular beneath the suit, you could tell.

It was like one of those awkward cinema moments: there are plenty of empty seats, why do you want to sit right there? I'm not comfortable having my personal space encroached upon at the best of times, but what could I say? We were all there for the same reason, the same passion. At least I hoped he was there for that. Maybe he was just lonely.

'Course. Help yourself.'

He parked himself down with a satisfied sigh, made himself comfortable. I was looking back towards the mat again when a sudden movement caught my eye, causing me to flinch. I glanced at my new neighbour, only to be faced with the demented grin of what might best be described as a cross between a water vole and a piece of old carpet on his lap. I'd left those idiots at work behind to end up next to the old geezer and his mutt. Fantastic.

'This is Arthur. Don't worry, he's not dangerous, as you can probably see. And I'm Jack.' He reached over the dog's back and we shook hands.

'Steve.'

'Good to meet you Steve. Been here before?'

'Not this place, no. I go to a lot of competitions though. You?'

'Oh, all the time. Ever been on the mat?'

I didn't want to talk about it, not with a complete stranger. I was a seasoned expert at lying over the phone, or during an expense-account lunch, but there, face to face? He would know something was up, I could tell. He had that air about him.

'Not for a couple of years.'

He didn't say anything, just looked at me, almost through me. This was judo, after all, a way of life. You need a good reason to stop. Uncomfortable now, I sipped my tea and then tried to make friends with Arthur, dabbing my hand in the general direction of his face, hoping he wouldn't lick my fingers.

'Anyone ever say you should get a fighting dog?' I asked, trying to change the subject.

Jack shook his head, like the spell was broken.

'Uh, no, they haven't actually. Although a couple of people have said I should get a boxer. What can you say to that, eh? Hilarious.'

The bouts soon began. Right from the off, Jack and I were commenting freely on what we saw, individual techniques good and bad. Like a couple of talent scouts. Although each contest lasts only a matter of minutes, you can tell a lot about a fighter in that short time if you know what to look for. And Jack knew his stuff, much more than I did, quietly criticising one person's grappling techniques, but happy to applaud what he liked. We saw what I thought were some fantastic throws, but on a couple of them Jack was less excited about the throw itself than critical of the victim's defensive stance. I was intrigued.

Even Arthur was excited. He sat fidgeting in Jack's lap, head swivelling all the time as the movement and noise battled for his attention. Every time the referee shouted *'Hajime!'* to start a contest, Arthur took it as his cue to stand bolt upright, eyes wide, facing the action. He was clearly an old hand too, and another expert, probably. Luckily he wasn't a yapper, or we might have received some unwanted attention, a referee's warning.

I remember on that first night that Jack didn't ask me what I did for a living, like most people do when they're stuck for things to chat about. As if it's so important, something to measure ourselves by, to check whether we're the right fit. We'd turned out for the fighting, that was all. The great leveller. Nothing else mattered.

Of course, the evening ended too quickly. I could have sat there all night, lost myself to it, even pretended that I'd only imagined having a day job all along, a sick joke. Jack looked as if he felt the same way, Arthur by that point snoozing at his feet.

As we put our coats on, Jack asked me if I would wait for him, said he wanted to have a quick word with someone.

I went and stood in the school's harshly lit entrance, trying to be interested in a display of kids' paintings. Lots of lions, tigers, a frog; some of it wouldn't have looked out of place in Tate Modern. After fifteen minutes I was tempted to leave, thinking perhaps he'd forgotten I was there, but something made me stay. Politeness perhaps, but something else too.

He eventually appeared, Arthur scuttling along on his lead next to him, claws tapping the wood floor.

'Got far to go?' Jack asked. He didn't mention how long I'd been hanging around, or apologise; maybe that was the first test. When I told him where I lived he laughed.

'I suppose it's fate,' he said. 'If you believe in that kind of thing. I'm guessing you know the Queen's Road Gym.'

'Yeah, course, there's a judo club there,' I said. 'I only moved to the area two months ago, but I've been past it a few times.'

'Well maybe you should come by some time – I own it. Only if you want to though, no pressure.'

And so it began. Two strangers at a fighting competition, on common ground. A handshake.

We took the bus together, talked about judo mainly. He didn't ask any more questions about me; that wasn't Jack's way, as I would come to realise. He got off two stops before mine, a quick goodbye, didn't look back. The rest would be up to me.

When I got home I closed my front door on the darkness outside and listened. Not having money to splash about, I'd bought a tiny house on the edge of one of south London's less photogenic estates, where something seemed to be kicking off most nights, and every weekend. In my mind the beast was always prowling, I just assumed that one day it would enter my place.

The house was silent. I went through and checked everything, my routine. Nothing had been stolen, all the windows were intact. I gave the kitchen surfaces a thorough wipe, then the hob, placed the cloth and spray cleaner back in the cupboard beneath the sink, and went upstairs to bed. In the distance I could hear a police siren starting to wail, louder and louder, until, like everything else, it too faded away.

2

Queen's Road Gym and Judo Club.

The local kids are always making comments, Jack said, when we met there for the first time. I'd come to have a look around, as he knew I would.

Hah, hah. Queen's. Is this where all the gay boys hang out?

Jack, I quickly learnt, had an answer for everything, when he could be bothered. Except that gem of a one-liner. A patient half-smile, or a nod of the head, is all anyone ever got. Maybe he had a comeback once but got tired of repeating it, never prepared to play the fall guy. Said he'd heard the joke, or something similar, more times than he cared to remember since he opened the place in the early 80s. That's a lot of forced smiles, a lot of practice putting your ego to one side.

I knew those kind of kids, I grew up with them; part of me was still there, running through the streets. Each one thinking they were the toughest, and everyone a comedian. Smart-arsed tykes grinning through greasy lips, chicken fat like Vaseline on their dirty fingers. Grinding their way through watery flesh camouflaged with industrial flavourings, a traditional blend.

Jack and I arranged to meet alone the first time. There were customers in the gym, but upstairs the judo hall, the *dojo*, was empty. We bowed together at the entrance. I felt like a lapsed worshipper.

It's a sign of respect, bowing, and every dojo across

the world will demand the same, and again when you leave. Oh, and when you're about to practise with someone, and when you finish practising, and when you greet the *sensei* – your teacher – and … see where we're going with this? If you're serious about the sport, respect is the one word you might want to keep in mind when you show up. And it extends outside the hall too, into all aspects of your existence, like a code for how you conduct yourself, as was originally intended. If you can't be respectful in your personal life, there's not much point turning up there either.

I wanted – needed – to fight again. I don't know how he knew, but he did, of course he did. Probably from that first night when I told him I'd been away from the mat, even without the details. An inflection in my voice, perhaps, or the way I looked. I was caught in my own web, despising what I did for a living and mystified as to how anyone else could possibly enjoy it either. There was no release.

But he didn't push me, just showed me the well. Thirst is more powerful than fear. Not many of us understand what we are capable of, don't even try to find out.

Straight away I started helping out at the gym in the evenings and weekends; not for anything in return, but just to be involved. After a couple of months I had become a fixture, chipping in with an hour or two whenever I had some time on my hands or they were short-staffed, someone gone down ill. Cleaning the equipment, sorting out items of overlooked paperwork, such as it was. Trying to make myself useful, any excuse. I just wanted to be in there, as often as possible.

It was a small place, just two rooms, plus an office and a tiny kitchen. The dojo was on the second floor, where Jack did his coaching, people of all ages. Quite a few youngsters were getting involved, both boys and girls. Jack didn't have any children of his own, maybe that's why he loved what he did, what he could give them.

Below, in the first-floor gym, was a good range of modern equipment, the sort of thing people expect these days. Plenty of free weights, but electronic stuff too. Machines. The kit that does a little bit of the work for you, in the background, making you feel like you're the one in control. Not many mirrors in that room though: just two, which is unusual for a gym. I suggested getting a few more in, told Jack that people like to look at themselves while they work out, but he hated that kind of vanity. Said if anyone wanted to step upstairs to practise some stances in front of the mirror, then fine; if not, go someplace else.

Often I would go up and stand in the hall on my own, learning its atmosphere, being open to it. I would stand and stare for ages at the photo of Dr Jigoro Kano, judo's founder. Every dojo has one, usually in what's called the *kamiza*, a sort of shrine. You feel a sense of reverence every time you're in front of it, as you should – it's like the head of the room, the top seat, as it were. The picture was in a glass case, which also contained trophies won by Jack's students. People who had stayed focused, stuck at it. People who hadn't messed up.

The gym was clean and tidy when I first arrived, but immaculate after I got stuck in. The non-judo guys seemed to find it amusing – someone should tell them that students of the art are expected to keep the dojo clean, so why shouldn't the gym be spotless too. But maybe they knew that. I didn't mind, I was Steve the cleaner, and happy to do it. Trying to make the place my own too.

For some reason I was really particular about the club's sign outside, above the door. More than thirty years old, and starting to show its age. Jack always refused to tart it up, replace it with a more contemporary version. He had a point, I suppose. Everyone thinks they're being different, he would say, but always end up the same. They just can't see it.

But the effects of time were there: dirt thrown up by passing cars, dust carried on the wind, the elements staking their claim. I cleaned it every week. The no-nonsense black lettering was from another age – like something you'd once have seen above a gentlemen's tailor or a proper old-fashioned hardware store – at odds with the other signage that adorned the rest of the high street. All those tarty, lurid fonts, a bit of leg to catch a shopper's eye, as if all the graphic designers from miles around had organised a parade but didn't invite us. Like Jack cared. He was happy to watch, I suppose, but not really fussed about joining in.

No, everything about the club was unassuming, like the sport that took place inside. Its blue door was squeezed in between a small stationery shop – 'Photocopies at two pence a sheet' – and a takeaway joint selling yet another finger-lickin' variation on Southern fried grub. The gift of heart disease, from Louisiana to London – revenge for all those trafficked souls. That place occupied the ground floor below us, which always amused me, like you had to walk the path of temptation first. Still, they'd been there a few years before I turned up, those relentlessly friendly boys in their stripy paper hats, so fair play to them. Whatever the market dictates.

Most of the day-to-day work came down to Jack, of course, on top of teaching five classes a week. He did have a couple of part-timers, but didn't pay them that much because they were allowed to use the gym for free whenever they wanted, which is all they were really after anyway. Besides, it's not like they were qualified fitness instructors, waving documentation around, being all continental and demanding the appropriate working conditions. The arrangement suited everyone, and kept the overheads down. After all, Jack was having to compete with the local leisure centre and a branch of a national health-club chain, both with their eye-catching logos, naturally. But he did well, couldn't complain, and money wasn't the motivation anyway. He had a steady membership, and that was without any branding or marketing. Or advertising – definitely no advertising. He would never shell out for that nonsense.

The place had an interesting mix of customers. For the gym it was your traditional types, muscle builders, some aerobic stuff thrown in. Mostly what you'd call proper blokes, assuming we're allowed to say that these days. They pushed themselves hard, one hundred-kilogram reps until they were risking an aneurism. Then a bit more on top, else what's the point? Working a different muscle group each day. A regime, their way of life, just like the judoka upstairs.

There were always a few of your metropolitan types

as well, pulled to the area by the rising house prices. Those who came to do a bit of rowing, then maybe twenty minutes on the cross-trainer and a few weights. Always focusing on the biceps. Chugging their bright-blue isotonics, head to toe in expensive gear, all pristine, getting home before the kids went to bed. Down the gym three times a week at first, and pleased that everyone in the office knew about it.

We didn't get many of them, it has to be said. But I'm not knocking it, trust me; I'd rather people made a bit of an effort than line up alongside the chicken chewers downstairs. It's just that they never lasted long. Never. They sensed the serious atmosphere of the gym as soon as they walked in, the lack of frills, exposed brickwork where most places would have paint, and then it was simply a matter of time. Or pride. Jack didn't even try to sign them up on a monthly direct debit, it seemed a bit cruel.

'Pay as you go sir, see how you get on.'

Of course, when the doubts started coming to life, the end always came swiftly. That first time when they go down the pub after work with Tom and Adam from accounts, swearing blind they'll only have a quick lime and soda, get to the gym by eight. Or the fatal lie-in on a Saturday morning when they'd promised themselves an hour on the treadmill; never mind, go for a run later instead. But the weather turns bad, the nights are drawing in. There's a good film on and Sally's made lasagne, some red wine left over. Tomorrow, I swear. Tomorrow.

Discipline has enemies, and one of them is you.

Maybe that should have been on the sign above the

door. A small concession to branding, like those council vehicles you see with a patronising slogan splashed down the side, the same old cobblers about community and striving together, the head of the PR agency smirking into his latte every time he sees one go by.

The casuals weren't made to feel unwelcome, far from it. But like I said, the guys there took it all very seriously. It wasn't just a hobby, something to do in the evenings to pass the time. Not a squash player among them.

I loved the place, right from the off, even while I was trying to pluck up the courage to put on my whites again. I loved the animal sounds of explosive exertion, the low growl of pain being embraced. The clanking and crashing of iron, the grunting relief when a bar fell back onto the hooks, endorphins coursing through stressed arteries. All that straining towards the common goal. Endless encouragement, fuelled by mutual respect.

And nowhere to hide.

Most of all I loved hearing Jack's voice coming down from the floor above, barking out commands in Japanese. I was always desperate to get back when I hadn't been in for a few days, even if I wasn't needed, or when I should really have been somewhere else.

I still miss all that, especially now, after everything that's happened.

That's also true of one or two other places, the ones I'm still drawn to but should leave behind. The world constantly changes, everything in flux; I need to be a part of that.

Jack and I quickly became good friends and would often head out together for a cup of tea – occasionally a bite to eat – nearby at Lucy's caff, or Lucy's Cough as we nicknamed it, such was the lack of respect for basic hygiene or, for that matter, the essentials of good cooking. On the plus side, she had no qualms whatsoever about letting Jack bring Arthur in. Lucy was fond of them both, always fussing, making sure they were well looked after and checking that they'd both taken their tablets – Jack's for hypertension, Arthur's for dermatitis – and sometimes she'd send a few chewy bits Arthur's way. Scraggy off-cuts from the kitchen, maybe even the bin for all we knew, he wasn't a fussy eater.

Jack and I would talk about the sport mostly. Rarely personal stuff, not at first, it didn't seem necessary. He never commented on me wiping the table with a paper napkin – my side and his – as we sat down; even tried to look as if it were the most natural thing in the world. Perhaps he respected the effort. He was a private man, old-fashioned, would never go sticking his nose in where it might not be wanted.

He just waited, like he was studying my angst, but leaving everything up to me. And my first step back, when I finally felt comfortable, was to tell him what had gone wrong, what I had done. This was my initiation, my interview, over builder's-strength tea and cheese rolls in a grotty caff. Thirst overcoming fear.

He didn't say a word, not one word, as I told him.

I'd loved judo since the age of thirteen; it was my obsession – pictures all over my bedroom wall, every book I could find, training videos, the whole deal. I attended classes every week in my local club, just outside Plymouth. I wasn't the best there, but I wasn't far off, going steadily through the grades until I got my brown belt aged eighteen. Happiest day of my life, that old cliché. Course, as I got older I started hanging out on street corners, getting up to mischief; but I worked hard in school too, not afraid to stand out. In fact, I endured all manner of grief from my mates when, after messing about for a couple of years, I went back to do my A levels and got a place at Royal Holloway, where I studied – for reasons that are still not apparent, even to me – medieval history.

Until, that is, I dropped out halfway through year two, the exact mid-point of my three-year sentence. I just couldn't make myself get along with it all, rankled by the privileges that fall so easily into some people's laps. To them I had the wrong accent, wrong clothes, wrong everything. They thought I was strange, and the more alienated I became, the more convinced they were in return. Plus I was a mature student – if starting a course when you're almost twenty-one counts as mature – and I don't think they liked that either, those wild teenagers. Kids from Ascot and Tunbridge Wells pushing their street smarts, until the holidays came around and their parents arrived to drive them home.

There are two kinds of students, as far as I could tell: the Sophisticates, with their bottles of mid-price red and classical concerts at dusk; and the ones like me. I rarely drank – the ultimate sin – plus I could string words and thoughts together, which the campus party organisers clearly didn't welcome. Getting an education against the odds rarely goes down well, so invites were always thin on the ground for me. But I wasn't there to win friends, didn't lie awake at night crying about how horrible it all was. Maybe that was part of the problem.

My own disquiet began to creep up on me more and more, as I knew it would. The beast at the door, determined to follow me wherever I went. At the end of year one we all had to move off campus, so I answered an ad that led to me moving in with three other lads, complete strangers to each other. Outcasts like me, from Africa and Europe. The peace lasted about a week. I made it clear from the outset that my room was strictly out of bounds, and I got very agitated with anyone who tried to ignore that rule. Christ knows what they thought I was doing in there. Then I started complaining about the state of the bathroom, and the overflowing ashtrays left on the living room table, getting upset if a half-washed spoon was put back in the cutlery drawer, as if their simple negligence would bring all hell down upon us. Before long I was a pariah among pariahs.

I had no refuge, day or night, other than a judo club I joined during the first year. It wasn't enough; my grades started to slip and I knew I had to leave. But I couldn't just walk away, having made it that far, it wasn't in my nature. I needed a push.

Ironically, the night it happened I thought I'd made a breakthrough, some form of contact. I was in the student union bar, a rarity for me, invited by some people from my course – an equally miraculous event. I got the first round of drinks in, made sure of that, but was still nursing my second beer as they sailed into number five. The louder they got, the quieter I became, the atmosphere changing. So subtle you could easily miss it, but I was an old hand. The shadow of a doubt.

The first couple of glances, a message in the eyes.

You go first.

I should have known it would be the one sat next to me, otherwise it would have been too obvious. Gary, a big guy, played rugby I think. And that was his disadvantage, ultimately, although he wasn't to know it: the confidence it gives you, subscribing to primitive laws.

He spilt a little of his drink on my part of the table, while I was in the toilet. Not much, but enough; they knew I'd have to get a tissue out of my pocket and wipe it away. Another couple of glances, the evening warming up. He waited, no doubt loving the attention. And the next time I wasn't looking, another small spillage appeared.

I had no idea how they'd found out; I couldn't remember telling anyone, but maybe I didn't need to. Just one time, that would be enough. Maybe someone had watched me in a lecture, discreetly rubbing at a mark on the wood in front of me, my behaviour more fascinating than some French monarch lost in time.

My irritation shifted quickly through fear and into anger. I had tried, I really had. I was there, wasn't I, feigning an interest. A few drinks, some conversation if possible, just hanging out. See you Monday, have a good weekend. It should be so easy.

After I cleaned up again Gary's hand moved forward, not even bothering to be sly this time. I grabbed it and he tried to stare me down, but making it look friendly, we're all mates here. As he pulled I did the same and the contents of his glass slopped onto the table. My chair screeched against the floor as I backed away from the puddle spreading towards me.

'Idiot.'

His word, not mine. Then another voice, and another, merging, like insects chattering at dusk.

Can't take a joke.

What's his problem?

Weirdo.

The first one caught me directly in the face, a slap of brown liquid, the sickly sweet smell of cheap beer. Cheap enough to waste on someone like me. And the dam broke quickly, our little part of the room descending into chaos, a torrent of exhilarated noise and activity. I was standing now, facing away from them, half-crouched and trying to protect myself. But they were swarming, moving in quickly, the bravery of the pack. Within seconds I was drenched. They all aimed for exposed skin, of course: my face and neck, or down the back of my shirt, for maximum discomfort. Someone even hooked their fingers inside my belt and I pulled away violently, to a delighted chorus that both welcomed and mocked my retaliation.

It ended quickly, a swift crescendo, half a dozen empty glasses. A lad from behind the bar came over, cursing. Told everyone to calm down, but stayed impartial, kept his distance from me in case I was the joker who had asked for it. The source of the problem.

All I could do was stand there, soaked, my face burning. By now the whole room was gawping at me, a hip-hop soundtrack blaring out from the high speakers, the backdrop to my humiliation, a night to remember. Everyone was standing to get a better look, straining to see over each other's shoulders.

My attackers were grinning, trying to gauge the level

of approval from the crowd, revelling in the attention. They regrouped at the table, looking around expectantly. The cheering had stopped, but everyone was still watching.

I tried to compose myself, saw my own hand shaking as I picked up my bag and coat, avoiding eye contact with anyone. I could have laughed, I suppose, tried to be in on the joke; but that would have been even more pitiful. Instead, as I turned to leave, I looked at Gary. He was happy, triumphant, although perhaps a bit disappointed that the two girls we were with hadn't showered him with kisses, gasping at his courage. I continued to look at him, waiting, waiting. And when he faltered, when his mask slipped just a fraction, I smiled at him. Not a big cheesy grin – *you're such a dude, Gary, such a player* – just the tiniest shift of expression, enough to register. Then I turned and left the bar, another resounding cheer sending me on my way.

I walked through the car park without looking back. A group of three girls giggled as they passed in the opposite direction, and I assumed it was directed at me. They hadn't been in the bar at the time, and it was probably too dark for them to see my soaked shirt, but that's what I'd become, assuming the worst.

I started to run, my body topped up with adrenaline, pumping legs devouring the pavement. I made it home in ten minutes and rushed upstairs to my room, changed hurriedly, then stuffed a couple of things in a small holdall. On my way back downstairs I could hear the TV on in the living room, but no voices. The smell of something herbal was seeping out from under the door. I didn't look in.

I knew he'd buy a kebab, the fat git. Most of them did, every Friday and Saturday night, the glowing grill in the window a beacon to guide them. I waited on the opposite side of the road for more than an hour, trying to let my thoughts fall away. I wanted clarity, an empty mind. The night soon started to cool, like a gentle hint, but I was going nowhere. Eventually, I saw Gary.

Three of them went in together, him and two of the others who had joined in the fun. One of them seemed to be with Gary all the time, following him around like a loyal lieutenant. There were no girls of course; it would be another lonely night for our Gaz, wrestling with his frustrations. I watched as they slobbed all over the counter, no doubt grunting out their demands for chili sauce and fistfuls of onion. Those lasses didn't know what they were missing.

When they staggered out and away from the shop I started to move, keeping in the shadows as much as I could. They ate as they walked, stopping only to hold one of the trio's food as he pissed against the side of a car, everyone laughing. Then they were back on their way, heading towards a residential area, but hopefully not to the same house – I wanted Gary on his own. At one point they all sat on a bench to have a cigarette, me about a hundred yards behind, hiding between parked cars. Thankfully they didn't chat for long, probably weren't able to, and after another short walk the other two peeled away.

At that point, oddly, I began to relax, watching Gary weave his way along, faltering as the pavement rose up to meet him. Not knowing where he lived, I began to close the gap between us just in case, until I was no more than ten yards behind him. I looked back to check there was no one else around, no one looking out their window.

Up ahead, in the middle of a row of houses, was a small forecourt in front of an auto body-repair shop. It was ideal; all that was missing was a mat in the middle. Never mind. And there would be no bowing, no show of respect. Not this time.

'Hey Gary,' I said, drawing up alongside him. He pivoted to his left, tottering backwards but managing to regain his balance. He looked at me groggy-eyed, as if his brain were shifting through gears.

'Oh. Steve. Alright geezer?'

Geezer. Jesus Christ. I didn't know you could hear the Bow Bells in Hampshire, or wherever it was he called home.

'Hi Gary, how's it going?'

He knew things had taken a wrong turn, I could tell, but he didn't want to show it.

'Why'd you leave mate? We were just having a laugh.'

'I know, I know. Not a problem.'

I said nothing else. He tried to look bored, wanting me gone, reaching into his jacket pocket and bringing out a can of lager. As he went to open it I reached forward and held onto his wrist.

'That can wait,' I said. 'I've got something else for you.'

I tapped the holdall that hung by my side. He looked at me dumbly, like he was being hypnotised. I took the can and placed it on the pavement at the edge of the forecourt, then walked to the back of the space, away from the streetlights.

'Come on,' I said. 'You'll like it.'

'Are you serious?' he asked, peering into the semi-darkness.

I didn't answer, didn't need to. He wasn't able to apply logic, not then, his ego couldn't allow it. Logic would have dictated that he walk away.

He moved forward slowly, looking at the holdall. Then he sighed, the weariness of the drunk, imagining that the advantage was tilting back in his favour. Just me and him, the big guy.

'Steve, really hammered mate. What is it, what you got?'

I put the bag down by the front shutters of the garage. He looked puzzled when I approached him and grabbed the material of his coat, but still he didn't know how to react. When I didn't let go, however, he didn't look happy.

'Steve, take your hands off me mate. Seriously.'

I moved him to the side, letting him stumble but keeping him upright. His face changed in an instant, the hatred only a split-second away. He grabbed my forearms and tried to break my grip, a waste of time. Our faces were inches apart.

'You motherfu —'

I blocked his right leg as he tried to kick me, then simply pushed him to his left, where his balance was weakest. The first lesson: use your opponent's moves against him.

He toppled onto the concrete, breaking his fall with his arm just in time. Fighting the effects of the alcohol, he struggled awkwardly to his feet. I wished he wasn't drunk, but you can't have everything. Not even his rage could help him now; if anything, it made things easier for me.

He threw a punch but I sensed it long before his fist lumbered through the air, using the opportunity to get behind him and drag him to the ground again. I thought it would be more difficult: it was like fighting a cuddly cartoon bear. But I couldn't get cocky, couldn't let my concentration slip – the hard bit hadn't started yet.

Again he got up and came at me, but again I stepped in close and grabbed his coat, pulling him around, toying with him like we were dancing. I wasn't going to be too adventurous and attempt a throw, so I just spun around and rolled him off my back. This time he almost stayed on his feet, lurching forward until gravity sucked him down onto his knees.

We were ready, I could feel it. He knew I wouldn't be letting him go home; his shoulders had dropped when he eventually stood, as if resigned to his fate. I'd expected more from him.

One last glance around to check that no one was looking, and I went in. He put his hands up again – a bit like someone getting showered with cheap beer – but didn't know what to do with them. This time I vented a little anger, moving him one way then tripping him up in the other direction, throwing him hard to the ground. He seemed stunned. It was time.

Gary wasn't getting up, he'd had enough. Sitting there on the cold ground, the world spinning too fast, chest heaving like he'd run a marathon. I crouched in front of him and pulled the zip of his jacket halfway down. When I walked around and knelt behind him he didn't move, couldn't even speak.

He did, however, try to revive himself when I reached over his shoulder with my right hand and grabbed the collar of his open jacket on the other side, so that my wrist was against the side of his neck. Then, moving quickly, I reached underneath his left armpit and across his chest with my other hand, gripping the material on the opposite side, a bit lower down. He started to wriggle but I ignored him. I'd been in his situation before, plenty of times, so I knew how it was about to feel: like a straitjacket around the throat. I was relaxed, my breathing steady. The hitman in the mafia film, way out in the desert, a shovel in the boot of my car. All in a night's work.

'What are you doing?' said Gary, suddenly finding his voice. It was high and pleading, almost feminine. As he tried to move I began pulling the two sides of his jacket together, my right forearm still tight against his neck. Not too much at first; I wanted to savour the moment. Again he tried to loosen my grip, silly boy.

'Ever heard of the carotid arteries, Gary? They lead up through the neck and into the brain, not that you'd care.' I spoke the words softly into his ear, like a lover.

'This is how it feels to be trapped, to know that you made a wrong decision, ended up somewhere you don't belong. You understand me?'

He tried to reply but my grip was slowly tightening; not how you do it normally, when you'd want to achieve the desired result as quickly as possible. I was breaking the rules, defying the code.

The only noise that came from his lips now was a wet hiss. Then, as I knew it would, panic set in. He began jerking, legs scrambling to get a grip on the tarmac, which only succeeded in pushing him further into my welcoming arms.

'Sshhh,' I whispered. 'It's alright, it's alright. Don't be scared.'

He was trying to scream, but the blood supply in his neck had dropped too low, the oxygen dwindling. Soon a clacking sound was all that came from his mouth. I almost didn't want it to end, but knew it had to. Still kicking furiously, he reached behind and was slapping at my face, trying to get a grip, but I kept out of range. His whole body was convulsing, and then, soon after, it went limp. It felt like a mercy killing, a pillow over someone's face. He stopped flailing, until at last his hands fell to his sides. I released my hold and his head lolled back into my lap.

I was slightly out of breath myself now. Mercifully no one had heard us, attracted by muffled groans somewhere in the half-light.

Bloody students. Animals.

Holding the back of Gary's head in my palms, I got up, lowered it gently onto the concrete and turned him over onto his side, as if putting a child to bed. I got a bottle of water from my bag and grabbed an old crate, placed it next to him and sat down.

He looked peaceful.

I thought of taking a picture on my phone, Gary lying there, but I couldn't be bothered. It wasn't necessary. Lording a photo around like a trophy wouldn't make it feel any better than it already did. Instead I just looked at him. I was feeling good, and I welcomed the sensation. Perhaps I should do this more often, I thought. Revenge therapy. Nice.

Eventually Gary began to stir, lifting his head, trying to place where he was. He looked sideways at me, as if I were a complete stranger, then sat up.

He was half-awake now, bewildered, like someone coming round after an operation.

'Here,' I said, offering him the bottle. 'Have some of this.'

He took the bottle from me without a word, drank one mouthful, then passed it back.

'Thanks,' he said.

'You're welcome.'

I got up and knelt behind him again.

'How are you feeling?'

He tried to turn, to look at me, hands resting on the ground to stop himself going over.

'I'm okay. Not too bad.'

He was a different person. The aggression was absent, the notion of supremacy over people like me, outsiders, evaporated. Like he was chatting to a mate on a quiet night in.

I reached over his shoulder and grabbed the other side of his jacket again.

'Don't worry,' he said, confused. 'I can do it, I've got it.'

As he fumbled with the zip my other hand slipped across his chest.

'What are you doing?' he asked, his voice urgent. 'No. What are you doing …?'

I brought the two sides together once more, pulling firmly on the material. As soon as he felt the restriction against his throat Gary panicked, but he was a little more sober now, which meant more effort on my part. He was like a training partner, it felt good to practise with him.

I tightened my grip, snuffing out his attempt to scream, holding him like a vice as he struggled furiously. Kicking, twisting, trying to punch the side of my head but connecting with nothing. The same guttural noises, the same choking sound, the desperation to draw in air. And then he was gone, fading, quicker than the first time.

I lowered him again, but this time I didn't wait around, couldn't risk it. I knew about the old resuscitation techniques, had studied them in my books, but had never been called upon to use one. I turned him over on his side, and, kneeling, put my ear close to his mouth. His breathing was faint. I waited. It was my turn for panic to start creeping in. Come on Gary, come on. You can do it.

Suddenly he twitched, took a rasping breath, then another. This time I threw the water in his face, bringing him round with a shock. He shook his head, brought his hand up to his eyes. As he wiped the liquid away, I couldn't believe what I was seeing. He was unable to hide it from me; maybe, deep down, he thought it might help.

Gary started to cry.

I didn't laugh – I'm not malicious – but it seemed like a fitting end to the evening. I waited while he blubbed, a chastised little boy, until his sobs began to ebb away. He even flinched when I moved.

The night was turning much colder. I looked at my watch: just after twelve, a new day. I went to the holdall and pulled out a towel. I handed it to Gary, who wiped his face and neck.

I stood a few feet back. It really would have made a perfect picture, and for a second I was actually tempted. But no, this was between me and Gary only; the world didn't need to be in on it. I knew I wouldn't hear from him again.

'Goodnight Gary,' I said, buttoning my coat. I put the towel and water back in the bag, then walked out into the street.

I didn't go in for any classes the next day, went to see the head of the humanities department instead. She was puzzled and disappointed, made us both a coffee and tried to talk me out of leaving. The don't exit interview. Told me I was easily in line for a 2:1, even a First if I really pushed myself. Being away from home can be hard, she said. She didn't know the half of it. Still, it was a pleasant enough half hour, for me anyway.

It was over.

I couldn't go back home to Plymouth, that was clear, and it took me ages to gather the nerve to tell my parents. I couldn't bear to hear the disappointment in their voices; working-class boy blows his one chance, slides back down the ladder, all that. Mind you, I'm fairly sure they didn't have a clue about what you actually do with a history degree, assuming you stick around long enough to get one. Teach history to other people, presumably. But it didn't matter, the certificate is what would have counted, the seal of approval.

They didn't say it to me directly, when I eventually did get round to confessing, but I knew what they were thinking. That was your window son, your opportunity

– the only person they knew who had gone to a university to learn, not just to deliver something. But we got over it, and they were delighted when I eventually landed a job in sales. The suit and tie clinched it, I reckon. They were relieved, and assumed I was too – I sold them that line, hid my own disappointment.

I was done. Jack caught Lucy's eye, got two more cups of tea in.

'Thanks for telling me,' he said. 'It wasn't easy, I could tell.'

I shrugged. 'Yeah, well …'

We didn't dissect it, didn't even go over it. Jack wasn't about to be my analyst, put me on the couch – he had all he needed to know.

Dr Kano, the man who created judo, started to learn martial arts because he was fed up with being bullied at school. So although I had strayed way off course, betrayed the spirit of what I believed in, there was a certain symmetry in what I had done that night. At least that's what I told myself. Having said that, suffocating someone twice because you don't like them is not acceptable, and of course the regret, the shame, followed swiftly. And the fear. Always the fear. I was scared of that side of myself, of what I was capable of. I had deliberately and carefully pulled the legs off a beetle, then discarded the body without the compassion to crush it.

Worst of all, that fear had kept me away from the sport ever since, had led me down a different path, one I wasn't meant to be on. Again. But what I didn't know was that Jack had another plan, a skill that was second nature to him: move me in one direction, a distraction technique, then make me go where he actually intended. The basic rule of judo.

'Come to the club next Wednesday,' he said. 'I might need your help with something.'

3

As it turned out, I met Jack just as someone else was about to enter my life. A little miracle, in its own way, all things considered. I'm not easy to get along with on a full-time basis, I know that, it takes a special kind of person. But I didn't go looking for her, she found me.

What do they call it? Serendipity? More subtle than just fate, something that isn't completely out of your control. Making your own luck.

But would I have called myself lucky at the time, knowing what I know now? Maybe. Life is theatre, and perhaps all you can do is welcome the opportunity to take part, to add to the sum of your knowledge. Maybe you can take it with you afterwards, who knows.

It's not good, it's not bad. It just is.

We didn't meet online, however shocking, however implausible that may sound in this age of virtual detachment. Real life does still happen, if you know where to look.

Don't get me wrong, I had been exploring the whole internet angle – although I didn't tell anyone, not even Jack. The results were disastrous. Actually, worse than that. The web, I quickly came to realise, is populated by liars and fantasists, and you join their little game at your peril. You can't know who – or what – you're playing with. Maybe that's the point for some people, the thrill, I don't know.

At the time, however, I had no qualms about

jumping in feet first. It had seemed such a logical step to join an online dating agency, prompted by an old friend who turned up unannounced on my doorstep one weekend. We'd worked together for a short while, right after I dropped out of college, in a job that involved selling coffee machines. It's an experience I've long since tried to bury. We lasted three weeks, the pair of us, schlepping all over London like a couple of beggars, and we didn't even get paid because the company was going under at the time but no one bothered to mention that.

Anyway, he came to visit me out of the blue, having moved back home to Warwick to set up a printing business. I opened the door on a bright Saturday morning to find him standing there, looking exactly as I remembered, except in a more expensive suit. He was doing well, it was obvious. Told me he'd come down for a few days to give his harem back home a well-earned break, a chance to get their collective strength back. Groupies regrouping.

Cue low moans of disbelief for most of the weekend as we wandered the parched landscape of my dating history, me totally embarrassed, him with the messianic look in his eye of one who can sense an oasis somewhere among the dunes. Beer, tequila and – very reluctantly, on my part – potentially lethal South African hash, these were the base elements tossed into our crucible, two alchemists seeking the gold that would enrich my love life. And I suppose our scheming did have a certain lustre; although if our situations had been reversed, with him in need rather than me, I suspect he might have condemned our foolish dabblings for what they were and skulked off back to the posh part of the Midlands.

No matter, point of desperation reached. You need professional help, he said.

For a long time there had been, I have to admit, a persistent voice in my ear, nagging me about those college kids I'd known who had now scattered across the country and were no doubt tucking into feasts of flesh every night of the week, stabbing their stout blades into everything from the finest venison to the cheapest cuts of pork, while I, well, I went hungry. And the hunger was bad, it really was.

Time to take my place at the table. I was ravenous.

Candlelight.

I picked the agency the traditional way, from the *Yellow Pages*, thumbing through lists of companies that promised far more than they could ever hope to deliver, like ads for celebrity perfume. I ignored the ones whose dainty little boxes, with their cunning phrases and Cupid illustrations, conveniently bypassed the fact that my piece of the pie – companionship, hearts entwined, semi-legal embraces in National Trust car parks – would be dwarfed by the giant slice earmarked for them. It was straightforward commercial gain, the counterbalance to which, in actual fact, could well be my splintering dreams and a long slide into a life of bitter regret, played out in a shabby flat with three kids forced to share a room because Daddy drank the savings.

So, Candlelight. Get to it lad, strike the match.

Should I have checked them out at Companies House? Probably, but that would have been too cynical, completely at odds with my grand romantic endeavour. The maternal voice on the other end of the line, no doubt originating from a magnolia-hued semi in High Wycombe, told me I would have to sign up for six months, on the understanding that if I hadn't found my true love (and presumably settled down with her in a plush riverside apartment) within that period, I would get the second six months free.

It struck me as a hollow offer: 'Should your time with us turn out to be a painful series of attempts at making a lasting connection among our hand-picked procession of divas and angst-ridden neurotics, we will line up another travelling carnival for you, absolutely gratis. And for this you should be grateful. Negotiations will not be entered into.'

Perhaps I was being too sceptical; after all, I may not have been born with the genes of a salesman, but I know the drill back to front. I did it every day.

Not any more though. I'm out of that game.

Needless to say, my cynicism about the whole quest was grounded in one of life's certainties: what you go looking for is seldom found. The entire candlelit experience was a bit like visiting a zoo for months on end, trying to tempt exotic animals away from the dense foliage with a bag of toasted pine nuts and some macaroons, only to be set upon by salivating beasts that kept creeping up on you unawares. At times I feared my safety was being compromised, a topic that elicited little sympathy from the voice at the agency.

Take Stephanie, an unnaturally thin and *very* intense lass who worked as a courier's receptionist, and who saw favourable qualities in me that had lain dormant since birth. I was like a god to her, which I found totally bemusing. She laughed like a hyena, but ate like a lizard, if you want an image to conjure with.

And she carried a small screwdriver, in her handbag, within easy reach.

For protection, she said.

The second web-date – Sarah – culminated in a wallet-draining visit to a burlesque club in Soho, while the third – Adrianna – bore all the hallmarks of your typical kidnap plot: a rendez-vous with the suspiciously pretty young lady in a Marriott hotel off the M25 one Tuesday evening, during which she kept glancing at her watch, and the door, as we tucked into nibbles and small talk. I bottled it, made my excuses and scarpered.

A BMW with foreign plates and blacked-out windows pulled into the hotel car park as I stood waiting for the bus, not daring to step too far from the lights of the foyer. Paranoia? Mistaken identity? Possibly, but a good story nonetheless to pad out at dinner parties: my CIA past, proficiency in hand-to-hand combat, a love of good tailoring.

The next date was also pointless. Kate was married, although she'd failed to mention that in her profile. Had to get it off her chest straight away when we met though, bless her, wedding ring no doubt shrouded in tissue paper, secreted away in her stylish, calf-skin purse. Not the sort of thing you'd want to wear on a romantic liaison, I suppose, like an ankle tag when you're out on parole.

She was married to an undertaker, of all things, and was a partner in the business. Slipping out silently every once in a while, into the land of the living, to meet people like me. It wouldn't have taken more than a couple of sauvignon spritzers for us to disappear into a pay-by-the-hour room, but Kate's eyes were too sad. They killed me. Glassy pools, her emotions too near the surface. I couldn't do it for pity's sake.

Her husband – she wouldn't tell me his name (you don't let details like that creep past the jars of fluid, the foundation cream) – offered those with no East End connections whatsoever the chance to make their final journey in a horse-drawn carriage. All Kray twins and salt-of-the-earth pretensions. Some people love that type of thing, I have no idea why.

The slow march of horses and black limousines. And Kate in the sombre procession, leading from the front, daydreaming of being held down, alive for an hour in a room with no personal effects.

I was tempted, of course I was. She was attractive, but desperation was dragging her towards pitiless middle age, the other slow procession. Say your goodbyes in private by the bedroom mirror, beneath the clever shading, the concealer.

Undertaking: a handy staff with which to beat off that temptation. As Kate and I sat there fumbling for conversation, I improvised her old man's working routine in my mind, imagining the tang of disinfectant in a temperature-controlled room, some light jazz to lift the spirits. It all served to stem the rising tide of need that threatened to drag me under. Of course, I have no experience of how such procedures are actually carried out, but when pressed I can summon images that would crush the libido of a rabbit fresh home from war.

But why didn't we? What harm could it possibly have done?

There were other similar situations, albeit without

weaponry or meandering through the valley of death, but still threatening nonetheless. Even to a thirteen-stone man who vents his frustrations on weighted iron bars, or runs towards a wall for half an hour, imagining that he's pounding the streets of early-morning New York.

Maybe I'd ticked the wrong boxes on my application form. The compatibility questionnaire was a test in itself, like being asked to look deep within to determine whether you're actually deserving of a mate.

I began to have doubts. If I'd made up the usual bullshit about loving independent films and quiet nights in, I might just as well have gone to a few evening classes at the local adult education centre and hooked up with someone there, saved myself the agency fee. As it was, I admitted that I worked in publishing sales and went to the gym a lot. Plus I Photoshopped my picture a little bit. You're supposed to, aren't you?

Just send me a girl with something between her ears, someone who looks nice in a dress but doesn't mind grabbing a hammer if I need a hand putting up a shelf. It isn't too much to ask, surely.

I heard myself whining. Complaints rained down upon the High Wycombe semi. She began to dislike me, I could tell.

To tell you the truth, I would have been tetchy in her position, trying to sell love to the lonely. People fly giant pandas halfway around the world for much the same reason; what's the point? If it's meant to happen, it will. So, two months in and I gave up, they could keep the other four. Candlelight's flame flickered and died.

And then, the gold that my mate and I had tried to conjure suddenly appeared, winking at me from the grime that seemed to cover my every path.

Of course, you stumble upon such treasure in the dark, on days when you're not even looking, but no self-help manual will ever tell you that. Just keep paying through the nose, and don't forget to play the soothing audio CD as you drift off. Sounds of the ocean breaking on the shore, the clattering of pebbles. Mantra-like confirmations of your inner strength, delivered in the calming tones of the kind of woman you will never meet: '*Unlock your inner confidence*'; '*Beauty attracts beauty*'; '*Go online for more products*'.

I was invited by another friend, Christina, to Sadler's Wells to see a showcase of modern dance. Three pieces by three different companies over the course of two and a quarter hours. Plus intermission. Without that interlude I might have choked to death, throat as dry as tobacco leaf.

The event had a suitably oblique name, of course, which I should remember but sadly don't. It didn't make it past my often over-zealous cultural border patrol, through which only a decent crime novel, Portsmouth FC and movies with that elusive combination of high-octane action and a decent storyline are guaranteed safe passage. Theatre and art exhibitions you can keep, ta very much.

But on this occasion, I did go to the dance. Someone must have laced the invites, chemicals seeping through the skin of my fingertips. No way would I have normally accepted. You Sophisticates can peer at me all day long through the barbed wire, fanning yourselves with twenty-quid glossy programmes, all smug inside the golden circle for *Swan Lake at Sunset*. It's your gilded cage, not mine. When you've seen what I've witnessed from behind the goal at Fratton Park, tossed into the firmament of the sporting arena, you'll understand what art means. Sit yourself down at the Milton End for ninety minutes, rain of biblical proportions lashing the gnarled turf and us die-hards staring a two-nil fightback in the face, and you'll wonder what you ever saw in those Greek turns. Genuine tragedy.

Sadler's Wells. A modern building, not peeking out from the gun turret of tired respectability like the places we were herded into as schoolkids. (All that burgundy, the heavy carpets, the crushing weight of expectation bearing down from rows of serious punters.) We were in the packed bar before the performance, dozens of animated conversations coalescing into white noise as I struggled back to our group, balancing a tray containing two ambitiously priced glasses of wine, a vodka tonic and two pints of Stella – one for me, the other for Graham, who I'd been introduced to five minutes before.

I was the odd one out, which should come as no surprise. Christina and her beau, Simon, were there, a decent enough fella (supported Chelsea, so no territorial or political threat); then there was Graham and his girlfriend, Helen, who I'd met once or twice through Christina. She was a journalist of some description; general arts critic, I think, for an esoteric magazine whose flexible remit seemed to cover everything from Sudanese warlords to recipes for baked apples.

At least we had publishing in common, dahling – although I never found out the name of her mag, which in my old line of work was a sin punishable by public flogging. She had told me when we were first introduced some months previously, but was wearing a semi-transparent blouse at the time and the hunger was very much upon me, so the words ended up on the floor between us. I kept meaning to find out, but didn't, so I suppose I couldn't have been that bothered.

She'd landed us all freebie tickets for the evening, and for a short while seemed to find my tales of advertising woe quite interesting. Mainly, I suspected, because the jobs of delicate editorial types depend on slaves like me pulling on the oars below decks, sweating on how we can drag revenue from cash-strapped companies who generally have other plans for their tight budgets. I am – was – every journalist's lifeboat, even if I was apt to loom out of the swirling mist like an iceberg.

It's not personal, just work.

Graham – so inanimate that his sole body movement was the non-stop dance of his lips, a flamenco of syllables that pranced around joylessly – began outlining in my general direction his doctoral thesis on ME. The 'lazy bug', or what people like me call 'a lame excuse not to hold down a job'.

Clearly that makes me sound like a heartless prick. I'm sure there's science behind it somewhere, fanning the flames, securing more funding.

Graham's lips kept moving, his dance card full. As he babbled on I found myself wondering for some reason about the threat of global terrorism, and what it would be like if a bomb went off in the theatre, right there in the bar, and then discovered I didn't care about that either.

Was he trying to be clever? Picking me off with sleek

darts dipped in research, theories on impaired social interaction and the role of genetics whizzing through the branches towards my treetop refuge. I could have mentioned the judo, just for the sake of something else to talk about, but it wouldn't have registered. I smothered a yawn.

I could see my mate Christina – Chrissie – smirking at me over the rim of her merlot, trying to catch my eye, make me laugh. I glared at her.

Eventually, thank God, a toneless Orwellian voice instructed us to take our seats in the auditorium. My glass was long empty, but I stood there like a patient sheepdog while everyone else finished their drinks, winding up conversations that could easily have waited until after the performance.

We eventually found our row and, mercifully, I was at the opposite end to Graham. Chrissie to my left, Joe Public to my right. Perfect. As we got comfortable I touched her forearm, moved in close.

'Thanks for introducing us. No, really, he's a bundle of laughs. I can see us becoming really good mates.'

A gentle squeeze of my hand. Old friends.

'Don't be like that. ME is a fascinating subject.'

I studied her face. Calm, assured. Serious even.

'Get lost.'

She laughed. 'We're going for Thai afterwards. You'll come, won't you?'

'Sure, love to. I'll go now if you like, get us a table.'

An exasperated shake of the head. And another smile, before the dimming lights took her away.

To be honest, my expectations for the event were hovering somewhere above zero: it was just a night out, something different. If I got bored I could look forward to Sunday's cup game against Everton. Away, unfortunately, so it would have to be Sky Sports in the pub. Or if things took a real nosedive, there was always mental homework. The life of a salesperson is a perpetual quest for target-busting glory, a crusade that won't ever be won despite high walls being breached over and over.

We never doubted the grail's existence. Nothing got in our way; everything was a sale.

I'm not particularly proud of it, I certainly didn't enjoy it, but there was a job to be done, a mortgage to pay. And there were always clients to be hunted down: those who didn't even know they'd been spotted, or those who had taken out ads long before and naively thought their silence was a shield, that we'd somehow forgotten about them.

As if. You're in the database forever. I will track you, and I will find you. Or one of my team would, in which case I was still able to claim my share of the kill. Bonuses all round.

Okay, the dance.

Three pieces. The first was all ghetto-style, sort of *West Side Story* with vials of crack. Drug wars, territory, plenty of posturing. Nothing for the audience to get too worked up about, I wouldn't have thought, a sea of white faces.

The second one I didn't understand at all. It could have been about ecology, it could have been about the arms trade; it might even have been about tennis. It seemed to involve at least two of these.

Intermission.

We had ice creams. *Ice creams*. Like the Famous Five. I started having bad thoughts.

Then back in for more, buffeted by the jovial banter of strangers all around me. 'Off to Henley this weekend'; 'You really must come over to dinner sometime'; 'Bridgitte's got into Cambridge, reading music, over the moon'.

Our lives supposedly improved as our arses gradually went numb.

Actually the final piece was a lot better than the previous two, despite it also being contemporary and therefore somewhat up itself. A romance, sort of.

Man and woman meet in Tube station; she's sexy and flirts with him; he quickly becomes obsessed and starts following her all over the place; her boyfriend gets jealous, wants to do the guy in but instead she leaves him, so he ends up killing himself as some kind of sad protest. A bit extreme, but there you go. Anyway, woman left on her own, shattered life and what have you, trapped in an endless cycle of guilt and remorse. Keeps going back to the Tube station – a slightly amoral touch, I thought, her boyfriend barely cold – but of course the other bloke's long since lost interest so she's all on her tod with no bloke. Serves her right. The End.

Yes, there was more to it than that, but in seat F28 all subtle nuances were missed: 'emotional touchpoints that drove the work forward', or whatever it was that Helen later put in her review. She sent us all a copy, which I knew she would, she was that type, and I guess she felt we could become her little theatre gang. No Helen, we can't.

Anyway, like I said, I missed a few of the subtleties because my thoughts did roam for a little while at one stage, scheming about how to sell a full-page advertorial to a special-effects company that had been avoiding me for weeks, ignoring my calls and appearing to be unschmoozable. Not to worry, I resolved to discover *their* emotional touchpoints, give them a good rub.

When we left the theatre I was ready to eat. Beyond ready. But, of course, we had to hang around in the foyer while Helen made a big show of talking to people she knew. Always networking, clutching at coat-tails. Eventually she said her exaggerated au revoirs and we headed off in search of south-east Asia.

The restaurant was trapped in the wrong decade, as befitting a jolly raucous bunch of theatre lovers such as ourselves, but the food was top-notch, I'll give them that. Sugar levels restored, I even found myself indulging Graham, who picked up our conversation at the exact point at which we had abandoned it earlier. The *exact* point, I'm not joking. It was almost admirable; I wanted to stop him in mid-sentence, tell him I understood his pain, but there was no holding him back. And he was probably busy counting my noodles as well. I focused on the delicious red-curry fire in my mouth, which I tamed with liberal quantities of Singha beer.

Halfway through, I noticed Chrissie and Helen exchanging a few hushed words and glancing in my direction. I smiled, feeling secretly pleased – you take what you can, don't you? Chrissie leant across the table.

'You're not seeing anyone at the moment, are you Steve?'

I wanted to invent someone, but I had nothing. Just

my pride.

'Well, you know me, if she's the right side of fifty I'm interested.'

Her expression was rooted in sympathy, but she wasn't giving up. 'It's just that we have another guest this evening. Helen thought you might like to meet her.'

Oh God no. Really? No. Just stop it. Honestly, when you girls get together it's either Weight Watchers or *Wuthering Heights*.

'Superb. Portsmouth fan, is she?'

'Ask her yourself – she just walked in.'

A presence behind me. Like a cold hand after dark.

I turned around, almost unwillingly, and looked up at a face that I recognised but couldn't immediately place. A girl I'd stared at while waiting for the train, possibly, or followed down the street until even I felt a bit creeped out.

If only she'd been leaping energetically, portraying the full range of human emotions through the contortions of her body, then of course I would have remembered straight away. She looked different up-close.

'Everyone, this is Emily,' said Helen, moving round the table like something predatory. The fragile-looking creature she was fixed upon was ushered into the empty chair next to me. I experienced the familiar sensation of my space being entered, of impending small talk.

She was beautiful, almost inhumanly so, as if she were drawn by hand. I felt as if I could look but not touch, that I'd be forced to pay if I broke her.

'Hello,' she said.

'Hi, how's it going?'

'Good, thanks.'

I needed more, that was clear.

'Nice dancing.'

Nice dancing. Genius. No doubt I had just validated in her mind those endless hours spent practising while her friends squatted in front of the television or brushed the golden hair of their dollies; patted her on the back for all the torture her famished body had to endure at dance school, a life of perseverance and denial bringing her to this moment.

Nice dancing. Bravo Steve, very well done.

'Thanks. It wasn't our best performance ever, but I'm glad you enjoyed it.'

I hadn't, not really, but it was the best of the three. I concentrated hard on saying nothing that could expose me.

'It would have been much better if Karl hadn't decided to have an off night,' she continued. 'And he's an egotistical twat at the best of times, so all in all ...'

She shrugged off the end of the sentence. I sat there humbled, having escaped the sword that she could so easily have plunged into my chest, cutting me down to size for my cultural failings. But she didn't. She didn't. Plus she'd used a rude word.

She talked softly, a gentle ripple that hinted at life's finer things: family portraits all over the house; obscene amounts spent on education; ski trips to Switzerland where she kissed a local boy but nothing more. I ran on ahead, making plans, not wanting common sense to win the race. I pictured a home for us both, full of velvet cushions and intellectual radio programmes, birds singing in the garden. A place where I could massage her feet with kittens when she got home from dancing nicely.

The hunger, always the hunger.

God, listen to me. It was a dinner with friends, not a wedding feast. Why would she be interested? I mean, don't get me wrong, it's not like I should be confined to a bell tower, but I wasn't sitting by the phone waiting for a call from any modelling agencies asking me to pack for a weekend in Rome. I tried to keep it together.

She was younger than me, but not illegally so. Nineteen perhaps, to my twenty-four.

Our waitress hovered, sour-faced, angry with life. 'More drink?'

Emily leant in. She smelt like citrus fruits, organic shampoo. Her hair, tied back, was still wet at the edges.

'What do you do?' she asked.

I hesitated. It actually occurred to me that I should make something up, or at least mention an ambition, my true calling, anything.

'Sales. Publishing sales as it goes, but, you know, still sales.'

She giggled, put a hand to her mouth, her slim wrist angled like a broken twig.

'You sound embarrassed.'

'Well, you know, it's not who I am. Oh God, did I actually just say that? What I meant was ...'

She reached out, squeezed my arm gently, just for a second, like she'd been teasing an older brother.

'It's okay, you don't need to explain. Or apologise.'

I felt hot, overwhelmed. I brushed a few grains of rice from the tablecloth into my napkin, folded the material neatly and placed it on the table. It was as if every move

I made was exaggerated, beyond my control. Like I'd been put on show.

'Do you mind if I ...?' Her hand was moving towards my plate, like a patient heron tracking movement behind its own reflection. I was entranced, oblivious to the danger.

'Go for it.'

I pushed the half-eaten meal towards her, watching with stupefied awe as she shared my plate, the food that had microscopic traces of me on it. We'd only just met; it felt more real than actual physical contact.

She ate delicately; in fact she didn't really take much at all. All I knew was that the room seemed to blur around us, as if we were alone on a stage, beneath a spotlight.

A performance.

An hour later the evening was winding down, the restaurant almost empty, people taking their last sips of jasmine tea from tiny painted cups and preparing to brave the chill. Everyone on our table had been chatting away the whole time, theatre talk mainly, so my contribution was negligible. Helen had steered most of the conversation, while Chrissie kept glancing at me, tipping her head ever so slightly to the side as if I had somehow forgotten where Emily was sitting. I kept frowning at her, trying to fend her off. She knew how rubbish I was in those situations, and despite her best intentions, she wasn't helping.

Everything slowed to an inevitable standstill. We paid the bill, got our coats and left. Outside on the street there were yet more extravagant gestures from Helen, the promise of tickets for some event or other, must do lunch, fabulous new restaurant. Emily discreetly rolled her eyes at me and smiled, then shook my hand.

'It was nice to meet you Steve.'

'You too. Good luck with everything.'

As she turned away Helen linked arms with her, and off they all went. Two happy couples and Emily.

I wanted to go after them. Something was urging me forward; but something else, far more powerful, held me back. So I simply stood there, fixating on one single thought.

I would never see her again.

4

'What do you reckon?' asked Jack, walking towards me. I was standing by the wall, watching. He gestured to the far corner of the mat, where a newcomer was being shown basic moves by one of the more experienced judoka, as part of his induction. I'd seen him at the club once before, a couple of weeks back, although he hadn't caught my eye.

But he had something. Jack sensed it.

His name was Cyan Richards. I watched as he was shown a demonstration of *tsukuri*, or how to apply a throw. He seemed keen to learn, watching everything, although he wouldn't be tested too much for a while. That's not how it works with the new ones, even those bursting with confidence. Especially those, in fact. Essential technique comes first, understanding the principles behind sleeve-holding, body contact, breaking your opponent's balance. And you don't get to swap your novice's red belt for a white one until you understand. When you're starting out you don't just bowl into a dojo and ask to be let loose on people.

Jack stood there, taking everything in, an artist considering a blank canvas. Despite his inexperience, Cyan was happy to fall. He showed no sign of tension. As I watched I realised what Jack had seen: that spark you offer the tinderbox and hope it takes hold. The kid looked exhausted, but jumped back up onto his feet every time and let himself be thrown again.

'Well?' said Jack.

'Got a live one.'

He shook his head in despair. 'Got a live one. God help us. That's your input is it?'

I laughed. 'Okay, sorry. He looks like a natural, that's what I meant. How old is he anyway?'

'Fifteen.' Jack turned away again, walked back around the mat, then stood sideways on to the boy. 'Put your feet like this,' he said. The youngster looked up, his face serious.

'Yes sir,' he said.

'Yes *sir*?' I said, quietly, when Jack came back.

'You heard him. Boy's got manners.'

I decided to labour the point.

'You giving it the sergeant-major routine, breaking him in?'

'Nope. And less of your lip sunshine, or you'll be cleaning the toilets.'

Like that was a threat.

We looked at each other, just for a second, enjoying the moment. The mat was alive with paired-off fighters, bouncing on the balls of their feet, readjusting their whites, then falling back into the grip like stags locking horns. I thought of that first evening in Deptford, me and Jack, feeling the surge when you think you might have found someone worth coming out on a cold night for. A shared discovery.

Half a dozen more practice moves and Cyan had done enough. When he came round to where we were Jack patted the side of his arm, said he showed the correct spirit. One more induction session and he'd be taking off his red belt.

Cyan remained expressionless, mopping his face with the sleeve of his judogi. He was unable to look either of us in the eye for very long, and barely glanced at me when Jack introduced us and we shook hands. But I was looking straight at him, staring in fact, aware that a hazy memory was slowly piecing itself together.

I'd seen him before – before the club, that is. I didn't know when, or where, but I was certain of it. Something made him stand out.

I tried to dismiss it. If he was local, there was every chance I'd seen him around. But there was more to it than that, a feeling starting to dig its way out of my half-formed thoughts, pulling towards the surface. Something out of the ordinary. Not just a passing face on the street, or someone on a bus.

I hadn't plucked my earlier sergeant-major comment out of the air, by the way. In the short time that I'd known him, Jack had told me a bit about his life, opened up a little. Showing me the way, I suppose, leading by example.

Royal Engineers, 1969 to 1974. Here, Germany, a few other places. Enjoyed the life. Plus he got really into boxing, which the services encouraged. Pretty good too, or so he told me, and Jack wasn't one for exaggeration.

Military competitions; a few pieces of silverware for the trophy cabinet when he got discharged. He made corporal though. Corporal Jack.

I watched as Cyan and the rest of the class did some stretching to warm down, Jack walking around discussing techniques with some of the guys, pointing out where they were going wrong, or what could be refined with a small tweak. Then everyone helped to break down the mat – the individual rectangles slot together like a jigsaw – creating a pile in the corner, after which they bowed and exited the dojo. Jack was left standing there, hands on his hips, looking satisfied with another evening's work.

'Time to go, I reckon,' he said.

'You got a minute, Jack?' I asked.

'Sure. Something on your mind?'

'No, not really. I was just curious, that's all.'

'What about?'

'The army. You didn't finish telling me the other day.'

He looked surprised.

'Oh that. Blimey. I'd forgotten we'd started on my life story.'

I sat on the edge of the pile of mats, and Jack joined me.

'Where did I get to?'

'Boxing. You were busy bashing heads.'

'Oh yeah, that's right. Well, there's not much I can tell you really. My army career hit the buffers, simple as that. We were up north, some grotty hall not far from Newcastle. I'd been volunteered for an inter-services tournament and came up against an animal from the Royal Marines. A monster, but, you know, you can't let yourself worry, and you definitely can't show fear. I gave it everything, but it was never going to be enough, I knew it before the end of the first round. I'm sure everyone else did too. In the third I left myself open to a right-hander that exploded against the side of my head, and that was it. Gone.'

He mimicked the action with a closed fist to his jaw,

head flying back in slow motion, eyes closed. 'I was like a dozy farm-hand being kicked by a horse. Never felt anything like it, not even when I sparred against the bigger guys from the regiment.'

He stopped talking, staring out across the hall, back in the north of England four decades ago. A different life.

'I went down badly, like I was freefalling in the dark. All I could see was hundreds of flickering lights, loads and loads of little stars. Didn't feel a thing for a few seconds, which was probably a blessing. That came afterwards. And of course, when I was struggling to get up off the canvas, our friend from the Marines was barely even celebrating – I think he was the least surprised of anyone there. Anyway, long and short of it is I tore a muscle in my neck and damaged a nerve, which for months meant I had bolts of pain shooting down into my shoulder if I moved even slightly the wrong way. Bloody nightmare.'

'Sounds nasty,' I said. 'I hope they gave you some leave.'

'Did they bollocks. After I came round in the dressing room they carted me off to a civilian hospital, where I stayed for a couple of days. Concussion, they said. After that it was back to the barracks. The stupid thing got a bit better, but wouldn't heal properly. For a while I tried getting used to the other duties they offered me – administration, supplies, that sort of thing – but I couldn't hack it. My world was shrinking, and filling in paperwork was not why I'd joined up. I'm no pen-pusher. So, anyway, I eventually accepted a pay-off and a half-decent pension.'

'Then what?' I asked. 'I'm guessing you didn't just open a judo club.'

'No, of course not. The thing is, I'd planned on having a decent career in the army. I liked the discipline, the physical work, even the parade drills that went on for hours, which most of the other lads hated. And I couldn't wait for the training exercises where they drop you on a moor in the middle of nowhere, pitch black, and then make it very difficult for you to find your way home. You don't get that sort of challenge working in an office, that's for sure.'

I didn't look at him, the sneaky bastard, and he didn't look at me. He knew what he was doing. We sat in silence for a moment.

'So, after taking Her Majesty's coinage, I was lost. I mean it. I had no idea what I was going to do, absolutely none whatsoever. I tried different jobs, but I just couldn't get excited about any of them. And then one day, quite by chance, I picked up a book on judo in the local library. It was an epiphany, like someone had opened a door for me. The stuff on those pages was unbelievable – the levels of endurance needed, the physical and mental discipline. I was reading about guys who dedicated their lives to it, training for hours on end even when they were injured, pushing through the pain barrier to achieve perfection. Living and breathing the whole thing, like true craftsmen. Well, that was it, that was the life for me. I knew they would wet themselves laughing at an injury like mine, and quite right too. It was exactly what I needed, so I did it.'

'Where'd you start?'

'The Budokwai. I meant business, I wasn't messing

around.'

Of course, I thought. Where else. West London's famous Budokwai club, Europe's first dojo. It opened in 1918, and practically all the big names have trained there, from all over the world.

'Bet that was fun.'

'Fun's one word for it. It was the toughest thing I'd ever done. A total shock. But after that first session I was hooked.'

He tapped my upper arm with the back of his hand.

'But look who I'm talking to. You had a head-start on me, you were a teenager. I bet you can still remember how good it felt, eh?'

'Like it was yesterday.'

He waited, let it sink in.

'So anyway,' he continued, 'I went for it big time, it was all I could think about, and after a couple of years I was third dan, and that was that, I was off.'

'Off?' I asked. 'What do you mean – you opened this place?'

'No, no, no. Tokyo. Biggest adventure of my life. Amazing. Like visiting another planet. I'll tell you about it sometime.'

I was impressed, of course I was, but Jack's words cut right through me. He knew that, and wasn't about to go into all the details of his adventure. All I could think of was everyone beavering away back at the office, the never-ending phone calls I had to make every day of the week, persuading people to buy something they didn't even want in the first place. Advertising – without it everything grinds to a halt.

Jack was looking at me now. I tried to not let my

feelings show, tried to stay positive, take pleasure in his story. But then he spoke, quietly, as if there were other people in the room. Maybe there were.

'You got your brown belt Steve, and it's a big achievement. Don't forget that. So you messed up a bit, so what? You're capable of going a long way, and I should know.'

He put his hand on my shoulder, made me look at him.

'It's not going to happen again, okay? You know the drill – forget that moment, move onto the next.'

I nodded.

'Now, there's some spare whites in the locker room, go and change. I'm in no rush to get home.'

It took me by surprise, so much so that I felt a bit choked. I didn't know what to say, sitting there mute like an idiot.

'Go on,' he said, almost a whisper.

I nodded again, got to my feet, and went downstairs.

5

'So what's the story then?' I asked.

'He just showed up, on his own, said he'd heard I might be able to help him,' said Jack. 'Seems like a decent enough lad. Respectful, as far as I can make out. Hopefully he'll stick with it, listen to what we tell him.'

We were back in Lucy's place, Arthur dozing beneath the table. I had to keep checking he hadn't moved in case I accidentally kicked him: he was prone to snappy little outbursts when poked. Lucy had brought out a bit of fried mince when we came in, which he wolfed down and then set about trying to lick the glaze off the saucer, pushing it around the floor until the noise got too much and I had to retrieve it. He sat there looking up at me, dragging his tongue across his nose as if I were somehow capable of pulling a string of sausages from my pocket. I put the wet saucer on the empty seat; he soon got bored and flopped back down.

In the far corner three lads were hunched over a mobile phone, sniggering at images on the screen.

Jack blew on his tea while I fiddled with my spaghetti bolognese, hoping that the meat had at least come from a legitimate source. Somewhere that received an unannounced visit once in a while, a piece of paper with a signature at the bottom. She liked to cut corners did our Lucy, playing roulette with our stomachs and her business. Luckily she'd never offered me a guided tour of her kitchen. I tipped a load of dried parmesan onto the dark mound and hoped for the best.

'So he's local then, is he?' I asked, talking through my first mouthful.

Jack seemed surprised. 'Course he's local. You don't think people come from far and wide just for my services, do you?'

I put on my serious face.

'Don't do yourself down Jack, you have a reputation. You command respect around these parts.'

'Yeah, well, whatever. Anyway, the boy's got something.'

'I think you're right.'

'He does need to channel that aggression though – at the moment it's controlling him. This isn't some daft knockabout on the street. But, you know, we'll see.'

Jack pursed his lips, looking over my shoulder, his forefinger lightly tapping the table. I could tell he was replaying what we'd seen, Cyan's attributes, and his flaws, like pieces on a chessboard.

'He's attack-minded, which is good,' he said eventually. 'The rest will be a challenge, but if he's prepared to put the time in, who knows.'

I stifled a belch, the pasta a solid, painful glob in the centre of my chest. I felt like a boa constrictor struggling to digest a goat.

'He's still young, Jack. He's got fire, that's the main thing. And like you say, he seems like a good kid. Not that I'm an expert.'

'No, you're right, but he is very quiet. There's something going on there. Maybe he's a bit shy.'

I pushed my meal to one side – the bolognese was half-eaten, but had become too much of an ordeal. Lucy came out of nowhere, swooping like a seagull to snatch my plate, something bordering on a dirty look also descending upon me as she considered the remains.

'Another tea?' she asked, her eyes now on Jack.

'Go on then,' I said. 'Spoil us.'

She ignored me. Jack looked up.

'Cheers luv.'

Lucy paused for a second or two, but he'd already looked away. I pondered the age difference between them. Ten years, maybe twelve. She sauntered off.

It was nine-thirty, almost dark. My insides weren't relishing the prospect of more toil, despite the fact that Lucy actually made a half-decent cuppa. But it wasn't time to leave, not yet.

I'd always got the impression that Jack hated going back to an empty flat, and I couldn't help but picture him there. Quietly getting ready for bed, pyjamas neatly folded on the pillow, setting the alarm for early o'clock. Maybe listen to a play on the radio for a while, or a late-night phone-in, lonely insomniacs curing the world's ills. I imagined that he sometimes just dozed in front of the TV, a glass of single malt perched on the arm of the sofa. Or maybe a refill if he knew he wouldn't sleep – screw what the doctors say, bloody tablets. Blood pressure's the modern disease; if it's not that it's something else. We're all carrying our crosses up the hill.

Arthur would be curled up on his special blanket in the corner of the room, a warm nest of moulted fur, the faint sound of his nose whistling.

And then there were the noises. Jack had actually told me about them, how he found it annoying sometimes but tried to blank it out. Live and let live. Music and voices in the wall, muffled, but there most nights. A bolshy type always making a toast to something or other. The occasional thud, something falling to the floor, more laughter.

There was one part that Jack left out of his story, that night we trained together in the dojo. But later on it would come out, little references here and there, piece by piece, until eventually it all slotted into place. He wasn't a great one for personal stuff, but these things find the light no matter how hard you try to smother them.

He wrote to her from Japan every week for two years, and she waited for him.

Gloria. Perhaps not the prettiest nurse in that Newcastle hospital ward, he said, but she came with her own celestial aura, cherubs heralding her many acts of kindness. Jack felt a lot better within a few hours of the fight but managed to spin things out a bit longer, staving off the spartan barracks that awaited his return, content to lie in his bed and watch her.

He didn't compete for her attention, not like the other patients. He just lay there studying her, fascinated. Later he would thank God every day for the hammer blow that brought them together, that much he did tell me. The slight twinges in his shoulder that he still felt, even in his seventh decade, were a reminder of how life can turn on a moment.

A thousand different directions.

I never asked about her, but like I say, over time things slip out. I suppose he couldn't help it. Thing is, I got the impression that no one else knew. Maybe it was therapy for both of us. His eyes would glisten whenever he mentioned her name. Then he'd suddenly become animated, start busying himself with a piece of equipment in the gym, or find something to put in the bin. Snapping at me to stop fannying around and do something useful.

He'd always find an excuse to brush past me afterwards though, touch me lightly on the back. Reassurance for us both.

Jack and Gloria. She'd been gone twelve years when I first met him and he still couldn't accept it. The other wound that refused to heal.

So, one more cup of tea.

When we did eventually leave – Lucy's chef-cum-executioner, Alan, ushering us out the door with his usual cheerful abuse, some sarcastic insight to send us on our way – I walked Jack home. Sorry, I mean I walked with him. It's not as if he was frail, faculties starting to slip. The complete opposite, in fact. Plus it was sort of on my way.

He told me he was going to meet the boy's parents, see how committed they both were to his judo. That was Jack all over; he liked to be thorough. A good judge of character.

6

The first date.

She got my number off Helen the journalist, then phoned up to ask me out. I was dumbfounded. It was like she knew I wouldn't be able to pluck up the courage, believing it was already over on that first evening, our worlds too distant from each other. Nothing to go on but my vivid imagination.

I was at work when she called, doing my best to marshal a team that for some reason wasn't in the mood to sell: the most heinous of all the transgressions. Someone, Claire my deputy, I think, had brought in a toy, a soft rubber ball encased in a net. It was green, but when you squeezed the thing it bulged through the netting and turned orange, like cherry tomatoes or a bunch of poisonous berries. Of course everyone wanted a go, their clamouring voices like the frenzied barking of seals, a bucket of fish by the pool's edge.

I had a couple of goes myself, because it was quite intriguing, but it couldn't keep my attention for long. Towering over us all was the whiteboard, our looming tablet of sales hieroglyphics, columns and marker-pen squiggles in blue and menacing red. Half-empty, yet fully expectant. While everyone tossed the new office plaything across the tables, squealing with delight every time they made it turn orange, I sat there juggling sums in my head, trying to work out whether we were actually going to hit target that month. We'd done it for the previous five, and our efforts had not gone unnoticed upstairs, which wasn't always to be welcomed. Get it right too often and they start expecting it all the time.

Sometimes you had to wonder where those targets, the numbers, came from. Were they the result of complex algebra based on an average of previous years' totals, then multiplied by statistics culled from the publishing sector, from rival companies? Or were they plucked from the air at random because someone on the board thought how exciting it would be to attain the unattainable, then factored in the cost of new Jags for everyone as well?

But it wasn't part of my role to argue, to show any form of dissent. And certainly not in front of everyone. Weakness from the team leader would quickly spread through the ranks, leading to who knows what. Mutiny? Quiet chats in small rooms? Spur-of-the-moment resignations? Probably not: my lot were as scared as I was about taking a chance doing something else. They existed within the framework of the office environment, like timid creatures held captive for so long that they could only cower at the back of the cage when the door swung open.

A couple of weeks previously, the sales manager of another mag in our company had sent out a group email telling us that if his team managed to hit their targets that month, they would do a conga around the building. Inside and out. Not because they had been ordered to, I presumed, but because they wanted to; and what better way to express your love of working life than a conga with the team?

But she called. The phone rang just as the rubber thing flew past on its latest voyage (they'd given up asking if I wanted another go).

'Good morning, ad sales.'

'Hello? Is that Steve?'

Her voice, like we were back in the restaurant. The words of a rescuer filtering down through the rubble.

'Emily?'

Two minutes later it was settled: the time, the place.

I spent an age agonising over what to wear, in my house two days later, as if people would be holding up scorecards, marking me out of ten.

I've always known that I don't suit pastels, which was a good starting point. They make me look vulnerable, like I should be taken advantage of in a prison setting, or brought to house parties by girls who will only ever be your friend.

Normally I'm a smart shirt and jeans type, nothing grand, but not scruffy either. And proper shoes, always polished, that's important. Trainers are for children, as my old man never tires of telling everyone. He would have got on well with Jack.

First it was a snug T-shirt to try to show off the hours spent in the gym while everyone else trawled the bars and bedrooms, before it dawned on me that Emily's dance partners propelled women through the air for a living. I didn't need to make that kind of impression. So, a suit then.

A suit? Come on, what was this, a business meeting?

I eventually plumped for a deep-red shirt and a new pair of jeans. Then I took that off, stood there in my shorts and socks, before putting it all back on again.

We'd arranged to meet at three o'clock in Leicester Square, on a bench in the little bit of greenery there. One of the worst parts of London, if you ask me, the capital's Benidorm. Strange place to kick things off, I suppose, but there you go. Maybe it was ironic.

I arrived first, sat there irritated by the crowds brushing past, like a squadron of bees throwing up doubt all around me like pollen. I was anxious, the back of my shirt slightly damp. I wanted to go home and have another shower. This wasn't an hour or two in a Thai joint, with friends around to bounce conversation off if you needed to, this was proper time spent in each other's company.

All that worrying, what does it achieve?

When she arrived, Emily kissed me on the cheek, held on to my arm and led me away. We had been lovers forever. Full Cinemascope.

Thankfully the afternoon was spent wandering the backstreets, not sitting opposite each other in a pub. I might have been found out, attempting to make a proper impression. Instead we sought out the interesting bits, tucked-away places, the city's murky history being overwhelmed by steel and glass. Real stories lost in the undergrowth.

We also dug up our own small piece of shared treasure: her family often used to holiday in Norfolk, as did mine, in villages separated by only a couple of inches on the map, although we as good as admitted that our paths probably never crossed. I don't recall my dad ever enjoying a round at one of the county's more exclusive golf clubs, content as he was to kick back and enjoy World Championship darts in the caravan I believe we rented about eight or nine hundred times.

But there may have been that one moment, outside a small bakery or a tourist office, as we sullenly dragged behind in our parents' wake. We settled for that.

First days are always the most stressful. School, university, new job – they each have that unique quality of otherness, of hours approaching that will need to be managed, people who must be deciphered and accommodated. But looking back, I can't picture that day without seeing Emily relaxed, laughing, holding on to me as if every moment could end up on a greeting card. She seemed to work hard at being happy. Perhaps a life of denial teaches you to squeeze every second.

The attraction of opposites, is that why it worked? Me, the poisoner, slipping minute traces of toxins into the collective bloodstream from my evil sales laboratory, breaking down the cells of a society already sick with desire. And then there are those like Emily, people who create, celebrate the intangible.

Jesus, listen to me. I was in deep.

I'm simply trying to manage your expectations; this series of placements will enhance your profile in the marketplace ten-fold.

There was one slight hiccup on that first day. Hardly worth mentioning.

Emily saw a top she really wanted in a small boutique around the back of Carnaby Street, but they didn't have it in her size. She pouted a little, was about to flounce, I think, but the girl behind the counter, clearly used to covering up for her employer's shortcomings when it came to stock control, took it all in her stride, possibly with a fist clenched behind her back. Emily was persuaded that she looked equally great in something very similar. We laughed about it later.

I put it down to her privileged background. Who was I to judge?

Piano lessons, private tutoring, art classes, drama – lots of drama – extra English. Enrolled at ballet school but allowed home some weekends. Horse-riding on Sunday mornings if time permitted, the borrowed animal cantering across a family friend's land, the bright lights of the city calling her back. And everything held together by the simple structure of dance, the one constant, underpinning the foundation of her teenage life. Emily in the centre of the web, feeling the sudden tug as something else landed nearby, prepared for her in advance, packaged and ready to be devoured. Ready to become part of her.

During our first dinner together she was wistful about the lack of long-lasting friendships while growing up. I appreciated her honesty; if anything, it made me more eager to fill the gap. Maybe she sensed that, overplayed it a little, the loneliness. That's what they do, isn't it, slowly break your heart, one story at a time.

Hers had not been a life punctuated by those easy days when you just hang out and do as little as possible, other than act stupidly and eat brightly coloured things that silently go to work on your teeth. She said she hadn't minded too much: sacrifices had to be made. She knew what was expected of her, what needed to be done. The pride of the family, so much riding on it.

I asked if she'd ever wanted to be anything else, but

she didn't answer. I wasn't sure she'd even heard me, so I let it go, and fell back on poking fun at another woman in the restaurant, sitting a couple of tables away with a much younger man. Her hair was stacked up like an extravagant dessert, once naturally blonde but now needing help. I felt bad when she looked over at us.

I confessed my ignorance to Emily about the whole dance thing, like she didn't already know.

'Are you well known?'

She speared a runner bean coated with a dark gravy. Sorry, *jus*.

'No, not really. Not yet,' she said, looking at her plate. 'But apparently I have a lot of potential. People keep telling me that. When I was doing ballet I was in the corps, obviously, but I knew people were already starting to talk about me. I was taken aside a couple of times, given a bit of praise. They don't really do that sort of thing in front of everyone else, but, you know, it meant something.'

I went to speak, but she cut me off. Almost defensive, the speech already prepared.

'It isn't what most people think, grand openings at the Royal Opera House, the big performances and everything. That's just what the media go for. There are plenty of other things happening, smaller companies, contemporary productions. For some people it's all ballet, ballet, ballet, which is ridiculous – they won't even look at modern dance.

'At the moment I'm contracted for eight weeks with a company in north London. We're doing a piece on human rights, written by this amazing guy from Chile. He's so talented, but most people wouldn't give him the time of day, what he's doing is just too controversial. It's not Covent Garden, but I don't care. There's more to life. And I'm classically trained, I practically grew up in ballet school. I can always go back to it.'

It was all there, everything I needed to know. Not just the steak that was a little raw. Her words buried among the polite thrum of conversation, the noise from the kitchen intruding on us when the door swung open. Black-trousered waiters dancing among the tables, their own rehearsed moves.

She was so matter-of-fact about her achievements; I would have been dead excited. She was breaking through, finding employment in what I soon came to appreciate is a highly competitive business where hard work and devotion are not always enough, not always rewarded. Yet they keep plugging away, prepared to damage their bodies, prepared to attempt the impossible. Whatever it takes.

At the time I was impressed by her coolness. I was sold. Discipline extended to the emotions, clearly.

Art is still a job: do the overtime, get the promotion. People forget that.

We kissed, later that night, on the street outside the flat she shared with another dancer, a posh girl who had about eight surnames. West Kensington, for heaven's sake. Even the pavement was extravagantly wide, like a European boulevard. I was an interloper.

I won't describe that first kiss. Who can?

I watched her climb the stone steps and push open the heavy door. She grinned back at me, framed like a portrait by the light from the entrance hall, the glossy red oak slowly shutting her in.

I stood there for a few minutes staring at the door, not a single thought troubling my empty head. As I turned to go I noticed a black glove on the pavement, its bent forefinger pointing away from the house, back the way we'd come. I looked at it, thinking maybe I should put it on a railing in case the owner came looking. Instead, I stepped over it and headed home.

I felt like I was in the basket of a hot-air balloon, the stillness deceptive. Dead air. Sooner or later she would tire of me, surely? I couldn't compete with her people, that background; perhaps I was merely a plaything, an amusement.

Should I jump while I still could?

I didn't, of course I didn't, and for the next few months I was condemned to the role of hormone-fuelled teenager. I looked forward to her daily phone calls, agreed without hesitation if she suggested going to an exhibition or a museum, and was generally compliant as she attempted – with some success – to inject a little sophistication into my life. Best of all were the fleeting moments we spent in my house, snatching precious time in between her endless rehearsals and performances; or the evenings when I went to the small theatre to watch her dance, feeling a little spaced out by the fact that my girlfriend was up there on stage and people who knew about these things liked what they saw.

And I won't deny that I enjoyed the looks we got, basked in the warm glow of having Emily Dashwood, future star, standing beside me as if she actually needed me to be there. I'm no premier-league conversationalist, despite what my job demanded of me, but at least when we were out and I couldn't avoid talking to strangers, the starting point, the middle and end, was Emily. She was all I needed. Christ.

I still can't look back and be okay with those days. Not yet. Like those images you see on the news, of people just before something terrible happens – a random murder or a natural disaster, some early-morning catastrophe on the commuter train from Guildford. They have no idea what's about to happen, sleepwalking through the routines they've grown comfortable with, enjoying their final thoughts. Watching the familiar world rush by.

I can't think of my other self, the salesman, lost for words among the wreckage.

7

I remembered where I'd seen him.

I was passing the same spot and it started coming back to me. I stopped and looked, like holding a divining rod over the past.

I was facing a pedestrian subway, staring right down into it, a stained concrete void. As I stood there trying to drag up the memory, a bloke in a suit, carrying a tan leather briefcase, slowed his pace right down like a mime act as he walked by. I think he was about to ask if I was okay, but I suppose he thought better of it, given what I was doing. The thousand-yard stare, only one can of cheap cider away from a sub-species, in his eyes. No doubt he was afraid of getting mugged – which is understandable, round here – or being caught in a stunt and ending up online. Still, nice of him to slow down.

The walkway was long, uninviting, and, with only one light left unbroken, faded into filthy darkness. But it didn't matter, I could still see Cyan. His face, and others, drifting half-formed out of the haze. Bringing old sounds with them. Harsh voices, a dog snarling.

It was a while back, months before. I was on my way home and had intended to go through the subway. But it was late, and the closer I got the more wary I became, to the extent that even as I was about to enter it I changed my mind and decided to go a different route. Bravery won't help much when they're circling the wagon.

But as I retreated I happened to glance back and see a

group of lads about halfway along, five or six of them, barely visible in their regulation black clothing. One was struggling to keep hold of a heavy chain, on the other end of which was a vicious-looking beast, a squat, angry ball of dark-brown muscle in a studded black collar. It kept rearing up on its hind legs, straining its neck against the leather, its young owner barely able to keep his grip.

One of the others had the lower part of his face covered with a piece of red material, like he was about to join a protest march. Price of broadband, maybe.

They were all facing one lad – Cyan, as I knew now – who stood with his back to the wall, everyone else having formed a tight, bristling semi-circle around him, a little knot of energy aching for release. At first it didn't seem as if anything too serious was going on, just kids hanging out, a bit of show, some well-rehearsed bravado.

At the time it occurred to me that the kid against the wall could be an up-and-coming leader, briefing the stormtroopers on his plan to take the next street corner. Whatever. It's not my life. But as I started to walk away something caught my eye, something out of place, through the tangle of legs.

An Adidas kit-bag, bright green. It was open on the ground, lying on its side like a gutted fish, the insides spilling out.

I was instantly curious. It's natural I suppose: who wouldn't want to know, deep down, if there was perhaps something in the bag for them, a place in that little gathering. Contraband, maybe, something sweet, forbidden.

I stepped back a few more paces and put my foot up on a low wall so I could fiddle with my shoelaces. One of the gang, picking up the scent – how do they do that? – looked out at me, his eyes set in their default mode of contempt. The cold glare of someone who has back-up. But, satisfied with what he had seen, he quickly lost interest and returned his attention to the negotiations, while I fussed with my laces.

As I watched, head bowed, the mood began to change. Gestures became more animated, words were spat, not spoken. Cyan had gone from potential leader to victim of a lynch mob, staring at the ground, at his feet, at the bag. He looked like he'd changed his mind about something, wanted to leave.

One of the group stepped forward and jabbed at Cyan's chest, an exaggerated movement, like he wished his finger was the barrel of a gun. He leant in close, as if issuing a warning, an ultimatum, before bending down and tipping the holdall completely upside down. The rest of the contents scattered everywhere but he was in no hurry, considering the objects like someone at a boot sale, convinced of treasure among the trash. I was too far away to see everything that had fallen from the bag; it looked like schoolbooks mostly, but it wasn't long before our angry friend lifted something from the debris. It was swiftly passed to other hands and secreted away into the depths of a huge, quilted coat.

The interrogator seemed to be taller now, his authority confirmed. He stood with his shoulders back, smug and scowling. Then he leant in once more, but Cyan still couldn't look at him; he had the downcast expression of the bullied, the tormented, forced to hear yet more syncopated threats from the troupe surrounding him.

And then it was all over, the gang dispersing quickly – two disappeared down the far end of the tunnel, while the others, one trying to restrain his now hysterical dog, swaggered in my direction like I was shooting a music video for them. I froze. I couldn't pretend to still be doing up my shoelaces, and no way was I getting my mobile out to fake a call. Might as well just toss them my wallet as well, give them my bank details.

Luckily they had other priorities. Mission accomplished, they needed only to be somewhere, anywhere, else. They knew they didn't have to worry about me as a witness, not in this postcode. I released the air from my lungs, felt the pounding in my chest begin to ease.

Back in the tunnel, Cyan was stuffing the rest of his belongings back into the bag. When he had finished he seemed uncertain about which way to go, or even about what had just happened. He looked dazed, numb, everything you'd expect. But upset as well, trying to hold himself together. Thinking of things he should have said, perhaps, words that flow easier when the moment has passed. The wisdom of the stairwell.

He looked out and saw me, a stranger, standing there under the streetlights, and it seemed to make his mind up for him. He turned swiftly and began walking in the other direction, the blackness enveloping him like a cloak. I watched him disappear.

Now, months later, replaying the incident over in my mind, I felt sorry for him. Who wouldn't? But at the same time I respected him for coming to the dojo. He wanted to do something about it, make a stand – and I wasn't about to reveal his secret. There are victims in every classroom, every walk of life; was there anything to be gained by me getting involved, telling Jack what I'd seen like some little gossip-monger poking around to get a story going? He could make up his own mind about the boy's potential, as well as his weaknesses. The last thing he needed to hear from my lips was something to taint his opinion, make him doubt what we'd seen.

So I let it go, didn't say a word. Cyan could work out his problems at the club, learn how to defend himself. Jack would help him with that.

8

'Haven't seen you in a while. Everything okay?'

'Fine. Been a bit busy.'

I'd started judo classes again. Back on the mat two nights a week, knackered, hurting. Everything I'd missed.

But I'd slipped up, already. Missed a couple of lessons. One because I had a cold, the other because Emily took me to see a play. She bought the tickets without telling me; there was no getting out of it. Whatever the reasons, I knew Jack wasn't impressed. But now I was back, raring to go.

'Sorry about last week,' I said. 'Something came up.'

I didn't bother to make up an excuse. I couldn't say I'd been tied up at work, he knew how much I hated the place, so I said nothing. I didn't mention her name. And there was no way he'd bring it up – Jack preferred to confront things by leaving them alone, let people figure it out themselves.

I'd been seeing Emily all the time, either grabbing an hour when we could, or going out for dinner, a drink, something cultural if she could persuade me. And whereas I once couldn't keep away from the club in my spare time, now I couldn't keep away from her. But I didn't think it would matter; I just wasn't there every day, hanging around like I had been doing.

It turned out to be a tough class that evening, with a heavy session of *randori* – floor work – at the end. It's sort of like sparring in boxing, and extremely tiring. You're not repeating certain techniques over and over, like throws and falls, just fighting with different partners. I tried to appease Jack by asking one of the most experienced guys at the club to practise with me; after all, you're supposed to ask senior players, else how are you going to learn? And he didn't go easy on me. If I were being paranoid I might have thought Jack told him to let me have it; either way, I was battered and bruised at the end. I couldn't get anywhere near the bloke, and by the end of it I was dizzy with having been tossed around so much, spending most of my time pinned to the mat, subjected to various elbow locks. He was stony-faced as we bowed to each other, then partnered up with someone else.

I'd had enough, and went downstairs to shower. Afterwards I looked in at the gym, said hello to a couple of the guys. By then the class upstairs had finished and I wanted Jack to come in, to act like nothing was wrong, so I'd know we were still alright. But he didn't come down. I didn't get the chance to explain myself, to tell him I'd lied earlier, when he asked me how I was.

Everything was not okay.

A few days before, I had arranged to meet Emily at lunchtime in a café near her rehearsal studio in Islington. I arrived early, like a good boy, and when I was about fifty yards away could see her sitting out front with someone else. I assumed he was a dancer, but as I approached something made me hesitate. I hung back and watched them: the easy laughter, the casual touching – hunched close like a couple of conspirators.

That was how we were together; it was like looking

at us.

I walked past, pretending to look in shop windows. Why shouldn't she be out enjoying herself with someone else, who just happened not to be a girl? I was being possessive already, holding a blade against the throat of our relationship.

I wasted some time, then returned to the café. He was still there. As I approached, Emily got up and gave me a hug.

'Steve, I want you to meet Alex. I've known him for, well, forever.'

Alex stood up and we shook hands. 'Good to meet you Steve.'

There was a bit of small talk but he didn't hang around, said he had to be somewhere. I caught the waitress's attention as I sat down.

'I'll have an apple juice please,' said Emily. 'One coffee is enough for me.'

'Been here a while?'

'Yes I have, actually. Our choreographer got called into an urgent meeting halfway through rehearsal, so we're having a very rare break. No doubt the production is running out of money and we'll all be unemployed by the time I get back.'

She laughed. I wondered what it must feel like, the thought that if the work stopped for a while it didn't really matter, you could always curl up in the comforting warmth of your family, wait for something else to come along. By the time our drinks arrived I could feel a bad mood descending.

'Your other friends not here?'

Emily's eyebrows bunched together. 'No – I told

them I was meeting you. Is everything okay Steve?'

'Yep, fine.'

I was being defensive, the familiar mechanism turning. I shouldn't have been there, the situation was ridiculous. She would soon get bored of me and I'd end up back where I'd started. I would go crawling back to the club, try to convince Jack, promise not to miss a single class. Maybe it was too late, and he had seen right through me. You don't waste opportunities, not in his world.

We chatted for a while, this and that. Emily told me a little about Alex, the bare bones. They'd been at ballet school together, but he'd dropped out and now worked as a physiotherapist out in the sticks. Next thing I knew, she was nudging my arm.

'Are you listening to me?' she asked.

'Sorry. What were you saying?'

'I was asking if you're free tomorrow night.'

I paused. I wanted to be with her, to go where she wanted to go, I really did. I could almost taste the words as they crawled stubbornly from my mouth.

'Can't. Sorry. I have a class.'

'Right,' she said. 'Of course. Well, never mind.'

Sometimes I felt as if I'd stumbled into the wrong town, that I should always have one hand poised over my holster, just in case. It was no way to be.

'How about lunch on Friday?' she asked. 'My treat.'

'Well, Emily, as you know, I only ever drink champagne on Fridays.'

She grinned. 'Strange, I hadn't noticed.'

'I'm good at hiding it. Got a bottle stashed in my desk at the office. Popping the cork quietly is a challenge, but, you know, a loud cough does the trick.'

She reached forward, took hold of my hand.

'Champagne it is then. Which should be quite fitting, hopefully.'

She was holding onto my fingers, caressing them like worry beads. 'I've had an idea.'

'Really? I'm intrigued. Want to give me a clue?'

'No. It's a surprise. It's why I was meeting Alex today.'

I conjured up a smile, squeezed the hand that held mine, our fingers intertwined. It was time for me to go, to make an exit while I could still look cheerful and be vaguely affectionate. Maybe it wasn't her fault; maybe I was supposed to learn new rules, for a different league.

We got up, and I waited while Emily put her cardigan on and got her stuff together. We hugged. I held her for longer than she probably expected, but she didn't resist.

'I'll see you on Friday,' she said, when I eventually let her go. 'Don't be late.'

'I won't. You just make sure that bottle is chilled.'

She turned and headed back to the rehearsal room. I watched her go, then went in the opposite direction. I would have done anything just to sit there for the afternoon, screw the office. The rest of the day was about to drag; I'd have to dig deep, pretend there was some point in me being there.

I checked my watch at the crossing, realised I was going to be late. When the lights changed I moved quickly, side-stepping to avoid the people walking towards me. I didn't look at any of the faces, but when I got to the other side I stopped.

He didn't look up, despite the fact that I was standing stock-still no more than ten yards away. Sitting in another café, drinking another coffee, in no hurry to 'be somewhere'. He was deep into a book, staring at it a little too intently, perhaps, engrossed – or was that my imagination too?

II

DENIAL

9

Emily tapped the screen with her forefinger.

'How about here?'

I shrugged.

'Maybe. I guess so. Why that place?'

'Alex says it's nice, he lives nearby. He could show us around.'

It was all there. Everything I needed to know. Buried.

'Do you have to do that?' I asked.

'What?'

'That. Touching the screen.'

I pulled the sleeve of my jumper over my finger, dabbing at an almost invisible smudge on the laptop. I'd cleaned the house from top to bottom before Emily arrived, my hands desperate for something to do, my brain craving order. I was unsettled, but excited.

'Is this how it's going to be?' she asked. 'Admonishing me every time I leave my bra on the back of the bathroom door?'

I sighed, mock gravitas.

'No, because bras are fun, so they basically don't count. Other stuff, such as general detritus or the non-appearance of fresh coffee at my bedside on a Sunday morning, is a different matter entirely. If you neglect these areas the punishment will be ruthless and memorable, and will act as a genuine deterrent. And if you carry on using words like "admonishing", you'll also be in a load of bother. Be warned.'

Emily's eyes moved from the screen to me, as if fascinated by a small bug.

'But words like "detritus" are okay, is that what you're saying?'

'Yeah, it is. My rules.'

She was frowning, looking right into me.

'Nob.'

She pecked me on the cheek. I barely felt it. A tiny bird.

Everything was happening so quickly. Her idea – which she explained to me without champagne – was to buy a place together. It came completely out of the blue, I had to bluff my way through it so as not to appear uncertain – maybe the only useful skill my job had taught me. I ladled the enthusiasm on thickly, tried to extinguish my doubts, but it was only over the following days that I managed to half convince myself. I was earning decent money, and between us we could scrape a deposit together, especially if I made a bit on my place. So why not? Be decisive for once.

That hold she had over me, like I wasn't in control of my own thoughts. I couldn't help myself. I was possessive, but at the same time possessed. Barely able to focus on anything else.

She brought up the subject while we had lunch in Hyde Park, sitting in the café next to the Serpentine. Wildlife causing havoc around us, strung-out parents watching every move. All that anxiety: never allowed to switch off, an unremitting electric current, the humming of nerves.

Emily was twitchy, dying to tell me. And when she

did I knew it could only go one way. Maybe there was a hint of relief as I agreed to start looking for houses, see what was out there. But it wasn't what I wanted, not one hundred per cent. Despite my efforts, I think she sensed something, but chose to ignore it.

I hadn't even met her parents, and the situation was bound to concern them; the speed of it, who I was, all that. But she didn't seem to care. There had always been something unspoken between the two of us, like those holidays in Norfolk, an acknowledgement of our differing backgrounds. I wasn't the type they would have chosen, not their first choice by a long way. In fact I wouldn't have figured in their calculations at all, but why poke the slumbering beast?

'So,' she said, returning to the map, finger deliberately teasing the space near my screen. 'A Sussex village is not objectionable to you?'

'I guess not. Good commuter links, decent pubs I imagine, a short trip down to the stadium of the gods. It might be the perfect spot, only with loads of off-road vehicles. Mind you, at least they'll have proper mud on them, not phony transfers like the ones your Chelsea friends stick on their Range Rovers.'

I'd meant it as a joke. That was all.

'I don't have any so-called "Chelsea friends", thank you very much.' A flash of steel, not in my imagination. Something cutting the air.

'Yeah you do. Maybe not specifically from Chelsea, but your dancing pals weren't exactly hauled from the barrios were they?'

'That's not fair Steve, I can't help where they come from. And for your information, there are plenty of dancers from deprived backgrounds.'

Of course there are. I backed off. A mound in the dirt with wires sticking out of it.

Hold your nerve, cut the right one. Green or red? Breathe.

'Fine,' I said. 'Sorry. I thought you liked me as your bit of rough, that's all.'

She manoeuvred herself into my lap, limbs everywhere, like a Hindu deity. Warm breath, lips sweet from Coca-Cola, and the perfume I still catch sometimes in the street, even now, a phantom presence.

'True,' she said. 'And if we move to the country, you might end up labouring in the fields, coming home all hot and bothered.'

'You're not so keen when I get back from the gym like that.'

She nuzzled the side of my face. 'That's different. You'd be a provider, breaking your back for me all day long.'

I kissed her.

'I'll give him a call tomorrow,' she said.

'Who?'

'Alex. For God's sake Steve, I mentioned him, oh, let's see, about five minutes ago. Before your little rant about that precious computer screen.'

'Right. Of course. And that wasn't a rant. It was … something else.'

She wasn't listening. She eased herself off me and began checking her kit bag. She'd be leaving soon for rehearsal, something new. They were reworking Shakespeare, *A Midsummer Night's Dream*, I think it was. The company had extended her contract for this new production, given her a bigger role, and there was a chance they might tour. Plus it was the Bard, so Mummy was pacified, although Emily hadn't broken it to her yet that it was another one of those modern interpretations, the set made out of giant Perspex boxes. Even I laughed out loud when she said it was set in Nebraska. That went down really well; I felt myself drop a couple of rungs on the ladder of civilisation.

I had the rest of the day to myself, but was at a loose end. Filling the whole afternoon could be a problem. A couple of hours in the gym, of course, but what else? There were no judo competitions on to go and watch, I'd already checked.

I was trying to be positive, for her sake. I'd always known that one day I'd end up in the countryside, just not so soon. I'd kept it to myself, because where I worked that sort of non-urban state of mind marked you out as a bit of a freak. Concrete and cocktails was the general philosophy, whereas I grew up on the coast, and that small-town feeling doesn't leave you, no matter how far you think you've come.

We would be living somewhere nicer though. I hadn't been in my place long, but already I knew it was a mistake. I kidded myself that I could fit in, and that my attempts to be friendly weren't a handicap, something to be exploited by feral creatures who stared defiantly at me as I walked home from work through the estate (they were never around in the mornings), waiting for me to be stupid enough to stare back. They could sense that I wasn't one of them, even when I tried to look moody.

My house squatted in the middle of a row of tired-looking 1930s buildings next to the estate, and it was quicker to walk through sniper alley to get to it than to take the road that went round the back. Plus if somebody spotted me going the long way home they'd know I had The Fear. It would be fatal.

For a long time I had done my best to accept the continual noise outside, which at night became a no-go zone, the prison-compound atmosphere punctuated by shrieks, squealing tyres and the occasional siren, all ricocheting back off the walls of the tower blocks built to contain us. Harder to ignore was the regular tapping on my window, courtesy of the little tyrants who came to bother people in what they inexplicably viewed as the 'posh houses'. They all had the look of innocence when I opened the door, delighting in the sheer thrill of tormenting the man who had a strange job and didn't sit out front drinking like their mums and dads. And I could only imagine what they would think if they stepped inside, everything looking like it had never been used. That really would have been the end for me. As it was, I began to obsess more and more about privacy and found myself working out at the gym whenever I could, burning off the hatred, building up my defences.

The power of those children was seemingly without limit, like in some weird horror film. If they wanted to kick a ball against my wall for an hour, or keep knocking at the door to ask if my non-existent dog wanted to come out to play, I was expected to rein in my frustration, put on my gang face, pretend I was part of the game. No way was I allowed to threaten one of the little terrorists; that would only get me pushed up against the wall, humiliated by one of their goon fathers.

I wore a tie during daylight hours, which probably

marked me out as a potential police informant, and I preferred decent beer and the occasional vegetable to sunset-yellow alcosugar and two courses for a fiver. Was I becoming a snob, turning my back on 'my' people? Possibly, but it was their fault, those garrisoned lunatics with their barbecues that smelt of petrol, their unbreachable class barriers.

Emily and I, sitting at the computer together, the maps, the estate agents, the floor-plans and furnishings – it was a break for freedom. It had to be.

She returned from the living room and put her pink mobile on the kitchen table.

'We're seeing him next weekend.'

As easy as that. Let's all meet up, pub lunch, somewhere nice. Get a feel for the area.

'Really? He's a bit keen.'

'I know. I told him what we were looking for and he's going to pick up some details about properties. I think he's excited about us being neighbours.'

'Neighbours? Steady on.'

She sensed my anxiety. Like the thugs outside picking up a scent.

'Does he have a boyfriend?'

A crass weapon, my blunt blade.

'You,' said Emily, approaching me slowly and prodding my chest, 'sound a little jealous. Admit it Mr Hollis, you are, aren't you?'

'Rubbish,' I lied. 'I just wondered, you know, what with him being a dancer once and everything.'

'Oh I see, of course. Because footballers are so much more manly, right? No hidden secrets from the lads in the dressing room, eh? No fashion tips, no sharing the conditioner. "Ooh, is that jojoba?" All one hundred per cent above board.'

She laughed, standing defiantly, one hand on her hip. I had been reduced to my basic components.

'Tell you what,' she continued, 'I'll see if Alex can squeeze you in for one of his deep-tissue massages. Maybe you'll relax a bit, perhaps even bond a little. Would you like that Steve?'

The good ship *Envy* was taking in water, tossed around, harbour walls receding into the distance.

I decided not to rise to it, to act maturely (never my strongest hand). I closed the laptop and went to the fridge in search of something comforting. A bottle of beer, that reliable phallic support system for men like me. I took a proper swig, like they do in films.

'I'm very much looking forward to seeing your friend again,' I said, wiping my mouth with the back of my hand. 'I'm sure it will be an absolute pleasure to spend some time with him.'

She couldn't help herself, collapsing into laughter. I sucked hard at the anaesthetic.

'I'm off,' she said, grabbing her stuff from the floor. 'The guys want to bake some cupcakes before we put the hours in. You know how it is.'

It's a skill she had. Mocking, but still holding my hand, leading me. But to where exactly? I didn't know, of course, but I would have gone anywhere.

She called from the front door, me still leaning against the kitchen worktop, perfecting my stubbornness.

'See you tomorrow.'

'See ya,' I mumbled.

Try again, or you'll regret it.

'Bye,' I said, louder now, moving out of the kitchen. 'See you later. Have fun.'

I went to the window, watched her step lightly through the litter towards the communal recreation area, where a group of hooded gentlemen were no doubt expressing their ongoing concerns about the stability of the Eurozone. She seemed to transform the wasteland, in her baggy sweatshirt that reached down over tight black leggings. Hard muscle hidden beneath, carrying her with a feline suppleness. Those nearly-men were in the presence of something they couldn't possibly understand.

One of them called out to her, standing there in urban wear that looked more like pyjamas, baseball cap to the side, an unreadable logo on the front of it, some kind of code. He filled his palm with his crotch as Emily passed. I knew he wouldn't last five minutes down at the club, but could never admit that to himself. Wouldn't even dream of taking on the challenge, too scared of being exposed.

I often wished I could talk to them, those skulking figures waiting for the dark. Make some kind of connection; tell them about the things we do, how hard it is. People going far beyond their limits, drawing on reserves of stamina they didn't know they had, teasing out that last bit of strength. The sensei shouting harsh encouragement from the edge of the mat, urging his pupils to go further than they ever thought possible. I wanted to tell them about the months, the years, of dedication to something you believe in, a way of life that you're happy to subscribe to, and which teaches you everything you need to know. Describe to them how it feels to be ready, finally, to be judged, to put yourself on the line, test yourself against a line-up of opponents. Forcing them to the ground, one by one, more strength sapped with every move, every combination. And all that just so you can change the colour of your belt.

But no, you're right, hanging around in your jim-jams and talking South Central is where it's at.

Emily glanced behind at our friend but kept walking. Smiling. Her weapon.

The lad made another gesture with his hand, still hopeful of charming her, then sat back down on the swing. One of his mates was grinning, the empty bluster of the terminally lost. They watched her disappear behind the launderette, heading towards the Tube station. I willed them to stay on the swings, to remain in their little dominion like good children.

Do not follow her.

The moment passed in an orchestrated performance of cigarettes and spitting, the comfort of ritual. I relaxed, put my half-full bottle on the coffee table, then went to the bedroom to get my kit.

10

Alex began seeping into my thoughts over the next couple of days, like water collecting, turning its host to rust. I told myself he was just a friend, someone who could help us, like friends are supposed to. On the other hand, it wasn't as if we were emigrating to the Urals. This was something we could handle ourselves, surely?

Perhaps she was right; perhaps I was jealous.

To try to take my mind off him I sought refuge in my job. That was a first. I even put in a few extra hours, managing to secure a new account worth twelve grand for the rest of the financial year. I almost felt like one of the team.

On Thursday we had our regular mag meeting, a jamboree of simmering tension, pen-tapping and oversized cappuccinos. Representatives from the editorial and sales teams – mutual enemies since fish first crawled onto dry land – always got together with the publishing director after one issue had been put to bed and the next production schedule was about to begin.

A ticker-tape parade of over-embellished achievements; oiled-up muscle-flexing on office podiums. The relentless beat of profit, targets, projections, then more profit, just for good measure.

All that cutting and thrusting. It's like a duel, both combatants back to back in the first light of the forest, unable to back down, and yet unwilling to admit that if they kill their adversary they doom themselves. A weirdly symbiotic relationship where each species mistrusts the other but knows they have to co-exist. Was I the only one who saw it that way? Sitting there with my mug of tea, making other plans.

I suppose the meeting went well. We'd had an extremely successful month, way beyond expectations, so we all stroked each other and I singled out one of my people, Aaron, for special praise. It was part of my job description. Sometimes it was even my decision as to who got their fifteen minutes; other times I received an email in advance from upstairs about who the golden child needed to be. Aaron was new – a junior classified sales assistant, his first job in the media bubble – so this was like a welcome mat.

Step into our world. Honours degree in oceanography? Never mind, forget everything you've learnt, it's not needed here.

I glanced out of the meeting-room window and saw him reading the Tottenham FC website, unaware that he was being watched. Golden child my arse.

On the opposite side of our table, Glenn, the editor, had to have his lap around the stadium. The pride in his voice was unmistakable, going way beyond the work itself, like it really, really meant so much to him. The magazine was his life, and he was defensive about everything connected with it. I could imagine him still there in years to come, after the publication had finally been shut down, gazing across dust-covered desks while still purring silky words of encouragement, hearing the tap, tap, tapping of keyboards long since packed away.

I took a gulp of tea, and noticed that Aaron was now

on the phone. Despite my deep reservations about all things spiritual, I had to acknowledge that Jesus had, in fact, quite possibly descended and contrived to work one of his miracles. With my next thought, however, I conceded that the chances of Aaron's phone call being work-related were marginal. For a few seconds I felt an unfamiliar sensation: vague affection towards a fellow worker. Because, if I were in Aaron's position and everyone else was sucking tongues in the meeting room, I would no doubt do exactly what he was doing – naff all.

I think I may have been smiling, judging by the way Chris, the sales director and therefore my boss, was looking at me. Having said that, our Chris was more than partial to a hit of something extra-curricular before those meetings – *'Puts me right in the zone, Steve'* – so his mind could well have been marching in a few different directions. What a joke that place was.

I dragged myself back to the proceedings, only to find that Glenn was still droning on. I sighed, my mug now empty.

'I'm especially pleased about Jenni's interview with Ian Jackson from One Stone Communications,' he said, opening up fully now like he'd accidentally got through to the Samaritans. 'He was very reluctant to talk to us, but really gave up some gold about the company's prospects going forward. I'm amazed she got it all out of him. So much so that I'm putting her forward for this month's Frontline Award.'

Ah yes, the Frontline Awards. The publishing company that owned our mag also owned four others, and every month an outstanding member of staff, chosen from between all the departments, became the lucky recipient of a bottle of cheap bubbly and a voucher to the tune of twenty-five quid. That's what you got either for conning people over lunch, or leaving the trenches with a fully loaded dictaphone. If you stayed at the company long enough they'd get round to you eventually, that was pretty much guaranteed: prize-giving days for every boy and girl.

Incredibly, I was once chosen as the winner, for one particular month when I pulled in an advert from a supplier who was deemed impossible to lure. I did my best to enthuse about the plonk, which tasted like someone had pissed in a barrel of weed killer, but the promised token never materialised. A neat little microcosm of the company, I suppose.

I felt like a jungle explorer on a flimsy rope bridge, gaping reptile jaws in the water below me, prehistoric brains willing me to fall.

I eventually left the meeting with a head full of new targets and returned to my desk, feeling more trapped than ever before. The sound of ringing phones filled the office like a plague of chirruping locusts.

Sunday took its time arriving, but when it did it was a scorcher, even though we were only in April. It was as if all the coming days of summer had been rolled into a ball, doused in petrol and set alight.

Emily and I drove south with the sunroof open and the windows down, her hair twisting freely in the wind. I couldn't stop glancing at her; she could probably tell. She looked relaxed and happy, content with life. Like we'd reached a turning point, a meaningful junction on our journey together.

As if to complement her mood, our surroundings gradually changed, with fewer houses spread out along the roads, many partially hidden by trees. A lot of them had ancient beams, set in proper old brickwork. We were in a forgotten land of tiny villages, where everyone had rose bushes.

'This is the place,' Emily said, pointing to a country pub up ahead. I pulled into the car park and killed the engine. I was about to speak but she was already getting out.

'There he is.'

She pointed into the garden, towards the only table that wasn't fully occupied. Alex was reading a magazine, a half-empty pint glass in front of him. Before I'd even locked the doors Emily was weaving her way among the busy tables as if she'd forgotten I was there.

I watched as he got up, obviously pleased to see her. They kissed and hugged, exchanged a few words, then hugged again. That easy way they had with each other. Emily turned around, looking puzzled, as if wondering why I wasn't right behind her. She said something to Alex and they grinned at each other. Friends forever.

I got a round in, coming back to find an Ordnance Survey map spread over our table. I drank half my pint in one go, then began scraping a bit of dirt from the table with the edge of a beer mat. Emily put her hand on my leg, brought me back.

'Okay,' said Alex. 'Down to business.'

I didn't know what to make of him, couldn't tell whether he was putting on a sunny disposition just for my benefit. I tried to let my concern go, knowing it would manifest itself in other ways, at least until I could figure out the rules. He wasn't a camp ex-dancer, just a normal one, which didn't help.

I knew he'd left the dance game early, but I didn't like to ask why. Maybe he was just no good. He'd used the experience and contacts to get retrained as a physiotherapist, doing well for himself tending to all those crocked rugger boys out in Sussex. I bet they strutted confidently into his converted spare bedroom, polo-shirt collar turned up, but feeling that first pang of apprehension when they saw the massage table. Something they didn't want to admit to, perhaps. The touch of a man, all professional of course, and the wife knows. One or two extra sessions wouldn't hurt though. The pain's gone, but you can't be too careful.

Alex quickly put my lack of focus, my shunning of ambition, into sharp relief. Not an exceptionally difficult task, I will admit. The thing about being around people whose livelihoods depend on positive energy is that it's always on show, making you feel like you should be doing a lot more, that what you put in you get out, all that. The kind of thing that's always drummed into you at corporate team-building days, except you don't feel the same urge to walk up to the enthusiastic guy down the front and shoot him in the face.

Within half an hour of meeting Alex again I decided that I would step up my visits to the gym and really knuckle down with the judo. I even thought that I could set up a new business if we moved, cutting people's grass, something like that. There had to be thousands of affluent country couples who couldn't be bothered to tend their own lawns, so why not pay me to do it for them? How hard could it be to push a mower around? I could learn about horticulture, maybe even do a course. Grab a spade, dig my way out of sales.

In an effort to break the ice, I suggested a football team that Alex could support. Bournemouth. Not the finest team ever to grace the leagues, but south coast, which meant we could have a little banter. He said okay, he'd keep an eye out for the scores. That was it.

'We're heading here,' he said, his finger on the map, beer glasses acting as paperweights against the occasional drifts of a warm breeze that barely troubled the pub garden. The place was really busy, full of boisterous families with their well-adjusted offspring; dads tucking into steak-and-ale pies, mums toying with the idea of sneaking off home to bring up the grilled-prawn salad.

'There are a few villages I think you'll love, Emily, and I've got details of eight properties from three different agents.'

She was leaning against him as we looked down upon the contours, all the little symbols denoting parish churches, historic buildings, roads too small to have numbers.

'You're a star,' she said. 'We're so grateful.'

And she meant it, the gratitude.

How perfect it all was.

Everywhere we went was like stepping into a painting. Constable – wasn't he the one for pastoral scenes? We kept finding ourselves in locations that seemed to have evaded the industrial revolution: great pubs, tiny butcher's shops, post offices, all propping up the rural way of life, and people who said hello to you in the street even though you'd never met. Some kind of common humanity that I assumed had long since disappeared. It made me realise I hadn't visited my parents in ages, hadn't bothered to leave the city.

I suddenly wanted to live in a place where I could get to know everyone, be part of a community. Go on litter drives and not be laughed at by some kid leaning against his scooter, flicking a cigarette nub in my general direction.

Emily was enraptured, like she'd found the missing piece of the jigsaw. If I was curious as to why she would want to move away, to leave the cocoon of west London, I didn't ask. We were setting up home together, why jeopardise it?

One place in particular stood out. A two-bedroom cottage, the fourth property we looked at. And of course our visit coincided with the spring village fete. Perhaps Alex had arranged that as well. It was a glorious setting, all tug-of-war and Pimm's tents, the whole thing kicked off by a little speech from the local celeb – a TV presenter – gushing about her love for the rustic way of life, how it had kept her grounded in a world that seemed to have lost its way. Right on, sister.

I remember watching that tug-of-war, mesmerised by the rag hanging limply in between the two straining teams. First a couple of feet in one direction, then slowly forced the other way, until one team began to get the upper hand. Everyone cheered when it was over.

After standing outside the cottage, which looked perfect for us, we took a short walk down one of the many lanes that reached out from the village like veins across the body of the countryside. Makes you wonder if all this green-belt erosion is actually a myth: there seemed to be a hundred trees for every building. It wasn't long, however, before I said to Emily that we should leave; I'd heard too many horror stories about people trying to move, the heartache. If it went wrong and we couldn't get the house, I didn't want a stack of memories to take away with me. She thought that was sweet.

'Okay, but look up there first,' she said, pointing towards something behind me. I turned and squinted into the distance.

'Over there. I want us to walk up it together, one of the first things we do.'

When my eyes adjusted to the sunlight I realised what we were looking at. A hill, heavily wooded. A local landmark no doubt, like a far-off land, still overgrown. I was surprised I hadn't noticed it.

For centuries it would have watched over the daily life of the village: every stagecoach depositing strangers at The Royal Oak, every joyful couple that came blinking into the sunshine from the tiny church next to the pond, every funeral that separated them.

Emily took my hand; I leant forward and kissed her. Alex looked away.

'I'll phone the estate agent tomorrow,' I said.

She threw her arms around my neck, whispered thank you, thank you, in my ear. We started heading back, towards the happy throng on the green, towards, maybe, a new life.

But the happiness wouldn't last, of course, at least not for much longer.

I should have known.

11

Life turns on a moment. The good, the bad – it's a question of balance. Always. But you don't plan on things going wrong, sparks on the screeching rails, the shock of impact.

Just one drink. Thank God. She probably said to me, laughing, poking my arm, 'Have another, go on.' I don't remember.

But no, just the one. Stay under the radar.

I'd wanted more, I'll admit it. One of those evenings, struggling to seem interested. I hadn't even wanted to come out, but Emily wouldn't listen to my protests. Her friends were irritating, with their excited chatter: supposedly famous names I didn't recognise, labels hung on people I couldn't care less about. They were like crows, gathered to squawk over life-changing topics – the new avant garde, who was holding back contemporary dance, who was cutting-edge. The weirder the better, as far as I could make out. I would never understand.

All that energy, normally so refreshing, seems banal if it catches you off-guard, every sentence a variation on what I'd heard enough times already.

I wasn't in the right frame of mind – the stranger again, unable to make myself fit. I had little to say, no contributions to make. Maybe it was noticed, remarked upon. Afterwards, when the phone calls started. *Have you heard what happened? Oh my God. I can't believe it.*

'Another drink?'

It might have been her, or someone else. Either way, I said no again, no thanks.

We left the bar early. It would be at least half an hour's drive back across town to my house, and we never stayed at her place, even though it was usually closer. Emily had the following day off, a rare thing, and we'd planned to get up early, make the most of the time together. Go to Spitalfields Market and browse the stalls, then eat giant burgers, proper ones, maybe a lunchtime beer.

But it turns on a moment. You don't give it much thought when you're young, there are so many moments to choose from, so many to casually discard. Plenty more on the way if you make a mistake, don't worry about it, they're lining up. There's always time to make amends.

She was off-hand with me, her evening dampened by my attitude, or something else. A word out of place maybe, or my silence. She hadn't said no, no thanks, to the third drink, or the fourth. Who could blame her? A couple of nights away from the stifling pressure, all that back-breaking work. *Run through it again; now do it again. Again. Feel the passion. Try to look like you mean it for once. I'm wasting my time, everyone, wasting my time.*

As soon as Emily got in the car she cranked the CD player up loud, too loud, but didn't seem to be into the music. Sitting perfectly still, staring out the window as the city went by. I didn't make it to the end of the first track. As my hand moved forward she grabbed it, telling me I was so sensible. I turned it down anyway.

The senses. She started talking about the senses, about being open to everything. If I went deaf I'd always be desperate to have my hearing back, she said, like having a limb torn off. And what if I went blind, had I thought of that? Of course, I replied. Who hasn't? She was rambling, muttering words I couldn't hear. It was my turn to be irritated.

She reached across. Fingers together, palm flat, in front of my face. Turned upwards, like a shield, to blind me. So I would know what it's like. I didn't see it coming.

'Emily, for Christ's sake!' I shouted, grabbing her wrist.

There was something wrong, the way she was behaving. A different Emily, a stranger. Humming along to the music now, but quietly, a little girl with a nursery-rhyme.

The hand suddenly darted back again, all part of the game. But this time she grabbed the steering wheel with the other, as if to defy me, the car swerving towards the white lines, me struggling to right it. Part of that game, the one where the rules had been kept from me. She pushed again at the wheel, more forceful this time.

Laughter, I can still hear her laughter. High and wild, but joyless, defiant. Sometimes it wakes me up.

I remember calling out, but not what I said. There weren't any real words, just a sound, something primal. The time I was given was too short, and I was busy trying to see, turning my head to one side, before it was too late.

But it was, of course it was. Too late.

You don't brace yourself for impact. Not if you don't see it coming.

She must have though. The white van approaching,

our car veering across the road to meet it. Did the driver flash his headlights, or try to avoid us? He didn't hit the horn, definitely no time for that.

There was a brief moment, maybe a couple of seconds, where I knew what was happening but not where I was. An emptiness, a total lack of anything physical, of anything remotely like sensation. As if you step outside your body. Jack must have felt something similar, taking a punch from a Royal Marine. Like falling through space, or being hit by a horse.

And the noise. An explosion, followed by the sound of things shattering. Glass, bits of plastic, casings. Fragments tinkling to the ground, almost musical, a gentle finale. Then the stillness, except now you know exactly where you are and what you've done. The silence is inside you.

She sprained her wrist, I would find out later, as her hand flew from the steering wheel and into the windscreen. But there was more than that. I knew it as soon as I turned to look at her. She was leaning into the seat, facing me, but at a strange angle, cheek pressed against the headrest.

Like someone relaxing, taking it easy – only expressionless. Eyes open. She could have been anywhere, the shock of it.

'Emily,' I said. 'Emily. Are you okay?'

She didn't reply. Didn't move.

I turned to get out, but a face at the window made me jump. He was angry, but that quickly subsided when he saw me. The panic in my eyes, I couldn't hide it. His van was practically unscathed, one of those models that have extravagant bars across the bumper in case you hit a moose, or perhaps a wolf, wandering through a busy English city. Or a careless driver.

Don't admit liability, the small print always tells you. Say as little as possible. Let the lawyers deal with it.

'It was my fault mate,' I blabbed as I got out. 'I'm really sorry. It was my fault.' Walking away from him, around the back of the car. The pulsating flash of his hazard lights in all the shop windows, the hiss of my broken radiator, like it was ashamed of me. The bonnet bent and contorted, a useless piece of tinfoil.

Everything so vivid; I'd never be allowed to forget.

Other cars began pulling over, offering help to the van driver, amplifying the situation, my guilt. They saw where my car was positioned in the road, had already made up their minds.

I didn't blame her, later, or tell anyone what she'd done. The girl who temporarily blinded me.

I heard sirens. He must have made the call while I was busy with Emily. Crouched beside the open door, holding her unresponsive hand. A wave of paralysing heat moved across my body: she hadn't put her seat belt on.

I leant right in and said her name, over and over, like coaxing someone awake, trying to reach them as they dream. But she was still staring the other way, as if I were sat next to her. I kept talking but there was nothing, no response.

Just Emily. And me. Among the wreckage.

12

The hospital was a hive of controlled activity, with barely suppressed fear haunting the corridors. It was almost eleven, yet the place was busy, even on a weekday. Emily had picked the wrong evening to be admitted, coinciding as it did with a pile-up on the Westway and a shooting that afternoon in Fulham, of all places. Someone's portfolio must have bottomed out.

The police had kept me at the scene, decided I was fit enough to answer a few questions. I was breathalysed, of course, and found to be just below the legal limit. I didn't know if that was still bad, a reflection of character. The slight doubt, the question mark.

I lied about the seat belt, said I unclipped it afterwards, worried that it would restrict her breathing. I couldn't tell if they believed me or not, one of them making notes.

The van driver was sympathetic, said the insurance companies could sort everything out. Go and see your bird, mate, he said. Gracious, considering what he could have said. But then, I was the one whose car had folded into itself, not him. Still, a nice gesture, of sorts. He knew I couldn't shift any blame, said he hoped Emily was alright. I thanked him.

The police finally gave me a lift to the hospital, dropped me off on a side road. I went the wrong way, had to double back, struggling to focus. I then walked straight past A&E and into the main entrance, as if instinct alone would take me to her.

I stupidly ignored the person at reception when they looked at me, and instead began walking hurriedly through the building, the smell of cleaning fluids and school food wafting out from side doors, from specialist wards. I couldn't get my bearings, it was as if all pathways were deliberately misaligned to heighten my confusion, make me malleable for some reason. I became more confused and more stressed, and ended up near where I'd started.

Retracing my steps, trying to decipher the colour-coded symbols like a learner driver, I eventually had to butt into a conversation between two doctors. One, a smoothly good-looking Indian, seemed offended by the intrusion but quickly registered my body language. I was dealt with swiftly.

When I eventually got to A&E it was like a scene from Dante's *Inferno*, I imagine, not having read the book. I asked for Emily Dashwood and waited while the nurse, her face flushed, turned and looked at a chart on the wall behind her. I, meanwhile, did what we all do in hospitals: look for tell-tale signs from the custodians of our loved ones – facial expressions, hesitation – anything that might offer a clue as to whether they're telling, or concealing, the truth.

'Miss Dashwood is in cubicle C. This way. Are you related?'

'No, I'm, well, we're going out.'

It doesn't sound right, not with the playground a long way behind you.

'I see. Right, follow me.'

She must have guessed: she was looking at the

driver.

Nothing by way of warning, no reassurances that what I was about to see was run of the mill and all would be well. Nothing. I followed, mute and scared, to cubicle C.

A metallic rush of curtain rings revealed Emily, looking back at me. She was deathly pale, with a tube running from her arm that ended at a hooked-up bag containing clear liquid, and what looked like a plastic clothes peg on her forefinger, a machine in the corner flashing green numbers. She had been crying.

'A doctor will be with you shortly,' said the nurse, from behind me. 'Please bear with us, we're extremely busy this evening.'

The voice, professional, dispassionate, faded away as she retreated back into the underworld. I was left staring at Emily, who tried to smile, an impossible task as her face disappeared beneath a landslide of emotions. A girl, long-protected, tossed into real life. I approached and sat on the edge of the bed, gently cupping her cheeks in my hands, kissing her softly on lips that looked like a crumpled worm. She tasted of salt.

'How are you feeling?'

She tried to compose herself, but the words kept getting choked off, her chest pounded by spasms as the shock returned once more, trying to kick itself free.

'Steve ... I'm sorry, I'm so sorry. It's all my fault.'

'It's fine, honestly, don't be daft. You gave me a scare though, afterwards, in the car.'

I pulled a fresh tissue from a box by the bed, waited while she wiped her eyes.

'What did the doctors say?'

'Not much really. I'm supposed to have an X-ray, but apparently there's a long wait. Busy night.'

'I know, it's all kicking off. Where does it hurt?'

She winced as she lifted her right side, moving her hand – the one not bandaged – down behind to show me the source. 'Here,' she said, gingerly touching her hip. 'And along the bottom of my back. And my neck, but that's not quite so bad.'

I nodded, adopting the reassuring manner of the bedside sage. When it comes to health, everyone's an expert.

'Sounds like you've pulled something, muscles probably, or a tendon,' I said. 'Footballers get that kind of thing all the time. Or whiplash maybe. They'll have a proper look soon. Don't worry about it, honestly.'

Don't worry about it. Brilliant. Why not just apply the roots of a forest herb to the wound at midnight, tell her not to cross a raven's path.

She didn't speak. Neither of us wanted to articulate what this might mean, to get ahead of ourselves. Like pagans peering into the flames, compelled, yet terrified of interpreting the images.

We sat quietly for a while, Emily staring at the ceiling, her eyes wet. She sniffed occasionally, wrinkled her nose. It was tickling, she said. I stroked her arm, her skin hot beneath my fingers. I looked at every nurse who walked by, but was reluctant to bother them for an update, not wanting to cause a fuss. So very British.

It was a long wait, tailing frustratingly into the small hours. Eternity seemed to pass between each fleeting visit of a doctor, different faces as time dragged by and people clocked on and off their shifts. They were friendly enough, but each so-called appraisal was brief and unhelpful. Like a fool I asked if Emily could have a scan, but was told that it was out of the question and would only be necessary 'at a later date'. They all but laughed at me, the befuddled pleb. I tried to explain the situation, told them what Emily did for a living. That may even have pushed us further down the list, such was the wordless disdain with which my pleadings were met. She eventually had an X-ray at just after four in the morning.

It revealed nothing.

This should have been positive news, but wasn't, strangely. Even the most medically illiterate can comprehend a broken bone when it's pointed out to them, and the thoughts that flow from such a diagnosis are reassuringly simple: it's broken, but it can be fixed. Plaster of Paris, some time off work, physiotherapy. But the absence of fracture pushes the victim towards the dark arts of modern medicine, into the realm of sacred texts: cells, muscles, nerve endings, chemical reactions, all configured in ways that are harder to understand than the shifting republics of eastern Europe. A confident guide is needed if you are not to lose sight of the path.

Unfortunately, those guides have spent years at medical school studying the intricate routes to health, and they don't want you following close behind, whining about a possible wrong turn or asking to look at the map. If, as we were about to find out, you are unlucky enough not to have a straightforward fracture, you'll feel like you've been kidnapped in some remote jungle, hoping against hope that you'll soon hear helicopters.

They wanted to send her home, simple as that. A conclusion was proving elusive, it was too early; we were officially in the way. Bed numbers, accountants – the whiteboard didn't only tower over people like me. Emily was wheeled into another cubicle, hidden away behind a different curtain.

The A&E department's night doctor, a large African with a proud belly, who was almost horizontal on his swivel chair when I approached, looked at me with yellow bloodshot eyes as I peered over the counter into his kingdom. The impassive stare of a white-coated dictator. I did my best to keep calm, but there was desperation in my voice. I pointed out that despite being allowed to lie down for hours, Emily couldn't even walk yet, let alone get from her bed and into a taxi.

The doctor was unmoved, sipping from a steaming plastic cup as those of lower rank busied themselves around him, not looking at me, trying to pretend I wasn't there. He looked like he was deciding whose life to spare and whose to sacrifice, as if it made his job more intoxicating.

Eventually I began to lose my poise, and he realised I wasn't about to give up, that I was on the verge of doing something irrational on his watch. Perhaps the thought of having to call security, all that paperwork, proved to be the stimulus needed. He rose lethargically from his chair and padded past me, like a grumpy fairy-tale giant.

'Lift the leg.'

Emily looked tired, her eyes puffy, a hospital sheen

on her skin. She winced with the effort of putting even a couple of inches between her right calf and the mattress.

'Now the other.'

This she did with relative ease.

'Sit up.'

She struggled, and something caught in her back. She cried out. My head began to swim.

The giant looked at her. Not at her leg, or the related parts of her body, but at her eyes, as if he was assessing something else. All part of the training. Was she one of the little rich girls who fall from their pony, and then demand that it be sold for dog food?

I heard noises from the cubicle next to ours. Terse voices, someone shouting, others trying to pacify. I stepped back a bit and peeked through. A drunken lad of about nineteen or so was in there, demanding to see his mates, no doubt the same ones who had left him on the pavement outside before driving off into the night laughing. He moaned theatrically as a nurse told him to lie still so she could inspect the damage. I looked away.

'She will be admitted. Tomorrow we decide what to do with her.'

He sounded like a bored soldier sifting out the weak from the strong, empowered by the suffering. Emily, however, looked as if she had become trapped and might panic, and I probably looked as scared as she did. After our friend left I sat on the edge of the bed again and held her hand. It was hot and damp.

'I really need a shower,' she said.

'Don't worry, you get one first thing in the morning, followed by a choice of full English or Continental between seven and nine, then a couple of hours in the hot tub. In the afternoon you can do some watercolours or learn Italian. I'd make the most of it if I were you.'

She squeezed my hand.

'I love you Steve.'

I faltered. It wasn't too soon, but simply that we'd reached the moment. I was the bloke, unprepared, floundering. It felt clumsy, emotions brought on by circumstance.

'I do,' she said. 'Very much.'

Her voiced sounded hoarse, her throat dry. I unhooked the oxygen mask next to her bed and held it to my face, pleased that she was able to laugh a little. But why, instead of hiding, couldn't I just say it back, tell her I felt the same way?

Because I did, I really did. She had me in the palm of her hand. I'd known it straight away, but hadn't dared to think she might want to end up with someone like me, the salesman.

But there was no getting away from it, I just couldn't say the words.

Rescue came in the form of two porters dragging the nylon curtain aside. It was time to go. I moved out of the way while they gently explained to Emily what was happening, then released the trolley wheels and took her out. Her eyes were closing, lips slightly parted, tiredness finally asserting itself.

As we passed the next cubicle I glanced in again. The lad was disappearing into intoxicated sleep, his grazed face and hands flecked with dried blood, dirty smudges on his jeans. One eye was badly swollen and turning purple-black. I thought of his friends, unconscious after the pub, having made the most of a lock-in.

*

Emily's cries as they moved her from the trolley onto the bed in the overnight ward will stay with me forever, some heartless staff nurse standing over her like a character from the colourless 1950s.

Emily rarely swore, I'd noticed that early on. All part of her upbringing. I used to more than make up for the both of us. I thought she liked it.

I couldn't look as she was being moved, wishing she would curse them all, spit, rail at the pain. It would have made it easier on both of us. But she absorbed it all, thanked them when it was done. Afterwards one of the nurses smiled at me, touched my forearm as she walked past. It's not just the wounded who suffer.

I went to get a coffee, something to do as Emily settled, the nurses trying to make her comfortable. I wondered if they hated their boss as much as I hated mine. When I returned, Emily was losing the struggle to keep her eyes open. She looked disorientated, as if trying to rationalise the situation, and couldn't give me her attention at the same time.

I leant in and kissed her. She seemed to come alive momentarily, reaching up to pull me closer, her arm around my neck.

'Thank you Steve,' she said. 'I'm so sorry.'

When I left the ward I looked back at her. A mistake. She raised a hand, the narrow tube connecting her to the life-support system of the building, like someone chained to a radiator. I suppose I should have spoken to someone at the desk, clarify what I was supposed to do later that day, find out the visiting hours. But I didn't. I walked blindly back down the corridors, only half-registering the multitude of happy arrows that move the terrorised through paediatrics, oncology and phlebotomy, until eventually I found the main door to the warren and stepped out into the night. The realisation that I had to work out which buses would get me home hit me like the cold air. I swore, a bit too loudly.

I started to hurry away, moving quickly through the bright lights of the hospital entrance. Past two patients standing around in their dressing gowns smoking; past the window of a franchise coffee place; past a few waiting ambulances and down towards the main road. Only then, in the safety of the semi-darkness, did I give in. I don't think anyone saw me stop by a charity shop, raise a hand to cover my trembling lips, my clenched teeth. As I cowered in the doorway there was, thankfully, not enough light to reflect the stream of tears, which ran down my face and seeped like blood through my fingers.

13

I woke up on my sofa, fully clothed apart from my shoes, which were kicked across the room. There was an unopened bottle of gin on the floor, a clean glass. For a few precious seconds I was oblivious, nothing was wrong. But it was a fleeting luxury, quickly stolen. In its place, an image of flashing lights, uniforms, the accusing stares of onlookers. A buckled bonnet, that feeling of despair edging closer.

I phoned work and spoke to Chris, told him what had happened, said I wouldn't be coming in. He sounded genuinely concerned, but it was a corporate environment so you can never really be sure. Told me not to worry and to take a couple of days; he would oversee things that end.

'We look after our people here Steve.'

He actually said that.

I shivered as I put the phone down. No doubt someone would step up while I wasn't there, move quickly out of the shadows.

A short while later, after a quick shower, I left the house. As I walked away I pulled a crumpled piece of paper from my back pocket – a mobile number written in Emily's shaky hand the night before. I hadn't intended to phone Alex, but I knew she would appreciate it. Plus, in his new line of work, he was like a connection between us and the medical profession, had seen some of the maps.

I walked towards the Tube station, pressing my mobile to my ear, turning up the volume against the background noise.

'Hello?'

'Alex? It's Steve.'

'Steve, hello, how are you?'

'I'm fine. Well, actually no, that's a lie. I'm not fine at all.'

I wasn't looking where I was going, too wired to deal with more than one task at a time, walking and talking for example. A chipped slab on the pavement had been deliberately left unmended to catch me out, and as I clipped it with my toe I lost my balance, only just managing to stay on my feet as I fell forward. I must have looked like a sprinter trying to chest the finish line.

'Jesus Christ Almighty!' I shouted, unconcerned about people looking at me. 'Anything else you want to throw my way?' Directing my anger skywards, furious at thin air.

'Steve? Are you okay?'

'Yeah, I'm here. Being a clumsy idiot. Sorry.'

'Don't worry. How's Emily?'

'Well, that's why I'm calling, as it goes. She had an accident, she's in hospital.'

'It's okay, I know what happened. Emily told me.'

It was all there, everything I needed to know. The closeness.

I stopped walking. The blank expressions of weary commuters quickly changed to annoyance as they were forced to walk around me, a crippled ant blocking the ceaseless progress of the colony.

On the opposite side of the road, in his glass

sanctuary, a white-haired bloke in a green cardigan was adding a radio to his window display, a shop that sold second-hand electrical gear. He reminded me of a hamster, working away. A handwritten sign to the right of his head declared that he rented out televisions, minimum period one month. I'd never heard of such a thing. Practically everyone on my estate had dishes clamped to the buildings like some marauding fungus, so who on earth still rented televisions? I wondered if you would need a licence. I guessed you would, but still, this entrepreneurial angle struck a chord with me. I watched transfixed as the man leant over his arrangement of gadgets, adjusting the position of the radio until, satisfied, he disappeared again.

My ear was warm.

'Steve? Steve?'

Someone calling to me through a dream, like I'd tried to do for her.

'Steve, are you there? What's going on? Say something.'

'Sorry Alex. I'm sorry. Not concentrating. So you know then?'

'Well, yes. Emily phoned me about two hours ago.'

I looked at my watch. A quarter past eleven.

'Oh God, I'm really late. Emily will be ... could be ...'

'Listen, stop worrying, get yourself together.' Alex's voice was almost motherly. 'I think you're probably still in shock. It's perfectly natural. I'll be coming into Waterloo in about ten minutes, why don't we meet outside the hospital and go in together. Emily will like that.'

14

What must it be like for a boy to fight his father? Not just a few harsh words, empty threats, some growing-up stuff. I'm talking about proper confrontation, when you're in danger of taking a beating, but giving back what you can. Circling each other around an upturned Formica table in a tiny kitchen, mother shielding the girls, everyone's heart breaking.

A broken bottle, chairs as weapons.

Imagine that, wanting to destroy your creator. The source of you.

I studied him. Just for ten minutes, keeping out of the way. He was on the cycling machine, breathing hard, legs working like pistons. Beads of sweat trickled down his cheek, along his smooth jawline and onto the floor. It was hard to tell whether he'd even started shaving yet. I thought of myself aged fifteen, eternity still on my side. Cyan came to the club to learn, ended up teaching me a lesson.

It was as if we'd been gifted a foal, a thoroughbred in the making.

Jack wasn't around that afternoon, wouldn't be back until late. He'd taken three of his under-14s to a competition in Hackney. He'd been dropping hints to Cyan about coming along to get a taste of the atmosphere, but got little response. The invitation wasn't repeated as the day drew closer. I knew he was trying to make a point.

We had a problem, one that took us both by surprise. Right from the off Cyan sometimes turned up late, or not at all, dredging up some excuse about homework or having to run an errand for his mum. It didn't happen all the time, but enough for Jack to be disappointed. Without total dedication a judoka is limited, held back. If you want to progress you have to give your all. If not, stay at home, live out those fantasies by jabbing your thumbs into a games console.

Jack had spoken to Cyan about the situation, and it was the only time the lad ever really got verbal with him, showed any disrespect. Said it couldn't be helped, he couldn't be in two places at once. Got quite shirty, so I heard, like a switch had been flicked. Jack was upset, and didn't bother trying to hide it from me, although he held back from giving Cyan a talking to for fear of putting him off, pushing him towards another club or giving up altogether. He was fond of Cyan, I could tell, and couldn't bear to see talent pissed away. And he certainly didn't want to waste time with a potentially great judoka who went on silly little errands when he should be training.

Anyway, come the day of the competition, Jack thought he'd show him what it felt like when other people didn't make the effort, didn't beg. They just went without him, nothing said. Cyan didn't mention it either.

To his credit, he got on with his gym work, putting in even more effort even though Jack wasn't there to witness it. Maybe he thought I'd report back, although I'm not sure he gave a toss about that either. He was more than capable of working himself to exhaustion in an empty room.

I'd never seen him smile. Not even when Jack praised him, told him how good he could be. He had his own agenda, which we didn't understand, not then. Despite Jack's encouragement he showed no interest in competing, kept saying he wasn't ready. We had no idea what we were dealing with, didn't have a clue about what was at stake.

Troubled, if you need a label.

Jack, as promised, had been round to visit the parents early on, but found only one. A proud Christian woman, Violet, holding down two jobs to raise Cyan and his two younger sisters while Jerome, their old man, whored it up somewhere, caning the Jack and Coke and spewing out the big talk. For all Cyan knew he might even have half-brothers or sisters he would probably never meet, sharing a father none of them ever saw.

Jack spent the whole evening with Mrs Richards, learning about her boy and the family background, drinking endless cups of tea but (he promised me) fending off the plate of cakes. I bet they enjoyed the moment, a man in the household, if only for a short while, the prospect of something new happening in their lives. They both had expectations of each other.

He didn't tell me all the details of what they talked about, as if doing so might betray Violet's trust; but he told me enough. She was very open with him – perhaps she'd been waiting a long time to talk. And Jack, with his old-fashioned ways, well, I guess she felt comfortable.

Violet spoke about her family the way someone might describe a garden, a place where beautiful things need help if they are to rise from the dirt. Her husband may have planted the seeds, but she had long since given up wanting him to return, to see what had grown up in his absence. Jack told me they didn't know if he was still in the country, or even alive, it had been almost three years. Three years since he turned up drunk one night without warning, after longer and longer periods away, to shatter Cyan's world. The overturned kitchen table, glass crunching underfoot.

According to his mother, her son became withdrawn and secretive after that, but prone to outbursts, little shots of temper that gradually took on a more sinister edge. She didn't ever feel threatened, and put his behaviour down to what he'd been through, combined with the usual trials of being a teenager. She was still waiting for it to pass. But word began to filter back to her, fragments of gossip culled from other parents, as well as things her daughters heard at school. A phone call from a concerned teacher showed her that the situation had gone too far. She was summoned for a quiet chat.

Half an hour in the head teacher's office. Is everything all right at home?

He excelled in some subjects, especially maths and technical drawing, but made little or no effort with the rest. And I don't suppose his teachers had the time or the inclination to wrestle him back. This wasn't Eton; they had wandered into an arcade game, a war zone.

Violet was happy for Cyan to come to the club. She hoped the environment, the life principles of judo, would be good for him, grounding. It had, after all, been his decision, not something recommended by another authority, an instruction. He seemed to have no real friends, lacked social skills, but would often go out in the evening without saying a word, coming back an hour or so later with nothing to add. She had no idea where he went, or whether he just walked the streets, and, such was the look he gave her when questioned, she no longer dared to ask. She couldn't reach him – but perhaps Jack would be able to.

Despite everything, he seemed to be preparing for a few of his end of year exams, although he probably kept that quiet for fear of reprisal. He wanted to be an architect.

It was a miracle he'd made it this far.

We'd barely spoken, Cyan and I, even after he'd been coming to the gym for months. We were mainly on nodding terms, and he saved his conversation, such as it was, for Jack. He, like the rest of the class, listened intently to their instructor, as if secrets were being passed around. And his technique was improving quickly, very quickly. Jack's words were like water bubbling up from a spring, and the boy drank greedily.

He'd been raised properly, you could tell, which made his excuses about being late so exasperating. His attitude at the club mirrored everything Violet had described – the reticence when he was off the mat, the aggression when he stepped onto it. On the rare occasion when he did choose to open his mouth he was quietly spoken, articulate; put the whites on and something different surged through him, barely controllable. We'd never seen anything like it.

He fought like a cornered animal, the most dangerous kind. We were excited, and blinded, by what we saw.

As Cyan pedalled away, head down, I heard my mobile ring in the kitchen and rushed out to answer it. He didn't look up as I left.

'Hello?'

'We've got it!' she squealed.

'Got what?'

They'd worked out what was wrong with her. Thank God. It had been weeks since that day in A&E, and Emily's back was still bad. It woke her up at night, restricted her movements during the day. Dancing was out of the question, and strained phone calls from her mother had become an unwanted feature of our lives.

The woman blamed me, why wouldn't she? As far as everyone was concerned I lost concentration, fooling around, not paying attention. And that one drink would always haunt me, the stain on my character, while Emily remained unblemished. She said she would come clean to her family about what really happened, but I said no, don't do that. She knew I would never let on, knew I wasn't that sort.

Besides, I told her, I couldn't go changing my story, admit I'd lied to the police and the insurance company. Another can of worms; we had enough to deal with as it was.

The only person I told was Jack. He wasn't best pleased, but understood why I'd done what I had. Always be the gentleman, protect the lady. Put yourself on the line if you have to, if you think she's worth it.

But he never asked me if she was. He knew what my answer would be.

Besides, if you're not up to it you don't step onto the mat. You walk away.

When I heard Emily's excitement on the phone I felt an almost sickening surge of adrenaline, which oddly seemed to weaken me, the rush. We were about to take the first step back towards where we had started. A time when Emily was well, no pain, no stress. Returning to the life that she – we – wanted.

'The house,' she said, 'we've got the house. The other buyers have pulled out, so the seller's come back and accepted our offer. We've got it Steve, it's ours. Our home.'

It was good news, of course, the right direction, but I would have traded it all for a cure.

Emily should have been jumping up and down, turning joyful pirouettes around her posh London apartment. Yet even in all the excitement her voice sounded wrong, the words taut, as if trying to escape without jarring her body.

'That's brilliant,' I said, without much conviction. 'Fantastic news. Let's just hope no one pulls out of the chain. Plenty of people do.'

A girl excited, like it's her birthday. The happy face, the party balloons. All it takes is one prick.

'No, seriously, that's excellent,' I said, trying to find my way back. 'We should celebrate. I can leave here right now if you like, we could go for a meal.'

Her silence was like a punishment.

'Hello? Emily?'

'You know I can't sit down for long Steve, I seize up.'

'Course, sorry. What else would you like to do?'

'Well, something that doesn't involve sitting for more than half an hour, like I said, or trying to relax. You know, those things that everyone else enjoys doing.'

Her voice even thinner now.

'I need this Steve, I really do. I thought you did as well. Just us together, somewhere new.'

'Of course I want it, you know that. I'm being sensible again, that's all. It's just, you know, I don't want you getting too excited and thinking everything's going to be okay; we've got to be prepared, just in case it goes wrong. Plenty of house moves fall through. Loads.'

I heard her breathe in sharply; it sounded as if she had shifted her weight. She didn't try to hide it. Then a sigh.

'I need something positive,' she said. 'And you're just, what's that phrase you use at work, managing something?'

'Your expectations.'

'That's it. You're managing my expectations. I should have expected that.'

She giggled. I was surprised. The tightness around my chest eased.

'If you're really lucky,' I said, 'later on we could do some blue-sky thinking, really push the envelope. Check we're singing from the same hymn sheet moving forward.'

'My God, Steve, do people really talk like that in your job?'

''Fraid so. In offices all over the world, I imagine. It's a plague, a nasty little virus that's spread everywhere.

There's no escaping it.'

'There is for us.'

I heard a loud bang, followed by someone swearing. I looked out of the kitchen and saw one of our regulars standing over a barbell on the floor. He grinned and rolled his eyes at me, pulling at the cap of his water bottle.

'You're right,' I continued, 'this is good news. We'll think of something else to do tonight. I'll come round in a bit and pick you up.'

'You always do Steve.'

'Don't you start,' I said, secretly pleased. Most people would have cringed. 'That's the kind of end-of-the-pier line I get into trouble for.'

She laughed again, and we said goodbye. Back from the brink.

I returned to the gym and sat down at the desk, trying to be excited. Moving in together seemed so unimportant compared with getting Emily well again. Shouldn't we be concentrating on that? But I knew I wouldn't have the nerve to bring it up.

I noticed in front of me someone's application to join the gym, which Jack had put there for me to check. I looked at it briefly. The handwriting flowed neatly, little flourishes on some of the letters. Very business-like, the writing of someone who likes to make an impression.

Two months. Maybe less.

15

Moving house. The most stressful thing you can do, those in the know would have us believe. Either that or bereavement, I can't remember. Depends on your values, I suppose, and the market.

All that bureaucracy; buyers and sellers getting the hump and threatening to pull out, loaded guns held to people's heads. A total lack of honour.

The estate agent representing the bloke we were buying from took to phoning us up all the time, an unwelcome presence in our lives: have you done this, have you done that, you can make it happen Steve, keep up the pressure.

The power of commission, the percentages game. He forgot who he was talking to.

After it was all done, our solicitor told us the move had been one of the most difficult she'd ever had to handle. Of course.

Halfway through I really started to question what we were doing, buying a place together so soon. Why not rent for a while, see how things go? But Emily said she wanted me to commit, so I kept my gob shut. I was no different to the estate agent, seduced by the pay-off.

And her back was still not getting any better. She had shooting pains down her right leg and into her calf, a numbness in the foot, so we assumed it was sciatica, although that didn't necessarily explain the ache in her lower back. Mummy, true to form, was still floating on the thermals, carried effortlessly on vast circles of hostility above us. What with her and the estate agent, I began to feel I was under constant surveillance, that I should be doing more, always more. It was as if everyone was waiting for me to trip up again.

In the meantime, Emily stayed at my place a lot while the house stuff went through. She preferred not to see any of her company's rehearsals, said she couldn't bear to watch others do what she couldn't. That was painful too, she told me, not being a part of it.

I was selfish, I admit it. I loved having her there with me, but because of the pain she rarely slept through the night. Lying down for long periods was becoming impossible. She would keep waking up, disturbed by a throbbing in her hip, her knee, and of course her back. I did a bit of research, found out that people with bad backs used to be told to take it easy, stay horizontal for days, even weeks, at a time. Now, like everything else, the opposite is true.

She would get out of bed as quietly as possible, thinking I was asleep, and I'd lie there and watch her blurred form leave the room, listen to her go to the kitchen and place a chair in the middle of the floor. I knew exactly what she was doing: standing on it, a heavy book tied to her right foot, which she let hang down the side. She said it helped to ease the aching, as if the weight pulling on her leg made the muscles in her back more elastic, prised open the vertebrae, allowing something to flow back in, something soothing.

Other times I listened to her pacing around, like she was willing her spine to work itself free, for the stiffness to finally leave her. Conducting a séance of sorts; trying to conjure up the body she once had.

All the assurances we were initially given, that she would be as right as rain in no time, proved empty. Give it time to settle, they told us, as we left the hospital that first time, me, Emily and Alex. Let the inflammation die down, and if things aren't a lot better soon go to your GP and take it from there. Re-assess. What they failed to realise is that, for a dancer, 'a lot better' might be nowhere near good enough. And now, much later, we were always on edge, trapped, bound together by razor wire.

Re-assess. I quickly grew to despise that word.

Straight after the injury Emily made it very clear to me that she would not have private treatment, despite her family having the resources, and then some. It smacked of elitism, she argued, and would cause resentment among her dance company, not all of whom came from privileged backgrounds. That old chestnut. It was important to her, something I would have to understand.

She wouldn't even let the company's physio give her any treatment. He was allowed to have a look and ask her some questions – her employer insisted on that – but it was as far as she was prepared to go. I bet he was surprised, if not offended, but then what did I know? Maybe plenty of injured dancers get all narky about who goes near them. I had no idea.

The only person she trusted, she said, was Alex. He was a friend and used to be a dancer, so he knew what she was going through, had seen it all before. He would understand.

No one else was allowed to touch her.

I admired her attitude, of course I did, told her that having principles is to be encouraged. I didn't mention that it's the sort of thing that makes people leave university, throw away their chances, let others down.

Meanwhile, half our time was spent sorting out the house stuff – reams of questions, writing cheques, filling in questionnaires – while the other half, what I thought was the important bit, saw us spun around inside revolving doors that kept stopping at random to spit us out into a succession of bleached corridors. There we would sit, staring at the walls, the same cheerful floral prints everywhere we went. The metal nameplates on the doors, each with its mystical acronyms; rooms we were becoming more and more afraid to enter.

Self-assured men and women, specialists in this and that, who spoke loudly but told us little. As if their confidence itself was a step on the way to a cure, something they could give to us in a bottle so we wouldn't keep bothering them.

'Bend slowly from the waist. Careful now. Where in your back exactly? Right, I see. Well, Steve and Emily, I don't think you need to worry too much, these things tend to settle down, given time. Some people take longer than others, so try not to fret too much. I know it's difficult. I'm writing a prescription for a course of painkillers. On top of the ones you're already taking, yes. And as a precaution I'm going to book you an appointment with X, I think he should be able to help. I have some minor concerns, and this is more his field.'

Send us on our way, the next corridor.

Information was dispatched to us in a casual manner, as if we were buying train tickets, and only when the pain stubbornly refused to die – in fact went the other way – was Emily at last granted an MRI scan. It revealed a couple of slightly bulging discs in her spine, apparently not uncommon, and possibly not even the cause of the problem. Could have been like it for a while, they said. Scan the entire population and you'll find that a third have slipped discs, most of them with no symptoms.

The expert who went over those particular results with us was a scratchy-featured woman who looked like she ate mice. She gave herself an escape route, made sure to stress the enormous difficulty that doctors face when diagnosing back problems – as if to imply that Emily could have done the decent thing and picked something more straightforward. Millions of people are affected, she said, millions. They get on with their lives, have jobs, socialise. Deal with the unpleasantness as best they can. I wondered how many sick notes she'd signed that week.

She asked about Emily's background, and Emily revealed that she'd had mild pain in her lower back on and off since she was a teenager. Her dance teachers had therefore always focused special attention on her posture when performing certain movements. The consultant looked indifferent. Repetition of an incorrect movement will nearly always have long-term consequences, she warned, so hopefully they knew what they were doing. Another side road, another escape route. Bring strangers from the past into the equation, just in case.

I sat there feeling more and more angry with the arts world, something I knew so little about, hadn't really bothered with. Ever since we first started going out, Emily always tried to show me the importance of creativity in all its forms, took on the mission of making me understand. For a long while she almost had me; now I began to hate it again. It's like a demanding child that never shuts up.

And guilty; I still felt guilty. Slowly convincing myself that it was somehow my fault. I should have been more firm with her, told her to stop messing around.

Sometimes the fear of it all brought sudden waves of panic. I'd had a glimpse of happiness, the briefest of moments. But now I just wanted to grab the doctor's sleeve during the appointments, see if they could slip me a prescription too.

The consultant said there might be a tear on the surface of one of Emily's discs, although she couldn't tell from the scan. If, on the other hand, the disc was becoming badly prolapsed, surgery would be required, an operation that was commonplace but not without risk. Been doing it for more than a hundred years, she said. Piece of cake. It was usually very successful, although in some instances there were complications, especially if the damaged disc had been left untreated and been pressing on a nerve for too long. It could result in a slight limp.

I remember sitting there as if someone had packed me in ice. Dance, modern or otherwise, had clearly not registered with the woman as a legitimate profession, something that might have meaning for a person. It didn't save lives, didn't feed the hungry. It couldn't be quantified.

At least I bothered to hate it, to recognise its power. To her it was nothing, a distraction, there to amuse professional types on their nights off. And she seemed to have forgotten that a slipped disc was only one possible scenario being kicked around by her and her mates, but for that particular day it seemed to be the favourite. She needed to sound knowledgeable about something, and a prolapse would do. A pinching of the sciatic nerve; don't panic, it usually goes away.

She too wrote out a slip for more tablets, different ones this time, to supplement the ones Emily was already taking. Morphine-based, although she neglected to mention that.

A slight limp. Maybe. Don't worry about it.

In the meantime, however, she unwrapped a little gift for us, something shiny, a medical jewel. Emily could have a steroid injection in her spine, which, when combined with physio and stretching, would hopefully do something to keep the symptoms at bay. A fingertip pressed against the clock face, stopping the hands from moving, for a while at least. I made her write down the technical name for the procedure so I could look it up later; my mind was being flung around on a rollercoaster.

She never said it to us directly, but I knew what she was thinking: it's worth a punt. And if that doesn't work, fuck it, have some surgery. Now move along, you saw the queue outside.

Sitting in the car afterwards, Emily looked as if she might be sick. There was little we could say to each other. The enormity of what we were up against had been presented to us with the cold finality of a death certificate.

We felt alone. Utterly, completely alone.

16

Jack had to break us up. Well, mostly he had to pull Cyan off me, I wasn't doing a great deal: just holding on to him, adjusting my stance to maintain balance, hoping he'd come to his senses. Truth be told, I would happily have broken the little runt's arm. If he'd kept on for much longer I'd have pulled him to the floor and applied some real pressure, fifteen years old or not.

For a bloke in his sixties, Jack moved like a leopard – he still had it. Grabbed the boy by the back of his vest and yanked him away. For that fragment of a second, when his feet left the ground, Cyan seemed to lose all sense of coordination, limp as a rag doll as Jack spun him around and pushed him towards the door, yelling at him to sod off and get changed, or just sod off altogether.

Then he turned on me, shouting.

'What is going on here?'

My look of shock, both at what had just happened and then having Jack shout at me, brought him tumbling back down. He raised his hands to his head, then grabbed me by the shoulders. He seemed as surprised as I was.

'Steve, I'm sorry. I didn't mean to have a go, I was just …'

'Don't worry about it,' I said, tugging at the bottom of my rucked sweatshirt. 'Tell you what though, if you two are going to take turns I may have to find myself a new club.'

'What happened?'

'Oh, you know how it is. State of the economy, financial meltdown. No one seems to have the answers.'

'Steve, I'm not in the mood.'

We left the gym and went through to the kitchen area. A couple of the guys asked if I was alright as we passed. Fine, I said, but keep an eye on Jack, you might learn something.

A fight in a judo club: that doesn't happen too often. Cyan might have some apologising to do, I thought, not that I was looking to score any points. I assumed he'd gone home, although I didn't really care. I was beginning to get fed up with him, if I'm honest.

'So,' said Jack, filling up the kettle, 'let's have it.'

'I think I made the mistake of showing him my caring side,' I said, sitting on the kitchen's only chair. I leant forward, rested my forearms on my legs. I noticed the floor needed mopping.

'Meaning?'

I turned to look at Jack.

'Don't you sometimes wonder about him?' I asked.

'Who, Cyan?'

'No Jack, George Clooney. Yes, of course Cyan. Bloody hell.'

He laughed. For some reason Jack found me funny, like we were old mates, without the forty or so years between us. We only had the judo in common really, but it was enough, more than enough. It felt like a lifetime.

'Listen Steve, he's highly strung, we all know that, it doesn't take a genius to work it out. What is it they say these days, the PC brigade, he's got issues? Well, whatever. It's just something else for us – me and you – to deal with, okay? I'm looking for your help here. He's not had the easiest of rides as far as his family's concerned, no dad and all that.'

'Oh blimey, don't you start,' I said. 'I think that's what kicked him off.'

'Why, what did you say?'

I paused, wondering if I should have brought it up. Take it like a man, brush it off, move on. Jack waited for me to speak; he wasn't going to let it pass, that was clear. He'd stand there all day if he had to, leaning against the work surface, arms folded.

'He was on the loose weights,' I said. 'I only came in to see who was here. Thought I'd say hello, you know, see what was going on. Check the place wasn't falling apart without me. My house is spick and span, so I brought my duster.'

I waited.

'That was a joke, by the way.'

'Hilarious. Stop stalling.'

'Right. Well, he was lifting the barbell with his head down, facing the floor. Obviously you're asking to do your neck in, lifting like that, and I stupidly thought it would be okay to tell him. You know, a bit of friendly advice. I was only trying to help.'

'And?'

'He just went off on one. Saying what would I know, I don't come to all the classes, don't fight in competitions anymore, all that type of thing. He worked himself up into a right old lather, just like that. It was weird. I thought he was supposed to be the polite boy, brought up proper. But then he starts asking who I thought I was, his old man or something. Moving towards me, like he wanted me to take him on.'

Jack was kneading the skin of his forehead with his thumb and fingers.

'Then what?'

'I told him not to be such a child, to grow up. And then he went for me, simple as. Tell you what Jack, he's learnt a lot since he's been coming to see you, I'll give you that. He was right in there, it was like fighting a flippin' octopus. He didn't get me down but he gave it a good shot. But then I suppose he's lucky you happened to walk in. I had no time to work some of my moves on him.'

Jack snorted. Shook his head.

'Don't even think about it,' I said.

We were silent for a few moments.

'I'll speak to him,' Jack said. 'Next time he's in.'

'Assuming there is a next time,' I replied.

'There will be a next time, I guarantee it.'

'Oh yeah?'

'Yes, absolutely. I know he's not always here, but something's driving him. I can tell.'

'Excellent,' I said. 'The first step to greatness. When's the next Olympics?'

'Well, you can joke, but he could really achieve something. Seriously. Just as long as we continue to support him – and that's where you come in, young man.'

'Me? What do you mean? He doesn't even like me.'

Jack looked like he wanted to give me a slap. And not for the first time.

'Don't be an idiot,' he said. 'Of course he likes you,

you big fairy. He's had a tough time, that's all. You can deal with it. I wouldn't say he's wild exactly, but he's, oh I don't know … untamed, maybe. He acts on instinct, I've seen it a thousand times with these kids. And that instinct is telling him that you and him are two of a kind. You might not have noticed it, with your head up your arse, but I have. And you've had your problems too Steve, so I reckon it's time to use that experience. All the more reason to stick by him, if judo has taught you anything. You need to be there, to make him realise we're all behind him.'

The water in the kettle started to hiss and bubble. I was trying to take everything in, still a little high from my spat with Cyan. I took a deep breath.

'Right,' I said. 'Well, of course, yeah, whatever you say. I'll do what I can.'

Jack finished stirring the tea, then handed me the mug.

'Thanks Steve,' he said. 'I appreciate it.'

17

A few weeks before our moving day I had the deep pleasure of meeting Emily's parents. I'd spoken to her mother on plenty of occasions, thanks to her ceaseless demands for medical updates, but now it was time for them to see me in the flesh. I think we'd all been deliberately putting it off. I know I had, although they probably thought we'd never have to meet, that I'd be gone when the wind changed.

We went for lunch at some stupidly expensive restaurant in St John's Wood called Belzar or Bell Boy, or something similar (I've wined and dined clients in some pretty serious places myself, but I know a second mortgage when I see one). They paid, of course. I think that was the test, to see if I would offer – to see whether I could risk offering, in fact – so in that sense the afternoon yielded results.

A five-course meal, portions so small they'd make a child cry. But at least the place was immaculate, cutlery and glassware shining. No smudges. I was stressed enough as it was.

I didn't get the inquisition I was expecting though: these people go on instinct. And one thing did surprise me: I got on well with Emily's old man, Michael. He had that home-comforts aura about him. Elizabeth – Mummy – was a different beast entirely, like a cunning but confused bird, never venturing too far, still fussing over an empty nest. She didn't have an ounce of fat on her, reduced to a collection of angles. She'd been a dancer too, back in the day, but only ever at an amateur level. Gave it all up when Emily's brother came along.

Michael worked at the Ministry of Defence for thirty-six years. Told me he loved every other minute of it, even though he'd always wanted to be a vet, an equine specialist. But then the possibility of early retirement was floated. Modernisation and all that, old boy, the field of modern warfare is evolving fast, ruddy internet. He grabbed the opportunity like a missile launcher and stormed out of the building, no looking back.

Michael and I talked about sport mainly. He didn't know anything about judo, although he did show an interest, asking about the club and Jack. Cricket and rugby were more his thing, and football, surprisingly, Arsenal man through and through. I wanted to make a crack about him being a gunner, but held back, there being a strong likelihood that he'd heard it once or twice before. He was sympathetic about me supporting Pompey, without being patronising, as supporters of big teams often are. He'd been to Fratton Park in the early 90s for an FA Cup match, loved the atmosphere.

'Family-style club, Steve, old-fashioned values. What the game needs.'

Emily and Elizabeth didn't talk much. There was history, I could sense it. Christ, even the waiter could probably tell. When a mother and daughter are that polite to each other you know something's up.

I thought it was because of me. I said to Emily later that I should have been more enthusiastic about my job, given them the spiel about ambition and prospects, let them think their daughter was in safe hands. She looked at me as if we'd just been introduced, told me not to be so ridiculous. Without a five-grand Rolex and membership of the Hurlingham Club I stood no chance anyway. She thought it was funny. No, not funny, amusing.

On the day of the move they put their hands in their pockets again, shelling out for the removal company. This time I did protest, but Elizabeth wouldn't have it. A little gift, she said. Not for me, I assumed, for her little girl.

I thought of Violet, Cyan's mum, the small presents she must occasionally give her son and his sisters. Saving bits of wages from her cleaning job. A CD; something towards kit for the gym; or a day out up in town, the whole family. Where shall we go?

Elizabeth brought it up on the day, a simple ceremony among a landslide of labelled boxes and second-hand furniture in our new home. She acted like it had only just come to mind.

'Oh, Michael, have you got the necessaries dear?'

The more you have, the dirtier the word becomes.

Still, at least she didn't arrange to meet me on an industrial estate somewhere, armed with a stuffed envelope, trying to send me back to my world. Save us all the embarrassment, the inconvenience of having to pretend.

With everything off the lorry, Michael and I went to the pub, left the girls to unpack a bit. We were role-playing, I suppose, but I didn't care, I was gagging for a pint – my tongue felt like a peach. Plus I had to get away from that stabbing beak. Emily shot me a look as I grabbed my jacket, but I still didn't care. Feed the woman, get her sugar levels up, do what you have to.

'Don't take it too personally Steve, she's like this whenever Emily meets someone.'

I bet she bloody isn't.

'And she's in a desperate state about the injury and everything.'

We clinked glasses.

'Cheers.'

'Cheers Steve. Best of luck. I hope you're both very happy down here.'

'Thanks. Me too.'

We took big mouthfuls. The first one's always the best.

It was a welcoming pub, if a little stuffy. Wealthy village attitude. Plenty of low beams, little hideaways in the corners, framed reproductions of ancient documents showing coats of arms. This is our history; now, think carefully: will you ever really fit in?

Michael let me get the drinks. I'd chosen the local bitter: support your community, hope someone notices. Pretty soon I would be going to the village hall cinema, making new friends. I took another big mouthful.

'How is Emily, would you say?'

A dark cloud on the horizon. Was the military man acting under orders, filing reconnaissance reports? I took my time, trying to huff the little doubts away. He was just a concerned father, and we couldn't talk about sport forever.

'Not good. The pain isn't getting any better. She seems to place a lot of faith in Alex, but I'm not convinced he's much help. In fact, last time she had a session with him she could barely walk properly for a couple of days afterwards. But, you know, all part of the treatment, so she tells me. She tries to hide it, but I know she's terrified, her career and everything.'

He didn't know what to say, almost shrinking into himself, a little boy whose pet guinea pig won't wake up. Our moving-in day, and I'm sitting there wanting to reassure my girlfriend's father that everything will be okay. Jesus, I was scared too.

'She's got the injection coming up. And if that doesn't work they're talking about surgery.'

It was like I'd pinched him. He visibly jolted.

'Surgery? Really? My gosh, why didn't you say?'

'Well, you know, what with the move and everything, we didn't want to worry you. We thought it'd be far better to be bright and positive. It's all so vague. She's even had acupuncture, but that did absolutely nothing. Total waste of time. So if she has to have surgery it'll be mainly exploratory, and if they find something they'll fix it.'

'But Steve, a back operation, that's a serious thing. Especially for a dancer.'

'I know. That's why we didn't say anything. You and Elizabeth have both been really generous, why spoil things?'

I was winging it.

Michael had gone pale, staring out the window across the village green. A small boy and girl were attempting to kick a bright orange ball to each other, lunging at it like two stumbling marionettes. Michael seemed to be looking past them; I'm not sure he even realised they were there.

He had a scar. Very fine, about an inch long, behind his right ear. I hadn't noticed it before. His hair, thick and grey, was pushed back like that of a rugged politician and mostly hid it. Despite having sat behind a desk for a third of a century he looked healthy, although those sneaky gin and tonics had begun to camp out on his pink cheeks, tiny capillaries rupturing just below the surface. Keen golfer, of course, and told me that he was a promising rugby player until he too, like Elizabeth, had to bow out, this time through injury.

Always the way isn't it? Rotten bad luck, pass the baton on to the children, let them have their turn.

'We wanted her to go private,' he said, 'right from the very beginning. Did you know that?'

'Yes I did. But you know what Emily's like, she's so stubborn it's ridiculous. She sees it as some kind of principle not to have special treatment, because, you know, not everyone can afford it. I can sort of understand what she's saying.'

I swallowed some more beer, hoping he'd step in, insist on helping us. But he looked almost catatonic.

'I have to say though,' I continued, 'the NHS is like the busiest circus in the world. You can all see the Big Top but there's a queue a mile long to get in.'

I was pleased with that, let it sink in. The sales boy can do metaphors. Or was it a simile? And who cares anyway?

Michael moved his head up and down slowly, as if vaguely acknowledging that he was involved in a conversation. I thought he was never going to speak again. Eventually he looked at me, weary, like the spirit had left him.

'We pushed her too hard.'

'Excuse me?'

'Elizabeth and I. Ever since she was a little girl. I've always thought it.'

I felt like a priest, two men in a pub separated by an invisible grille. Except I had no wise words to back me up, no recourse to sorcery.

'The Royal Ballet School, Steve, the Royal Ballet School. That really is something, isn't it? An achievement.'

I tried to smile, tried to be sympathetic. 'It certainly is, Michael, you're right. And I know she appreciates all the help and encouragement you've given her over the years. Honestly, she does.'

He continued as if I hadn't spoken. 'All this contemporary nonsense she's doing at the moment is a way of getting her own back. A little bit of rebellion. I understand that – but I'm sure she'll grow out of it though, eh? Shakespeare on giant plastic boxes. What were they thinking? Not exactly the Royal Opera House is it?'

'Not when it's set in Nebraska, no. Probably not.'

He shook his glass, swirling the remains of the beer, smiling to himself.

'I'm sure we'll look back and laugh at the irony one day, but really. Bloody hell, Steve, bloody hell.'

He drained the dregs. I felt for him, I really did. So proud of his daughter, wanting to give her the world.

We had another pint but were losing momentum. The silences weren't awkward, just a little reflective, getting longer. I think he felt that he'd spoken out of turn about the family, but I couldn't imagine he had too many allies in the huddle of repressed Hertfordshire society. One misplaced word down the golf club could find its way upstream like a determined salmon, domestic misery waiting to spawn.

One thing I'll always remember him for: he didn't try to push the blame onto me, the driver, the misfit. He was a gentleman, old school. Like someone else I knew.

When we got back to the house little had changed. There were two cups in the sink and a Victoria sponge with a very modest triangle missing, but I could see no evidence that Mrs Dashwood had got her hands dirty with any boxes. In fact she appeared to be sulking, something at which she apparently excelled.

Emily avoided looking at me. She gave the impression that her back was really aching, and seemed very keen for her mother to be somewhere else.

Fortunately, within half an hour they were gone. A perfunctory goodbye to us both from Elizabeth, a big hug for Emily and a hand on my shoulder from Michael, who followed his wife to the car like a dutiful hound. He still looked worried, but then so would I if I had to face a long trip back with that woman. God only knows why he didn't have a few more in the pub, give the journey more of an edge.

Emily was worn out. It had been a long day. She moved slowly onto the sofa, as if weightless, and with an effort brought both legs up so that she was at least lying down.

'Give me ten minutes,' she said, 'then we'll go out for a bit.'

She closed her eyes.

'I'll get my hunting rifle,' I said, but she didn't reply.

I went upstairs to give her some space, and make a start on some of the unpacking. Our stuff, scattered everywhere, was already making me uncomfortable.

'I've been dancing since I was six years old. I haven't treated it like a hobby, for heaven's sake. It's unbelievable. All those hours I put in when everyone else my age was out having fun. My whole damn life. Jesus.'

We'd strolled through the village, Emily supported by a grey metal walking stick given to her by the hospital, and were heading down one of the lanes. The occasional car went by, drivers acknowledging our efforts as we leant into the hedgerow to avoid them. Everyone's politeness was a novelty, to me at least.

'I don't think anyone's questioning your dedication,' I said.

'You don't know what she's like Steve.'

'I have a fair idea.'

We carried on in silence for a while, holding hands. Emily always told me that walking did her good, loosened her back. It was sunny, our moving day, everything you'd want.

Eventually we found ourselves leaning on a gate, gazing across a patchwork of green and gold, a few chimney pots peeking out here and there between clumps of trees. In the distance was the hill, the one we'd seen on that first trip down. I nudged her and pointed to it.

'What do you reckon, a few weeks?'

She looked at the hill, ran her gaze along it: the

inviting woods, somewhere to escape to. I wish I could recall her expression, but I can't. Maybe it's for the best.

'When I was nine,' she said, picking at a splinter in the gate, 'my friend Anne and I wanted the same bike for Christmas. We'd seen it in the window of a local shop, and instead of being all precious about it we decided we'd both get the same one so that we could ride around together. It was pink and white, with matching tassels on the handles, a total girl's bike. We were so excited, the pair of us, and made sure our parents knew which one to get. I realise that makes me sound totally spoilt, but the thought of going into the living room on Christmas morning and seeing the wrong bike, and the crushed look on their faces if I went into a strop, was too painful, so I had to be certain they knew which one to buy. I even made Daddy walk me past the shop a few times so that he'd keep seeing it. Anyway, Christmas comes and guess what happens.'

She stopped talking, picking harder at the beam. She reminded me of Lady Macbeth, in a production we'd been made to watch on a school trip, down at a freezing open-air theatre in Cornwall. She sighed, left the wood alone, and looked back out across the fields.

'I can still see Anne's face when she turned up at our house with her bike on Christmas Day, her father standing at the end of the drive, keeping out of the way, no doubt expecting to watch us share our delight. She wasn't horrible to me, just bemused, I think. Or maybe it was pity – we all had very middle-class emotions, even at that age. Anyway, I'd been given new ballet shoes and private lessons with a highly respected teacher. So all I could do was stand there at our front door, my face burning, trying not to cry in case my parents heard me and thought I was being an ungrateful brat. Anne said nothing, just turned and rode away. It was the beginning of the end for our friendship; every time I saw her after that she looked as if she felt sorry for me.'

'What's Anne doing now?' I asked.

She looked at me. 'I have no idea. What do they all do Steve? Have a few years partying, then look for someone to marry. Have his children, try to keep him interested, perhaps make some curtains if they're bored.'

She turned and put her arms around me, the side of her face on my shoulder.

We stood there for ages, just me and Emily and the quiet countryside, the occasional snatch of birdsong up above us. Eventually she pulled away, picked up the hideous stick that was propped against the gatepost. She rarely leant heavily on it – it was just part of the support, the psychology.

We started off again, eventually coming full circle back to the pub. This would be my second visit to our local, and on our first day as well. I was officially a regular.

If the lad behind the bar recognised me he was determined not to show it. If anything, he looked concerned when I greeted him like an old friend. I suppose I should have asked him for my usual.

I took the drinks to our table, and straight away I could see that Emily was uncomfortable. She would often sit with her weight on her left side. You wouldn't notice unless you knew it was something she did. She was always discreet, but whenever I saw it I felt a familiar dread rising up. All the frustration, the anxiety that we would be forever funnelled through a system that at best seemed over-burdened, at worse, callous. I'm not ashamed to admit it: I wanted her parents to call, to wave their wallet around again. I would happily beg, do a little turn, whatever was required.

Dancers live with pain. They try to work through it, which can be dangerous in itself. Pain is there for a reason. Only when an injury threatens permanent damage do they rest or have surgery. It's almost a matter of, 'If you're not hurting, you're obviously not working hard enough. Push yourself.' The same as judo. I never knew this until I met Emily. I thought it was all prancing around, look at my costume. Of course, everyone can see that the guy in the tights is made of muscle, and we joke about those tights, but secretly we're envious. Strength that few men possess. So we pretend they're all gay, which helps a lot.

The strain on the body is enormous, ridiculous even. Endless rehearsals when there's a production or tour approaching, pressure that you wouldn't believe. Like going to the gym for eight hours every day, your muscles on fire. Wrenching the joints, the tendons, over and over, forcing them too far, all in the name of beauty. Then bed early and do it all again the next day. They put our footballing fondants to shame – a couple hours of five-a-side in the morning, round of golf in the afternoon, maybe piss on the floor of a nightclub, then abuse a cab driver on the way home.

At that point Emily was still on a cocktail of painkillers, more than twenty a day. One of them had weight-loss as a side-effect, but of course that wasn't mentioned. She took them like communion wafer, solemnly, as if belief was part of the treatment. God only knows what it was doing to her liver.

It's not just the pain that's tangible, it's what you can't see. The damage being done.

Whenever people talk about a loved one being ill or in distress, they always say they would swap places with them in an instant if they could, that the other person doesn't deserve to suffer. Take their place, make a noble sacrifice. I would have swapped with Emily in a heartbeat, but it had nothing to do with heroics. When you live with someone who's in that situation, someone you love, you know what it means to feel truly impotent. You want to scream but you daren't, and inside your sense of reason is scrabbling to find a foothold. So you stay silent, try not to explode when the doctor looks at his watch. And that powerlessness is a horror in itself, like listening to someone being tortured in the cell next door.

They have their own pain to endure, they can't be taking yours on board as well. That would be even more unfair, more unbearable.

My advice to you is simple: don't fall in love.

18

I don't imagine the cottage would be everybody's dream house, but it was certainly ours. Small – modest, as the estate agent had put it, trying not to smirk – but with plenty of character. The kind of place where you could leave the door unlocked, or the windows open. Welcome the outside world, rather than wish it would go away.

I've been back to the house since, more than once. Can't help myself. Secretly, of course – I'm not daft. And always at night: the last thing I need is to get collared and find myself up on a trespassing charge.

I slip quietly over the fence at the bottom of the garden and stand there on the lawn – the grass kept nice and trimmed – between the two banks of shrubs that are far neater than when we lived there. We didn't cut them back much or try to tidy them, preferring the semi-wild feel. That was our excuse anyway. Maybe she was trying to help me, a bit of disorder in my life. We even allowed weeds to do their thing if they had a nice flower on them. That's changed as well, of course; it's all pristine now, everything in its place.

We did try our hand at some gardening though, your stereotypical young couple. I can recall Emily's instructions to me as she leant on her walking stick, pretending to be the demanding lady of the house, me the quiet, enigmatic gardener. She'd be almost wetting herself as I got all suggestive with the handle of the trowel in the soil, tears rolling down her face, hushing me in urgent tones in case next door came out and saw what I was doing. That just made me carry on even more, eyelids at half-mast, tongue lolling around like a senile donkey.

These days, when I go there, the moonlight somehow relaxes me, everything liquid silver and black, all the colour gone but the stillness comforting. Like a cemetery. One time I stood a few yards from the kitchen window. I'd had a couple of drinks and driven down, which was stupid. Again. Not me really, not me at all, despite everything that happened. Just one of those evenings.

The young woman was doing the dishes in the window, her daughter appearing at her side to ask questions before flouncing out dramatically each time in her puffy pink dress. The woman – she is attractive, I have to say, which would make things even more problematic if I ever got caught – smiled to herself, then looked up, straight at me. I stood there paralysed with fear, the sour beer starting to rise. I watched her, scared stiff but fascinated, as she pushed a loose strand of hair away from her face with the back of a wet hand, tilting her head to one side until, satisfied with how she looked, she carried on with the washing-up. I moved backwards, placing my feet down slowly like a hunting cat, into the safety of the garden. Back, back, then silently over the fence and away.

I'd gone too far. Lucky that time.

Emily liked greenery, but I insisted on a splash of colour here and there. Stuff I'd looked up in gardening books or on the internet: peonies, geraniums, jasmine, even a few nasturtiums, just to show that I could defy gardening convention. We compromised. We were good at that.

So a few things have changed, but apart from being tidier it's still pretty much as we left it. It hasn't been that long – they're probably focusing on the house. There are a couple of ornaments now, the sort of things we hated: a bird bath, a freaky-looking sundial, and a corny sculpture of two fat babies, artificially weathered to make it look like an artefact from a Tuscan villa. Romantic, if you're into that sort of thing.

The planting is essentially the same though, probably because Emily knew what she was doing, having that creative touch. The apple tree we inherited is as sturdy as ever, and the sound of a light wind moving through it at night could make you believe in higher things. We never tired of saying to each other that we had an apple tree. Such a simple thing, but thrilling. A tree.

We couldn't eat all the apples from that first harvest, there were too many. Kept giving them to friends. Jack got sick of the sight of them, said why didn't I just strap him to the toilet instead. Emily would make blackberry-and-apple crumble, the blackberries picked from the very same lane we walked down on our first trip to the village.

Thanks to my efforts to try to be more sociable, our faces quickly became known in the pub, which resulted in a couple of volunteers coming over one Saturday afternoon to help take down a small but dilapidated greenhouse, next to the shed. We removed the cracked remains piece by piece, carefully passing sheets of filthy glass between us like scientists handling radioactive material. Emily and I kept meaning to replace the greenhouse with a second shed alongside the old one, but never got round to it. Time was against us.

She took photos as me and the other two lads sank victory beers and posed, shirtless and smudged with dirt, like US construction workers who had just brought down a condemned tower block in the projects. I remember her wincing as she bent down to pick up the camera, the guys pretending not to notice. I couldn't go and help her: she'd always told me not to make a fuss in front of other people.

The shed is still there, its roof bowed, the whole thing threatening to collapse inwards at any time. I suppose the new people are as wary of doing anything to it as we were. Or maybe they can't afford to, still just starting out, young kid and all that. I've sat next to it for ages, beneath the stars, looking down the length of the garden at the house, the doors all bolted, sometimes a light on upstairs. Occasionally I think I want to go in, when everyone's gone away or fallen asleep; other times I just want to get back in the car and keep driving until I run out of road.

Eileen, the elderly lady next door, told me not long after we moved in that she'd buried two dogs beneath her roses years before, and, she thought, one of her daughter's rabbits, but she couldn't swear to it, what with it being such a long time ago. The next time the subject came up it was just the dogs; the time after that the bunny reappeared. She was sweet, but I sometimes wondered what she'd pull out of the hat next.

It's hard not to think of the bones down there in the earth when I'm back in the garden, everything so peaceful. I still think of the place as ours.

How much longer?

19

Most spies are recruited, I'm sure that's how it goes. Taken aside in an Oxbridge corridor by someone wearing nondescript clothing, intentionally forgettable. Average height, no distinguishing features. Miss a seminar on Nietzsche as they puff up your credentials, your suitability for government work, the lure of an exotic life of classified access and international travel.

Or there's the other approach: you're working abroad, a lively European capital, when a colleague suggests a Friday-night sojourn to a specialist dance club, a bit of after-hours release. Come Monday morning you find yourself in a café, sat opposite a man you've never met, rain trickling down the window as he passes you grainy photos taken from behind a mirror. And you stare at yourself in shame and horror, ploughing into a modern-day slave on a mattress that's far more filthy than you remember.

Me, I decided to work alone.

Cyan was up to something, I could tell. The way he acted was both annoying and troubling. Not just because of our confrontation, although that didn't help. But he apologised, sort of, and we moved on. Course, that would have been a good opportunity for him to start acknowledging my presence, but, shockingly, that rarely happened. So nothing had changed – we were back where we left off.

His behaviour didn't add up, and I wanted to help

him, but either he thought he was better in some way than the other people at the club, saving his limited repartee for Jack and Jack alone, or there was something seriously wrong. I knew about his background, had firsthand experience of his flare-ups, and had seen the lack of desire to connect with the rest of humanity. But I'm no shrink, no social worker. He kept being late for classes – not all of them, but enough to disappoint Jack. And yeah, that makes me a hypocrite, but I knew my reasons for sometimes not turning up. Cyan was different – he was lying.

Trust between a judoka and his instructor goes both ways, and Jack's hands were tied. Push Cyan too hard, test his commitment, and we might end up watching him leave. That fragile temperament underlay everything. But at the same time Jack was so keen to hone that talent, harness the aggression. The opportunity was there to create something devastating, the same thing all coaches want, what they always hope to find.

Cyan still trained like his life depended on it, that was the frustrating thing. He soaked up all the instructions Jack gave him, improving his technique, and wouldn't quit until he'd mastered each new element, piece by piece. He was moving beyond the basics, but no one dared mention him doing his first grading. He just wasn't interested.

He was still being bullied, to me that was obvious. But there was more to it than that, and I had to know, had to see it for myself. If I was wrong, the episode in the subway a one-off, Jack wouldn't think too highly of me spilling everything. I needed more to go on, so I decided to make Cyan my project. I wanted to help, that was all. Maybe step in if I caught him getting some grief, try to sort things out. The personal lives of kids who came to the club were nothing to do with me, but with Cyan it was different. Much as I hated to admit it, I felt the same way about him as Jack did, and I couldn't stand by while he threw away his talent. I should know, me of all people.

And Jack deserved better than to get dicked around. He and the judo club were practically interchangeable, it was like they shared the same DNA. You don't run a place like that for years without it taking on your personality. Judoka, from those who simply enjoy the sport for its own sake, to those who harbour greater ambitions, respond to the attitude of the trainer. He's the epicentre, the eye of the controlled storm. He can't afford to slip up, can't say, 'I don't feel like it today,' – and by the same token he'll sniff out the weak ones before they know it themselves, concentrate on those with the right attitude. Get it right or get left behind. A way of life.

So I became a spook, a ghost. Just for a short while. A week off work, trying to follow a teenager around the streets of south London. Nothing out of the ordinary.

I took up residence in a pub along the street from where Cyan lived, drinking vats of Coke and reading the paper, looking out the window after every couple of paragraphs. Getting far too acquainted with the menu. School had broken up for half-term, but Cyan rarely left the house. He'd finished his mock exams, Jack told me, so he was unlikely to be studying. Plotting revenge, maybe, drawing up plans. The architect.

I saw few visitors to the family home, save those who were obviously friends of his mum or her daughters. No one for her son, it seemed. I came close to packing the whole thing in early on. I'd seen Cyan only twice, once when he went running – and there was no way I could follow him – the other time when he visited a shop that sold cheap sports clothing. I didn't go in, just waited nearby. He went straight back home.

Undercover work quickly lost its shine. No one was after Cyan, he was just a loner, the kind who invites other kids to rob his kit bag just by having no self-confidence, talking a certain way. Getting a few equations right in class. A hard fact of life, nothing more to it than that – a single drop of fear in the water attracts predators from miles around.

The incident in the tunnel, I told myself, was nothing, boys' stuff. It brought Cyan to us, gave him some focus, that was all. We should be thankful.

Sick of dry steak, mountainous portions of scampi and chips, and running the risk of Coke-induced diabetes, on the fourth day I decided to drive in from Sussex to the city, armed with a packed lunch. I parked on a street adjacent to Cyan's estate and settled in. Flask of coffee, fresh newspaper.

I expected another dull day, but he appeared after a few hours, walking quickly, staring at the pavement. He looked different. Not his clothes, just the way he carried himself. Self-assured, confident. The result, perhaps, of his visits to us, of things finally turning around.

His hands were buried deep in his coat pockets as he headed towards me. I dipped down behind the *Daily Mirror*. When he'd gone far enough past I slipped out of the car, closing the door quietly.

As I walked I felt stupid, a character in a bad cop show, my attempt to trail someone surely drawing the attention of the whole street. They all knew what was going on, they had to, I was that obvious, even stopping to look in the window of a ladies' clothes shop when Cyan stepped into a newsagent's. An assistant watched me from behind a rail of dresses.

What size are you after sir? I see. You won't be interested in our petite range then.

When Cyan moved on I followed, praying that he wouldn't go down into the Tube station. It was too quiet, rush hour long gone. One glance along the platform and I'd be rumbled. Sure: I often take this train – just don't ask me where I'm going.

But he didn't, thank God. Instead we walked for about ten minutes, me hanging back, the area becoming unfamiliar. I tried to memorise landmarks, ready to reverse them for the walk back. A school, kebab shop, zebra crossings.

I eventually found myself on a busy road, opposite a church. It was one of those modern affairs, about as spiritual as an office block. Could this be it, Cyan's troubles distilled down to a crisis of faith, teenage angst over the meaning of life and your place in some unknowable plan? The passing cars seemed to be working in unison, acting like a shield, defenders of the faith. I watched as he crossed over.

He looked around then passed through wrought-iron gates into the church grounds. Through the railings I could see a paved area with a couple of wooden benches out front, a bit of greenery at the edges. Not exactly the

Garden of Eden. I waited to see what he would do, thinking it might be a short cut.

He sat down on one of the benches, hands still in his pockets, shoulders hunched. The determined expression was gone. He looked lonely again, deserted, the child with no friends.

I didn't have to wait long. A girl arrived, stopping outside the gate. Her dark-blue tracksuit had bold letters arched across the arse, but I couldn't make out the word. She too looked around before entering the grounds. I had taken up position at a busy bus stop opposite, trying to blend in, perched on the plastic seat. I watched as she approached Cyan, who looked up without smiling. She said something and he nodded. Then she sat down.

They started talking, but neither of them looked at the other. Cyan didn't move, kept his hands hidden. Then, suddenly, the girl stood up, and instinctively I did the same.

Two buses pulled up simultaneously, blocking my view. I walked along the pavement as the first bus pulled away, its toiling engine churning out thick blue ribbons of exhaust. Then I looked across towards the church.

The girl was still there, but the scene had changed, the balance shifted. She was leaning over Cyan, who sat on the bench looking up at her. He seemed calm enough, but his face was only inches away from a finger that darted like the needle of a sewing machine in the narrow space between them, just like I'd seen that day in the subway. He must be getting sick of it, I thought. One day it'll all be too much and he'll grab one of those fingers, snap it sideways.

She was shouting, gesturing wildly, moving away from him then turning back in, like bad over-acting. Except her anger seemed genuine, her range convincing, as she veered between fury and disbelief. I couldn't hear a word though, everything drowned out by traffic.

Cyan still didn't move. His face bore no hint of response to hers, no look of surprise, no pretence of being defensive. As if he'd expected all this, had done his homework.

Suddenly she made a lunge for him, aiming at his face, but Cyan was too quick and grabbed her wrist. I thought of Jack, of what he taught his fighters, to be agile and always aware. The girl tried to wrench herself free but it was hopeless.

As Cyan held her I saw his other arm rise slowly, eyes locked onto her as she struggled. As he reached for her throat I stumbled forward, my own arm raised to try to catch his attention. When I stepped into the road a shrieking horn to my right caused me to pull up sharply, the cab driver's eyes wide with shock as he slammed on the brakes. I felt myself losing balance, tipping forward, hearing only tyres screaming against the tarmac, rubber being burnt into the ground. Then gravity disappeared as someone behind grabbed my jacket and yanked me backwards.

I swung round, breaking loose from the grip.

'Jesus mate, watch yourself. You alright?'

The bloke who had pulled me back was big, but looked like an alternative therapist, all loose-fitting clothes and a generous ponytail. 'Did it hit you?'

'What?'

'The taxi, did it hit you?'

'No, no, it didn't, I'm fine,' I said, backing away, palms raised towards him. 'Thanks though.'

He shrugged, looking almost disappointed at what counts for gratitude these days. I could read his expression: the next one goes under the wheels.

I turned around again, but was still held back by the traffic. The cabbie was getting out of his wagon, sizing me up, wondering how far to take it. I looked past him, over the cars and towards the church, almost afraid of what I'd see.

Nothing.

They had both disappeared. I craned my neck, trying to catch sight of something through the railings, half-expecting to see her on her knees, bent double with her forehead on the ground, struggling to breathe.

I cursed myself. The wasted days, the boredom, crappy food in a crappy pub. The miserable barman. I'd missed the vital moment.

I eventually made it across the road, ignoring the cabbie, who raised and then dropped his arms, exasperated. I walked up to the bench but there were no clues, nothing conveniently left behind. There was more than one path leading to the church, as I'm sure the priest regularly pointed out to his flock: one led into a small public park, another went out onto the street to the left of the building, yet another went round the back. Cyan and the girl could have headed in any direction, either together or separately. Or they were still around there somewhere, the battle still raging. I picked an exit at random and went out onto a side street, only to be faced with rows of houses, parked cars, a woman pushing a pram towards me.

I must have seemed agitated as she passed, earning myself a worried glance, so I went back into the church grounds and had a look around. I circled the whole building, eyes scanning everywhere, then looked through into the park, but found nothing. I ended up where I'd started, the bench where they had confronted each other.

I am stupid. Inept. Unreliable.

There was nothing I could do. Angry now, I started retracing my steps back to the car, trying to absorb the details of what I'd seen. I walked slowly, too slowly, barely concentrating. Within five minutes I was on an unfamiliar street, walking past shops I didn't recognise. I should have carried on, at least until I reached a junction, got my bearings. But I didn't. I turned around.

He was looking right at me. He seemed surprised, shocked even, but above all, scared. It was like having a young deer in my sights, already startled. I began to move.

Without warning, he turned and ran. I knew I'd never catch him, not with his head-start. I watched him go, then brought my hands to my face, swore quietly into them. Cursed the day, cursed my life, cursed everything. Wished I was somewhere – someone – else.

I headed back the way I'd come, my legs like rubber bands, until I found the right road. I looked in all directions, but he was gone. As I got nearer to the shop that sold ladies' clothing I saw the assistant out front, sweeping dust from the window ledge with a small brush.

She smiled at me as I passed, sweetly, like she understood.

*

What did I really know about the streets? Plymouth isn't Baltimore, no matter what some of the lads I grew up with might like to think. Try leaving them in South Central LA overnight, or the Bronx, then come back in the morning and wipe their tears away.

My parents brought me up to be proud of my heritage, something handed down to them and then passed on, now slowly being dismantled by the world around them, by con artists, salesmen. But the whole un-working-class thing, and the gangs that grew out of it – well, that was new to them. Something had bloomed around the neighbourhoods and silently spread, the wrong kind of culture.

We all do it, pretend it isn't there. Not until it erupts, explodes onto our TV screens.

You don't have to put on a suit to make money, I knew that. I'm not an innocent. But bosses, whatever they're selling, still like an office. The back room of a pub, the street corner, a penthouse apartment in Docklands if all goes well. Somewhere to make plans, strategise. Before Emily and I moved I saw it every day on the estate by my house, without it really registering. You know it goes on, of course you do, but who stops to watch? The strict hierarchy, foot-soldiers and generals, all those little kingdoms. Game plans put into effect in front of you when you're busy not paying attention. Maybe you think they're only hanging around, doing nothing, learning how to intimidate. But the new trainers, designer labels – it doesn't pay for itself, does it?

Not everyone wants a seat on the train from

Guildford.

I was short-sighted, or blinded. One or the other. Cyan was mixed up in something, but I wasn't his keeper. He didn't want my help, maybe didn't even need it. He saw me and ran, that's how much he wanted me in his life. He had his agenda, just like everyone else.

People can get away with a lot, right under your nose. Maybe I should have had an agenda too.

20

Emily loved getting ready to go out, enjoyed looking good: a treat in itself. It was one of the things I loved about her from the beginning, something that we both understood. The attention to detail. She wasn't a show-off, didn't have to turn everyone's head, but enjoyed attention, like all performers. Yet she went about it gracefully, a magnetic force pulling covert glances towards her.

A few weeks after moving to the village we were invited to a dinner party, a small affair, at the neighbours' across the road. I guess they were intrigued by the butterfly with the broken wing, a delicious bit of intrigue for the village. I suggested to Emily that she slap some black and blue make-up around her eye, maybe put her arm in a sling, then I'd act like a vulgar slob all evening and hopefully get us kicked out early. She wasn't having it.

I didn't feel like socialising that night, but Emily was in a bright mood. Her dress seemed to reflect that – vivid splashes of turquoise set among a range of subtle greens and yellows; no angry reds or sombre greys.

'You look great,' I said.

She smiled. A twirl was out of the question, but a stiff sort of curtsey had the desired effect.

'Shall we?' I asked, offering her my sword arm.

She flashed me that look, the one that spoke of unrestrained physicality, of freedom. The life we briefly had, and which I craved. We went downstairs, turned off the lights and stepped outside.

The road, quiet now, felt like a moat between us and their house, which explained why I hadn't yet spoken to the people inside. Emily had, once, outside the village shop. Their place was about three times the size of ours, and I began to feel unsettled, knowing I would have to make dreary small talk. As we were crossing over I stopped and held out my arms like a crucifixion, facing the long row of cats' eyes.

'Let the gods take us,' I said. 'It will be less painful. I have no fear of eternity.'

Emily poked me in the back. 'Knowing your luck, we'll be hit by a cyclist and the eternal form-filling will most definitely be painful. Now stop misbehaving, they're probably watching us.'

She tried to look serious; I pretended to sulk.

We headed up the tarmac drive, past the name declaring us to be at Glebe Cottage, which said it all. Were they being ironic? Cottage my arse. Everything about it constituted a threat, a gauntlet thrown down at our feet.

It took the best part of a minute for someone to answer when we knocked on their fake medieval door. An attempt, I thought, to give the impression of distance travelled, of echoing corridors and seldom-used rooms.

'Hey, how are you both doing? Wonderful to see you,' said the master of the house, a little too excitedly, as if we'd just returned from a six-month jaunt across Africa. 'Come in, come in.'

He stepped back into the hallway to let us pass, eyes locked onto Emily.

'Jonathan,' he said, extending a hand that I grasped firmly. It's important, the grip.

'Steve. And this is Emily.'

'Emily,' he repeated, like someone under hypnosis. 'It's an absolute pleasure.'

He leant down so they could do that cheek-kissing thing. I estimated that our host was at least six foot five, which irritated me.

The interior of the house was a lesson in studied nonchalance. Everyday objects had been strewn indiscriminately around the hallway, as if to suggest that nothing was irreplaceable. It was messy, but the right kind of mess.

'This way,' said Jonathan. 'Everyone's in the kitchen.'

As we followed I tripped over a stray pink wellington, and then had to deal with the attentions of a border collie that came hammering towards us.

'That's Truffle,' said Jonathan, over his shoulder. 'Don't worry, all good fun.'

Walking into the kitchen was like entering something's lair. Jonathan's wife and the two other dinner guests stopped talking a little too abruptly, all trying hard to divest themselves of *that* look, as if attempting to work out what we might have heard.

Jonathan's missus immediately sprang into action, bounding over like the dog to greet us. She kissed Emily, then shook my hand.

'I've met your lovely girlfriend already,' she said. 'But not you, of course. I'm Daisy.'

'Steve.'

Her cool hand only emphasised the heat emanating from mine. She looked at me intently, a slight smile hovering at the edge of her lips, like a satisfied cat.

She was wearing a snug, baby-blue jumper and what looked like expensive jeans. She was slim, with delicate features unravaged by a life of toil, fair hair pulled back and secured with a delicate silver clasp. I tried not to stare while she introduced Emily to her more robust-looking friend, Penny.

Penny and Daisy. Even their names fitted together cosily, like their whole lives had been spent in a sun-dappled meadow.

A word about our fellow diners. She, Penny, looked like a try-hard. One of those who go power-walking every morning in the local park with ski poles and no apparent sense of embarrassment. A trophy wife, of sorts, but some of the sheen just starting to wear off. A few more pounds than he'd bargained for this early on.

Simon, her husband, struck me as the kind of person who drives past housing estates demanding to know how they can all afford satellite. His handshake was far too strong, like he had something to prove, and he wore a pink shirt. I was already in a bad mood, a slave to my inferiority complex, but that one garment only made things worse – no poor man has ever worn a pink shirt. He was also carrying himself in a bizarre manner, standing impossibly erect with his chest stuck out.

'What will you have Steve?' asked Jonathan.

Emily was cradling a glass of bubbly I hadn't seen arrive.

'Oh, uh, red please. Burgundy if you have it.'

Jonathan seemed to falter, no doubt assuming I'd go for beer. I would actually have preferred one, and cursed myself for trying to fall into line.

'Of course,' he said. 'Coming right up. Another Hooverfraulein for you Si?'

Simon barrelled his chest a little more, his lower jaw jutting out.

'Keep 'em coming chief,' he said, glancing at me like we were about to strip down to our jockstraps and get into a rucking maul.

'So, you found us alright?' said Daisy.

We smiled. Yes. Good one.

'Where do you live Simon?' I asked, offering a silent prayer that he'd say Maidstone or Crawley. Just give me something, anything.

'Little hamlet just outside Marlow. Very similar to here. Love it. Managed to snag us a place that came with a disused barn, just ripe for conversion.'

He seemed to be releasing swathes of pheromones into the air. I already felt like I knew everything about him. For a while we all fiddled with bits of chit-chat, punctuated by Penny's excruciating laugh. I'd been dumped into the cast of an opera.

Jonathan and Simon started talking about cars. Airbags, specifically. This was not ideal, seeing as how my knowledge of cars could fit into a Fiat Punto, along with all my belongings. I started to zone out, depressingly early in the proceedings. Simon must have clocked me.

'So,' he drawled. 'What line are you in?'

'Sales.'

'Uh huh, I see. Do we need to be careful this evening? Are you on the prowl, a bit of subliminal sweet-talking, catch us unawares?'

'No, you're alright, it's my night off.'

Simon was in hunting mode, I could tell. Some blokes are like that, always evaluating, from your shoes to your lawnmower. I felt glad he wasn't the one we lived opposite, especially as he looked like he enjoyed going out partying. The last thing I'd want to see on a Sunday morning was him and his Flight Of The Valkyries wife rolling back home bleary-eyed with their clothes torn. Mind you, I couldn't really see the point of Jonathan either. He was kind of foppish, always poncing around the village in his pretend country boots and red corduroys; but at least he kept out of our way.

Pretty soon we were ushered into the dining room. Daisy, to be fair, knew how to cook, and I tried not to spill anything down my shirt while everyone around us discussed property prices, holidays, wheat intolerance, school fees – all manner of endlessly interesting stuff. Emily dipped her toe in the water a few times; they asked about her family and Hertfordshire, and the girls seemed absolutely entranced that a trained ballet dancer was in their midst.

We got the injury out of the way early on. They seemed a bit deflated, short-changed. A muscle-wasting disease, or something eating away at Emily's central nervous system, would have given the gals much more to work with over their lunchtime cappuccinos.

Unfortunately I was opposite Simon, who ate with his mouth open, fork held in a mutton fist, forearms resting on the table as if negotiating the terms of a surrender. Above us an intricate chandelier glinted menacingly, glass shards pointing down at us like some ornate execution device.

Jonathan and I did what guys always do: try to find some common ground by talking about sport. Unfortunately he was a tennis and sailing man, and judo was completely foreign to him, as it is to most people, I suppose. I racked my brains trying to remember who had won Wimbledon the previous year, but it wouldn't come to me. We gave up.

When everyone had finished the main course, I offered to help Daisy with the plates. I began scuttling back and forth with crockery, placing things carefully on the vast expanse of kitchen worktop while Daisy brought something bright and creamy out of the fridge. The voices in the dining room seemed a long way off.

'Would you like to help?' she asked, gesturing towards a bowl of summer fruits, the decoration.

We both worked quietly for a few seconds; I had nothing to sell.

'I'm pleased you're getting on with Jonathan,' said Daisy. 'You boys should get together more often.'

She was joking, had to be.

'He and Simon go back a long way, they were at Charterhouse together. Jonny is a year older. Simon was his batman for a while, or whatever it is they call it.'

I'm pretty sure they have another name for it, I thought, carefully placing a blueberry.

'You should all play tennis together sometime,' she said.

Something I've noticed with the wealthier classes is that they possess this uncanny ability to have what they believe to be a two-way conversation, and yet no replies are necessary. Questions go unanswered, points unresolved, but the talk trundles on. It's a wonder they get anything done.

'How is Emily coping, if you don't mind me asking? Not being able to dance, I mean.'

The question seemed a little forward. Maybe she actually cared.

'Well, it's not easy,' I said. 'She's worked hard to get to where she is, but, you know, hopefully they'll get her sorted soon. What am I saying – of course they will. Everyone's rooting for her, her family and everything, and she's a fighter, so ...'

It struck me that I was talking to someone who'd never had to fight for anything in her life. Probably the only thing she ever cleaned was the shrine on which they placed her husband's wallet.

'She's a lovely girl; you're very lucky.'

Daisy had stopped working. She leant against the worktop and popped a berry in her mouth, coyly, as if she wanted to get something off her chest.

'It must be a comfort – having a friend who's a physiotherapist.'

I was a salesman, supposed to have an answer for any given situation, but I faltered.

'Um, yes. It is, you're right,' I said. 'He's been great.'

I was surprised. I thought Emily had been on her own when she met Daisy. My frown gave me away.

'He comes to visit quite often, doesn't he?' she said. 'I see them going off together. They seem very close.'

'Yes they are. He's been a real help. He understands what she's going through.'

I felt as if someone was sitting on my chest. What did she mean by 'often'? I suddenly had the sensation of everyone knowing my business, better than I knew it myself.

Daisy smiled, a little smug now. Then, almost ceremonially, she placed a fat strawberry in the middle of the dessert, like a warning sign. Don't mess with us boy, just because you struck lucky.

'Thanks for your help,' she said, softly. 'Would you mind bringing the bowls?'

We were halfway through pudding when Penny decided it would be a good time to open her mouth again.

'What I love about you, Daisy, is that you recycle so much.'

It was time for us to leave.

Daisy tried to look humble, as if saving the planet was the very least she could do with her empty days. Beneath those layers of self-contentment though, I had her down as a self-harmer. She was confident, of course, but a little edgy, despite the cordon of respectability around her home and family. One careless move away from being caught shoplifting in Waitrose, I felt, luxury chocolates she neither needed nor wanted nestling in the depths of her Gucci handbag.

'Oh, well, I try,' she said. 'But it's mostly Veuve bottles. Probably doesn't count.'

The room was filled with the orchestral clanking of silver on porcelain, as everyone deftly handled their summer fruits, feeling, if they were anything like me, desperate for an end to the evening. The lack of conversation was oppressive.

'So, Steve,' said Jonathan, 'Emily tells us she's planning to take the hospital to the cleaners when it's all over. I imagine the cut and thrust of a court battle would appeal to a salesman such as yourself. Getting excited?'

He had me, they all did. I should have known better than to enter their den and try to join in. I couldn't look at Emily, didn't want to see the expression on her face. I had no option but to bluff.

'It'll be interesting,' I said. 'She's got a good case. This whole thing is dragging on way too long.'

That was it: I had nothing else, and they knew it. I let Emily handle the rest of the discussion while I sat there in mute humiliation, trying to look as if we'd already been over the ins and outs a hundred times, that I'd been in on the plot from the beginning. Details tumbled from her lips that I'd never heard her mention before, but had to pretend I knew about: the name of the lawyer; correspondence she'd had with him; opinions and options traded back and forth. I felt acid sitting at the back of my throat as I tried to digest these revelations. I stared at the table, barely able to look at anyone. I knew Simon was eyeing me, sitting there like he'd reeled in a big one, watching it flop around on deck.

Eventually, after what felt like a decade, the discussion ended and the evening died on its feet. Any remaining hope of meaningful conversation became tiny talk, little crumbs easily swept away, before we all lapsed into a ritual of sighs and mutterings about the time and having important things to do next day.

Emily was sitting with her weight on one side again, trying to ease the ache that I had stupidly hoped would take the night off. I should have known. She gave me the look: take me home.

I kicked the evening into touch with one last

compliment about the meal and before we knew it we were out in the cold, Emily holding on to me as we made our way across the road. I could sense her tension, trying not to let the pain defeat her, but close to giving in.

Back indoors I went to the kitchen and poured myself a huge vodka while Emily grabbed a handful of painkillers from the bathroom. When she came back down I was ready for her.

'What the hell are you playing at?'

'What do you mean?'

'Don't give me that, you know what I'm talking about. You can't sue the NHS, it's not right. Why didn't you just go private in the first place?'

Her head dipped slightly, looking up at me, that playful look she liked to use. Then she came up and put her arms around me.

'Oh Steve,' she said into my shirt. 'You're too easy. It was a joke. I was bored out of my mind, all that talk of schools and property. And a second property on the way.'

'But you made me look like a dick, in front of those ridiculous people.'

I grabbed her shoulders, not tightly, but just enough to put some space between us.

She looked surprised and took a step back. The sudden movement caught her and she toppled sideways, grimacing, but steadied herself by grabbing my arm. Her face was screwed up, her eyes tight shut. When eventually she let go of my arm she didn't speak, didn't look at me, just went into the living room and stretched out awkwardly on the sofa. She lifted her hand to her forehead, like an old-school Hollywood actress, as if the pain had migrated there.

I stood watching her, took a mouthful of the vodka. It was bitter as I sent it down.

'You were very convincing Emily, I have to say. Even had the name of a lawyer.'

'My family's,' she replied, turning over to half-bury her face in the cushion. 'My parents have sued a few people in their time. It's like a bloodsport to Mummy. The rest I made up, okay?'

I didn't answer.

'Although,' she continued, 'Alex was going on the other day about taking legal action, so perhaps it was in the back of my mind.'

And there he was again. In the house with us. Standing behind me, sat in a chair, upstairs in the bathroom. Wearing my dressing gown. It was almost as if she knew which button to push.

I let it go. Alex had become a presence I was unable to shift, but I couldn't face a row about it, not while she was unwell, and not with wine and vodka swilling around in my stomach. A stony silence I could live with. Besides, we weren't one of *those couples*, systems clogged up with crap that needs to be flushed out regularly. Despite Emily's passion for life, for art, she always tried not to get angry or emotional. It's odd to think that now. Even at the end she didn't crack, didn't cry. Defiant, almost, part of the breeding: it doesn't do to make a fuss. I even admire her for it, which doesn't help.

Refilling my glass in the kitchen, I listened to her struggle up the stairs. My mouth was already stale; in the morning it would taste of charcoal. I went and slumped in the sofa, still warm from where she'd been, and reached for the TV remote. I needed a distraction, other people's lives. For a while I could hear Emily moving around upstairs, then the house went quiet.

21

I came to late the following morning, reluctantly blinking myself to life in the stuffy bedroom. It was rare for me not to wake up when Emily got out of bed, which she always did at least once in the night, but I was dog-tired, and now badly hungover. I'd had a couple more glasses while watching crap TV, and now I regretted it. If Emily had fallen I would have been worse than useless, unable to stand let alone drive. I vaguely remembered staggering up to the bedroom, but not much else. Had we spoken? Did she watch me struggling with my clothes, the sad clown?

We were approaching breaking point, despite the move, the idyllic surroundings. Any possibility of reclaiming our intended life seemed to be hanging by a thread as we shuffled between fear and dread. The threat of an operation was always in the background, like an impending court appearance: sentence or second chance.

It was less a question of fatigue catching up with us, more the fact that it never went away. I was irritable at work, totally unfocused. Shadows had appeared under my eyes, and hers.

I lay there for a while, the pain gathering, an advance unit preparing the full assault. I felt like someone was twisting a knuckle against my skull. An atmosphere was pretty much guaranteed when I went downstairs; Sunday could be wasted, and there was a fair chance I would be sick not long after standing up.

I closed my eyes and dug my fingertips into the clammy sockets, groaning as the circular motion eased me towards a state of semi-alertness. The house was silent, the stillness broken only by an occasional car whooshing by. Apart from that, nothing, not even Emily's beloved Radio Three. I assumed she was in the garden, looking at her plants, tending. Eileen next door must have spotted her – she was like a keen-eyed traffic warden – and they were keeping their voices low because of the poorly person upstairs.

But surely I would have heard Emily pottering about, the rattle of her watering can being filled.

I slid from the bed, groaned again, only this time with more urgency, and nudged my feet into a pair of threadbare Portsmouth FC slippers. I negotiated the stairs like an old man, gripping the wooden handrail, unwilling to trust my shaking legs.

What was I expecting to find? Emily had a back injury, not a heart problem. Her condition didn't lend itself to any kind of attack, some life-threatening seizure. Ours was a situation that drained rather than shocked, a steady drip of uncertainty. On occasion, though, my mind raced towards calamity, I couldn't help it; we were like two exhausted birds on a wire, instinct alone preventing us from falling off. But still I had a vision of finding her on the lawn in a crumpled heap, hair fanned out, one of those pre-Raphaelite depictions of romantic death that Emily had insisted I look at properly on one of our gallery outings.

She wasn't downstairs, a few unwashed dishes next to the sink the only sign of recent life, like the galley of a ghost ship. I'd been too drunk even to clear up. I opened the back door and stepped into the garden. Nothing. I wanted to call out but felt self-conscious, as if I hadn't learnt my lines for the scene, the abandoned shack in the woods. But the axe was safely locked away in the shed, and she probably wasn't in the compost bin.

I went back inside, not knowing whether to feel alarmed or annoyed. Was I being punished? Had I screwed up that badly last night? Even through the vodka-induced merry-go-round of my immediate memory, I was pretty sure I hadn't inclined our conversation in the direction of Alex when I came to bed, however tempting.

I grabbed the coffee jar to have something to do. Caffeine would offer my head no favours, but I'm a traditionalist. Spooning sugar into my cup, I had my first constructive thought: phone her. Obvious really. I clumped back upstairs and retrieved my mobile, phoned her number.

My spirits sank as the buzzing in my ear was echoed downstairs, the inanely happy tune mocking me as it rose towards the bedroom. I disconnected and returned to the kitchen, passing Emily's phone on a bookshelf. I picked it up and deleted the call. My finger was poised above her messages button, but I pulled back. She hadn't been taken against her will, hadn't left the house in the dead of night, sacrificing herself so that I might go on alone. Wherever she had gone, she had gone voluntarily. Perhaps I didn't want to know where.

I sat at the kitchen table and nursed my coffee. It felt odd to be alone. Emily and I had only ever had one real argument, a few months before, and we'd put very little effort into it. She'd wanted to go to an arty party and I had no intention of accompanying her. It would be full of pretentious types, as usual, and at that point I'd had my fill, even though Emily was adamant that she still needed to be 'seen around' until she got back to full fitness. In the end she went on her own, and when I picked her up later she was deathly quiet until we got home, where it all kicked off. I was a selfish git, apparently, a charge I would normally be happy to accept, but which on that occasion seemed totally unfair, so I let her have it. Just the one barrel though. It wasn't pleasant, but what the hell? Give and take, then make up.

After twenty minutes at the kitchen table I was starting to feel less benevolent. I'd finished two cups of coffee and my head was throbbing, so I had a shower. Afterwards there was still no sign of my beloved girlfriend.

I picked up her phone again. If I looked at it, would she be able to tell? Everything goes behind your back in the digital age.

Do it.

I pressed the button. Inbox. Four messages: Mummy, naturally; Rachel, one of her dancer friends; Chloe, her ex-flatmate, still living in West Kensington but with a Russian bloke who had as many cars as she did surnames; and Alex.

He stood out on the list like the results of a blood test. I didn't read the message. I wanted to, but stopped myself. Like poking around in someone's diary, finding things that won't help you in any way whatsoever. I didn't want to give in to doubt. Emily wouldn't lie to me, especially not in our situation, what we'd been forced into. When the time was right I'd give her the opportunity to explain herself. We'd laugh about it.

Her having physio with Alex was no big deal; she never tried to hide it from me, even though it still didn't appear to be helping. And yet her faith in him was unshakeable. I wish now that I could picture her face whenever she defended him, told me he knew what he was doing. It's pointless, I suppose, but, like everything else, I keep going back.

I was waiting, doing what I thought was right, it just doesn't feel like that yet.

I grabbed my coat and went to the front door. Emily's walking stick was leant against the wall. I stared at it, wanting it to be a clue, but it meant nothing. She didn't use it all the time, was afraid of becoming too dependent, she said. I think she enjoyed being courageous.

As I stepped out I saw Jonathan's Range Rover creeping down their drive. It stopped at the edge of the road. I almost didn't want to turn around and acknowledge him, but there were limits to how much time I could reasonably waste fiddling with my keys without looking obvious. I considered going back in, pretend to have forgotten something – they might be dumb enough to buy that. But I didn't. I turned and walked down the path, looking straight at them, Jonathan and the two organisms his loins had produced. I'd never spoken to them, but they'd stared at Emily and me enough times to indicate the boundaries they felt comfortable with.

I waved. Jonathan acted all surprised; the window

slid down and his head popped out.

'Morning Jim,' he called. 'Off out?'

Looks that way, doesn't it? And don't ever call me Jim again, you twad.

'Yep, just a little stroll to clear my head. Had a few more when we got in.'

He waited while a couple of cars whizzed past.

'You sly old devil. Me, I had to take Truffle out early, he was going crazy. Don't want a dog do you? I'm joking.'

See what I mean? Questions and answers, a whole conversation from the one mouth.

'Anyway, got to dash. Tennis lessons for these horrors. We must do it again some time.'

Up went the window. As the car pulled away I received stares from the back seat. I wanted to throw a rock, vomit blood, something special to induce night terrors.

I wasn't sure where to go. It was a nice day, fresh, and I had the Sussex countryside at my feet. I was still standing there trying to decide when I noticed Daisy watching me from a downstairs window, the room where we'd had dinner. Instinctively I raised my hand. She waved back.

Life changes on moments, all the time, tiny impulses pulling you in a thousand different directions. I knew I should walk on, hair of the dog in the pub, leisurely read of the Sunday papers. Exchange pleasantries with the bar staff, joke about getting old, my poor kidneys. The girl I loved would soon be home, accompanied by a friend I'd turned into a threat despite having only the bitchy insinuations of a neighbour and my own frailties to go on.

It was like I was someone else, an observer. Out of my body and mind, angry with everyone, everything. I saw myself walking across the road, up to the front door.

Cup of tea, Steve? Emily not with you? Oh, Jonathan will be gone for hours, they love their tennis. I'm so sorry if I made you uncomfortable last night, I really am. I thought you knew. You're not upset with me, are you?

A thousand different directions.

When I looked back at the window she was still there, still watching. Determined. My empty stomach began turning over, like wet clothes twisting in the wash, the water turning dark.

Who wouldn't be flattered? Even from a lonely woman. She could probably stare out of the window all day long, waiting to be noticed. I stared back.

Then a movement caught my eye, off to the side. I looked back down the road and saw her.

Emily. On her own.

She was quite a way off, and at first I was sure that she was walking, but then I realised she had stopped and was leaning against the low stone wall of someone's front garden. I moved off quickly, started running. She smiled as I got nearer, pleased to see me. She looked tired.

'Are you okay? Where have you been, I was worried,' I said.

She seemed a little out of breath, the effort of moving.

'Sore this morning,' she said. 'My back's really tight, I thought I'd come out for a bit, try to loosen it up a little. And let you lie in for once.'

She read my expression.

'Don't worry,' she said, holding my arm. 'It's not too bad, honestly. At least I don't feel any worse than I have been these past months. I'm going to get better, I know I am.'

'Of course you are. I was concerned, that's all. After last night and everything, you know. At least you're not using your stick though, eh?'

She shrugged, like that was a minor achievement. Dancers live with pain; when would I get that into my head?

I didn't know whether to believe her or not, about feeling better. I still wanted a miracle. Not too much to ask for. Divine intervention, something to make us not give up.

As we walked slowly back to the house I looked for other positives, which I had been doing, it seemed, on an hourly basis for a long, long time. I had so little to go on, but eventually spotted something. I reached up, stole its freedom with my net, then eased a pin through it, careful not to break such a delicate thing.

She hadn't been with him.

22

Emily didn't sleep at all on the night before the injection. Not a wink, and looked truly awful in the morning. Same as me. When she got up early I didn't follow; she'd been irritated by my presence the day before, like I couldn't possibly offer any comfort, didn't understand.

I lay there, as usual, listening to her downstairs making a cup of tea, moving around quietly. I thought she made a phone call, but I couldn't be sure. It might have been the TV, a low murmur.

She was scared, I knew that. Who wouldn't be? And if she'd known what was coming, she might never have gone at all.

Another step into the unknown, the same clinical attitude, a job to be done. Emotions only get in the way here. We'd ventured too far up the chain of command, strayed away from the front line, into the hands of generals.

I wasn't allowed to go in with her, had to sit it out in the waiting room. Anxious patients and their helpless relatives gathered together to wait, huddled in pairs against the icy nonchalance of the white coats. Those of us left behind when names were called either stared at the wall or flicked through magazines. I imagined it was the same for them as it was for me, sitting there skimming columns of text that meant nothing. Sentences floating away or merging incoherently: gardening tips, celebrity chat, gossip that never runs out, gorging on itself. I was desperate to leave the building, to go and get some air, but couldn't risk not being there to see Emily the moment they finished with her.

People glance at each other in those rooms, but they don't really look. Too scared to make meaningful eye contact, to admit that we all feel the same way, carved open.

When they eventually let me through, she was lying on her side in a bed in a small ward. It felt like a military field hospital, the worst cases. An occasional muffled groan in the background; you don't want to look but you can't help it. It's instinct.

Like the scene of an accident.

She was crying quietly as I approached, her face red, the gown drenched with sweat between her shoulder blades. She could barely talk.

No anaesthetic. That was the first thing I remember her saying. I went hot, then cold.

The pain was still too close. Agony, unbearable, excruciating; no single word to neatly sum it up. The man who did this was a ghoul, a criminal. A concentration camp doctor filling a child's veins with petrol, curious to see what would happen.

He had to hit the right spot first time, she told me later, no second chances that close to the spine. A male nurse, solidly built but still looking worried, held on to her tightly to stop any movement, the merciless steel spike easing its way through layers of skin and muscle. Emily admitted that she whimpered like a puppy, through gritted teeth, as the pain went to the centre of her.

And no anaesthetic.

I felt a fury I had never experienced before, but with nowhere to vent it. Twenty-first century medicine, best in the world. Slips away behind closed doors if you dare to ask questions.

Hopefully it'll work, Miss Dashwood. See how it goes.

23

'They almost took the entire bloody door off, the little sods. The lock's buggered, and we're on the high street as well. Heaven help us, I thought those cameras everywhere were supposed to help prevent this sort of nonsense. What's the bleedin' point of them if they don't do that, eh? Somebody answer me that.'

Jack lifted a mug to his mouth, then seemed to forget what he was doing, plonking it back down without it touching his lips. Some of the tea slopped out, running down the sides like candle wax.

I rarely saw him agitated, but when he did he sounded a lot like Michael Caine. I'd told him that before, but it probably wasn't the best time to go over it again, not with the front door nearly ripped off its hinges. Jack's normal demeanour was that of quiet determination and army discipline, which, he always maintained, rubbed off on his judoka. You set an example, not make one, that was his motto. But today was different.

'Is anything missing?' I asked.

He shook his head. 'Not as far as I can tell. They gave up pretty quickly by the look of it.'

'Any thoughts?'

He shrugged. 'Opportunists. Kids, maybe. Probably just curious, or kicked the door in for a laugh, had a bit of fun upstairs then ran off. Got scared, I suppose, or heard something, you know how brave they are. Christ, what's happening to this damn country?'

I liked that about Jack: he always talked to people as if they were the same age as him, with the same beliefs, as if we'd all witnessed the breakdown of society together.

'Bit odd though, don't you think?' I said. 'There's always a few notes in the till, and some things worth taking, something to show off, especially if you want to make a bit of a name for yourself. You know, a souvenir to prove they broke into –' I did an impression of open-mouthed astonishment '– a martial arts club. Wow.'

Jack didn't reply. He was staring at the wall, a deep frown creasing his forehead. Eventually he stirred, looked at his watch.

'Bloody locksmith. Even he can't turn up on time, just like the Old Bill. If he's not here in ten minutes I'll do it myself.'

Emily glanced at me, a questioning look suggesting that perhaps we should make ourselves scarce. I made a hidden gesture: give me a minute. She got up anyway, as if to re-emphasise a point – the injection hadn't really helped much, she was uncomfortable. At first she thought it had, but no. Sitting down for long periods was still impossible; like I'd forgotten, like I wasn't carrying it around with me all the time.

It was Saturday morning and I'd finally brought her up to meet Jack. I thought it would be nice to whisk her off for the day, do the sightseeing thing we did on our first date, take our minds off things.

We couldn't say it to each other, but we'd both been hoping for more, much more. A new start, an injection of confidence.

Jack had been banging on for ages that he wanted to meet her, and when was I going to introduce the pair of them? I'd always been wary, I suppose, about how they'd get on, but eventually I gave in. And besides, Emily was fed up, totally bored, unable to burn off her frustration.

We thought we'd pay a visit to the club, then head up into town. There was an exhibition on at the Barbican, a history of Scandinavian folk painting Emily wanted to see. My enthusiasm was kept in check by a total lack of interest in what people in Sweden paint, but there was the promise of a couple of beers afterwards, maybe an Italian. The deal clincher.

Jack eventually calmed down, as I knew he would. He'd experienced worse things than a broken door, a bit of mess. It was an inconvenience, he said, an irritation. I made a suggestion.

'Why don't you two take Arthur for a walk? I'll help out round here, man the desk. It'll do you both good, you know, stretch your pins.'

Jack and Emily looked at one another.

'Not a bad idea. Emily my dear,' he said, all mock-Victorian, 'would you care to take the morning air with me? The local park is spectacular at this time of year, the yobs are in full bloom.'

She laughed. 'I would be delighted sir. But do you think we are in need of a chaperone? One doesn't like to hear gossip.'

We all looked down at Arthur, curled up in his basket behind the desk like a very large, hibernating mouse. Something in our body language, or the staring, must have had an effect because he twitched, then raised his drowsy head. Jack grabbing his lead from the coat peg was enough to have him out of his pit and jumping around the room, barking, and whipping the air with his sorry excuse for a tail.

'That's that settled then,' I said. 'Have a nice time.'

They were gone for an hour and a half. An hour and a half. The park was only ten minutes away. After an hour I started to get very twitchy.

The locksmith eventually turned up, with a battered toolbox and an armful of rusty apologies about being late, so I just left him to get on with it. Far from the happy worker, he said he had a hangover from celebrating his daughter's eighteenth birthday the night before, apparently labouring under the misconception that I cared. Sitting at the desk in the gym, I could hear him moaning and groaning at the bottom of the stairs, dropping bits of kit as the complexity of the task threatened to overwhelm him. At one point he came up and asked to use the toilet, but I lied that it was out of order and we were waiting for the plumber, who was also late. As he moaned his way back downstairs I made the universal gesture of male contempt behind his back, a satisfyingly rhythmic motion, and the cosmos gently realigned itself.

People came and went, leaving the gym in better spirits than when they'd arrived, which made for a good atmosphere. Saturdays were always busy, both the gym and the dojo – Jack held two classes in the afternoon, one of which lasted for three hours. I think when we turned up he thought I would be attending, but didn't make a scene when he realised I was trying to cheer up Emily.

He had started badgering me about doing my first black belt, saying it would not only set a good example to Cyan, but was also, you know, *about bloody time*.

I chatted to some of the regulars while I waited, catching up on gossip, trying not to fret as the quarter hours rolled by. What were they doing, for God's sake, arranging a holiday? I hoped it was a good sign, that they'd made a connection, found things in common. Mostly, however, I just wanted Jack to like her.

Such a simple request, that we all get on.

When they eventually returned I knew things had gone wrong. Jack was too jovial, cracking jokes about the mess our security expert had left by the front door, threatening to withdraw payment unless he came back and painted over the scuff marks that had actually been there for years. He asked me if everything was okay in the gym – had I broken anything and was scared to tell him. He was over-compensating: something was up.

Emily wasn't going to pretend to be as happy, that was obvious. Her mood had darkened. She hadn't turned into a foot-stomping monster, but neither was she the same gay promenade partner she'd been when they stepped out. She was reduced to being merely polite, and clearly wanted to leave. The day suddenly seemed to get longer.

We said our goodbyes. Jack was about to take the first class, which included a few new kids who had so far demonstrated some commitment by turning up on time for the past three weeks and not giving him any lip. One of them, he thought, even had some potential, a confidence that went beyond his age. The other two would go nowhere, probably sent to the sessions by dads who wanted to impress other local fathers. The human equivalent of a fighting dog, tethered to the family. The workouts would do the boys good though, Jack said, teach them something about life. Maybe they could educate their old men in return.

When we started to go, Jack stopped me.

'By the way,' he said. 'I have some astonishing news.'

'Oh yeah, what's that then?'

'Cyan's agreed to do his first grading.'

'You're kidding me.'

'No. He took a lot of convincing, and I'm not even sure he'll turn up, but there you go. He's agreed.'

'Jesus, I didn't think you'd ever get him to do it. Blimey Jack, that's amazing. Fair play to you.'

He looked really pleased. Like a proud parent. He wasn't one for great displays of emotion, our Jack, but on this occasion he looked chuffed to bits. I was really happy for him.

I turned to Emily to explain what this meant, but she was already halfway down the stairs.

As we walked off down the street I began to wonder if Jack would sleep at the club that night, or maybe for a few nights, because of the break-in. It was something he often did anyway, although he didn't think I knew, so we hadn't talked about it. I was sure he did it just to avoid going home to the empty flat every night.

Charlie, one of his part-timers who regularly opened up first thing, used to fill me in. There might not be a breakfast bowl in the sink, and Jack's sleeping bag would be hidden away, but there were other signs. The shower room freshly used, morning post not on the doormat, Jack muttering about having come in early again to take care of some paperwork. Little details that gave him away. The nation should be thankful that his stint in the army hadn't included black ops.

I could picture them both, Jack and Arthur, bedded down in the corner of the dojo hall, Jack pondering the strengths and weaknesses of a judoka he'd been working with. Cyan maybe, the one he really wanted to help. A few snacks, a book, their medication close at hand. Like an old married couple. Arthur curled up next to him, occasionally looking up or maybe just sniffing the air, thinking he'd heard something scuttling, some big-eyed creature come to life from his dreams.

I never brought it up with Jack, never felt that it was my place to. A man is entitled to put his head down where he likes, and besides, I always thought it was enough that I knew, that being aware was somehow a help.

'So,' I said, as Emily and I waited at the Tube station, 'how did you two get on? You were gone for ages.'

'Fine,' she said.

'Just fine? You seemed different when you got back.'

'It's nothing.'

I kicked a cigarette butt off the platform and onto the tracks. 'Filthy habit,' I said.

'What is?'

'Litter.'

I smiled, she didn't.

'You need to tell me, or our day out will go down the pan. What happened?'

Emily stared across the tracks, as if deciding whether or not she could be bothered.

'He seems like a lovely man.'

That was it. I waited, but she wouldn't look at me.

'And?'

She sighed, energy being summoned.

'Look Steve, he obviously cares about you, about the club and, you know, everyone involved in it, which is lovely, it's just that I don't need to be lectured at the moment, I really don't. My back is either aching or stabbing me, neither of us has slept properly for months, I can't return to work and I'm just really, really tired. Okay?'

'Lectured? What do you mean, lectured? That doesn't sound like Jack.'

'Really. Well, he asked an awful lot of questions about my injury, like he's some kind of expert. Kept asking me about the symptoms, does it hurt here, does it hurt there? I'm not in the mood Steve, even the so-called specialists can't make up their minds; what makes Jack think he has some kind of special insight?'

'Emily, don't forget what he does for a living. He's been involved in judo for more than three decades. He's seen more injuries than you could shake your walking stick at, so of course he'll want to help, that's only natural. I don't get it, why should it bother you?'

She turned to me, her face pinched in a rare moment of spite.

'Well, aren't you his biggest fan? I do so envy your working-class solidarity. Does he try to tell you what to do as well, bombard you with questions?'

This wasn't the Emily I knew. The girl who refused private treatment, the one with principles. I was shocked, and took the bait without thinking.

'Be careful what you say to me, Emily. That is totally out of order.'

My turn to stare across the railway lines. A train rattled up to the platform opposite, packed full of early-morning shoppers returning from the West End, and it wasn't until it creaked and groaned its way out again that Emily spoke.

'Sorry.'

I let it hang for a few seconds.

'It's okay. You've got a lot to deal with. I understand.'

She slipped her hand into mine. 'We both have, Steve, and I appreciate what you're going through as well.'

'Yeah, well, don't you worry about me, tough as old ballet shoes.'

'No, seriously,' she said. 'I really am grateful. For everything.'

'Fine, whatever. You owe me though, I'll think of some way for you to repay me. And Jack, you know, he's just looking out for you. It's what friends do.'

'Either that or he works on commission.'

'What do you mean?'

'Steve, he must have said to me about three or four times that I should go and see his physio. Said he'd sort me out, like he was some kind of wizard.'

'George,' I said. 'Who actually is not far short of a magician, as it goes. Jack sends all his lads there when they get injured, or even just for an MOT. Decent bloke, you should think about it.'

'But I have doctors poking me from all angles, plus a fully qualified physiotherapist who understands my world and whom I trust implicitly. What makes you think Alex isn't up to the task? Why would I want to see someone else, someone who might have different ideas and end up undoing everything?'

I watched as our train approached in the distance, the rails sparking like it was under attack. I didn't know what to say. The last thing I needed was a conversation about Alex, those healing hands. My opinion of him might have been based on paranoia, my very own bundle of insecurities, but I still didn't rate him. Sometimes when she'd had a session she came back in even more pain. What anyone might 'undo' wasn't clear to me.

The manipulation of muscles, she kept repeating, is always painful, it's supposed to be like that. You should try being a dancer sometime.

Maybe, I thought, despite her champagne socialism, deep down she still retained a little bit of snobbery, as if a physio recommended by a gym in the East End is never going to come up to the mark. Like all he'd be able to offer her would be a bucket and sponge, an ice pack.

As the doors of the carriage opened I let her get on first.

'I'm sure Alex knows what he's doing,' I said, quietly, behind her back.

If she heard me, she didn't reply.

24

A face on a poster, one of hundreds up and down the country, millions around the world. Like the building blocks of a cruel monument reaching towards the heavens, more names etched into it every day. Families dreading the phone call when their little girl or boy is officially out of reach, beyond the clouds.

Have you seen this person, what information do you have? Were they troubled, keeping secrets, or were they led astray, looking for a friend in all the wrong places?

And what's the best picture to use, to capture someone's personality, their essence? Is it the party girl, her eyes bright, alive with the moment, but with the wine glass out of shot or erased altogether? Or the one taken on holiday, laughing at the camera, the turquoise sea crackling with life behind her. You'll assume she's headed for college, brimming with ambition. That's got to be the right picture, surely: convey the right message, make the compassionate folk far more likely to give a damn.

But still, you can't help but look at them and wonder if it's all too late, whether they were gone before the ink was even dry. Sociopaths get bored of their victims quickly, almost as if they're a let-down, a disappointment. They do what they have to, whatever it is that makes them feel powerful, then that person is dispatched, like twisting the neck of a kicking rabbit, or a struggling bird.

I stopped in the street, staring at the image, which stared back at me. They'd chosen the giggling party girl, taken indoors on a friend's mobile, the lighting poor, part of someone's arm in the corner. The whole scene slightly blurred, as if she were already becoming a memory.

The poster was curved around a lamppost, carefully placed at head height to catch your eye, the paper still so fresh that garish nightclub flyers had yet to intrude, to demand their turn, bringing her peers back to their preferred reality.

I felt like I was choking, the blood pumping hard in my neck.

Was it her?

Missing. One word sitting boldly at the top, like a wanted poster in an old Western.

I shivered, dug my hands further into my coat pockets. I didn't know her, couldn't attach a personality to the face, but to me she was more than an arrangement of pixels, a touch of red-eye. A person I almost had some sort of contact with, even though she never knew, couldn't pick me out of a line-up.

Missing. Please ring this number. Any information.

I wanted it to be a mistake. I'd seen her for a minute or two at most, and not close enough to make her stand out from any other girl on any street you'd care to pick. They all want to believe they have what it takes to be different, to be spotted, but to me they all looked the same, jostling for position until the effort becomes too much. Maybe we've all done it, fending off the inevitable as the years trickle by, preparing our excuses. Discipline has many enemies.

I remembered her snarling face, not a bit like the photo. The righteous indignation, the fury, as if she herself were capable of putting someone else's daughter on a poster.

And if she was still alive, was I the last person to see her, hopelessly held back by roaring traffic, denied vital seconds?

Or was it Cyan?

Standing by that picture I felt the strength drain from my body, the kit bag pulling on my shoulder like a dead weight. I turned and hurried away, glancing round to see whether anyone was checking me out, as if staring at the image for too long could somehow incriminate me.

It wasn't panic I felt. I don't know what it was, I really don't.

25

She went behind my back. I couldn't believe it. And now she was standing in our front room, leaning on her stick like Charlie Chaplin, enjoying my reaction.

'You're bullshitting me, right? Tell me this is a joke.'

She was beaming, her eyes bright.

'Holy mother, you did. You actually agreed to this.'

She began giggling, covering her mouth, the naughty princess in the fairy-tale. 'Oh Steve, don't be like that, it'll be fun. They're only being kind. I think it's very nice of them.'

'Yeah right. We'll see how they like it when I bury him up to his neck in the sand and pour honey over his head.'

She moved forward, pressed herself up against me like a small animal; the desired effect. I gave in too easily.

'When?'

'Tomorrow. Around ten.'

I looked at her. 'Emily, I can't, not tomorrow.'

'Why not?'

'Cyan's grading is tomorrow. You know that, I told you a while back. And I promised I'd be there.'

I thought she'd understand, be reasonable. Instead she took a step back and watched me, like she was loading a gun.

'Steve, I've already agreed to it. I can't be expected to remember everything you're doing, and I certainly can't just turn around and cancel at the last minute, how would that look?'

I shrugged. 'I have no idea, but try seeing it from my point of view.'

'Try seeing it from mine.'

We eyed each other, almost daring the other to go first. She had that air about her, expectant. *I'm ready if you are.*

'Look, Emily ...'

'Don't "Emily" me. Just don't, okay? You've got to start making some choices Steve, them or us.'

'Them? I presume you mean Jack, and the guys at the club. Jesus, Emily, that's not fair. Those people are my friends, I like going there. You just don't get that, do you?'

'And I'm trying to make friends for us down here, or can't you tell that either?'

'Oh come on, the Lord and Lady in their castle? Give me a break.'

Her face was flushed, eyes bitter and resentful, as if she'd reverted to childhood.

'You're such a rebel Steve, such a bloody revolutionary. The whole world is against you. If this is how it's going to be we may as well give up now, and you can move back and live among your urban gangsters. But oh look, you hate them as well. What *are* you going to do?'

My heart was hammering against my ribs, anger coming quickly to the boil.

'Thanks Emily, thanks a lot. Still the pampered little ballet star eh?'

'How dare you Steve, how dare you. All I want, all I

want is for us to …'

She began to lose it, her lip quivering, the tears already there. She brought her hands up to hide them.

Was it out of line, or did she ask for it? I couldn't tell; both, probably. But I wasn't about to comfort her, even though I knew I should. Not this time. I had a phone call to make, one she'd forced on me. She could dry her own tears for a change. I picked up my mobile and left the house.

I'd been to only one class in the past two weeks, in an effort to please Emily; on her own all day, waiting for me to return.

I was the limp rag in the tug of war.

'Jack? It's me. How's it going?'

'Oh, hello Steve, everything alright?'

'No, not really.'

He laughed. 'Trouble in paradise?'

I took a deep breath.

'Look,' I said. 'Tomorrow, it's about tomorrow. I'm sorry, something's come up.'

He didn't reply.

'Jack?'

'I'm still here.'

'Right, well, I'm really sorry. Honestly. Emily arranged this thing, I can't get out of it.'

'What thing?'

I stopped walking. It wasn't cold, but I was shaking.

'The beach. She's arranged a trip, with our neighbours. We just had a fight about it.'

'The beach? You're going to the beach?'

'Yes.'

'Right. Fine.'

'Jack, I can't ... she ... Look, next time ...'

'Alright, don't worry about it. Have a nice day out.'

'Jack, come on. I'm not doing this on purpose. Don't you be on my case as well.'

'Steve, just forget it, okay? I mean it, really, just forget it. I should have known.'

'Excuse me?'

'Don't play dumb, Steve, not with me. We're trying to give someone a chance, yes? And here I am relying on someone who takes being given another chance for granted.'

'What?' I said. *'What?'*

I was doing my best to sound incredulous, aggrieved even, but it didn't work. We both knew I was bluffing.

'Right, Jack, listen. Just let me get this stupid trip out the way, then I'm all yours. I promise. I'll step up my sessions, take my next belt, and do whatever it takes with that young protégé of yours. Alright?'

'Okay Steve, whatever you say.'

There was no emotion in his voice. He sounded cold, detached. A sensei, not a friend.

'I'll see you next week Jack, okay?'

'Sure.'

I waited, but there was nothing else. I looked at the panel on my phone.

Disconnected.

The following morning I got out of bed early, cleaned the kitchen, then went out for a run. It was Saturday, hardly anyone around. I saw only a couple of elderly people, walking away from the shop, newspapers in hand. They both had small dogs.

Twenty-seven minutes after leaving the house I was back sitting on our front step, leaning against the door. I had more than enough in me to run a lot further. I sat there for a few minutes, barely out of breath, looking at the house opposite. I wanted to be on the point of collapse, drenched in sweat. Cleansed. I tried to let the tension melt away, but it wouldn't. I wanted to be fitter, stronger, not sitting on a doorstep with more to give.

I was treading water, standing still.

After I'd showered we ate eggs on toast, which Emily wolfed down. She was chattering away, excited about the day. No mention of the night before.

Soon there was a knock on the door, and I opened it to find an equally buzzing Daisy, in a pale summer dress, sunglasses pushed back to hold her hair in place.

'Hi Steve.' We did the cheek-kissing thing. 'I am so looking forward to this.'

I wasn't sure what to say; it wasn't a question. That would have been easier. I glanced over her shoulder and saw Jonathan in the car. I tried not to show my gratitude that they were alone, make it too obvious.

'Be right with you.'

Unlike at the dinner party, there was no awkwardness in the car, no gaps in the conversation. I think Daisy was concerned about me feeling left out, and made a point of involving me all the time. Emily sat up front, and every once in a while I caught a glimpse of her face in the side mirror. She looked happy.

We drove for about an hour, to a beach called West Wittering. I'd never heard of it; it sounded like a made-up name, a private Victorian retreat where ladies swam in their clothes. The wittering classes.

Considering who we were with, it wasn't what I expected, some quaint little cove that only the locals and a privileged few knew about. Far from it. The place was massive, broken every hundred yards or so by wooden breakwaters that stretched from the pebbly back of the beach, all the way down across the flat sands and into the sea.

We walked away from the crowds, then set up on the pebbles. Daisy laid out a blanket before suggesting a stroll along the shore, which Emily declined, as did Jonathan. He said it was his day off so he would rather sit around and be lazy for a bit.

'Fine,' said Daisy, taking off her plimsolls. 'Looks like it's just you and me Steve.' She reached into a rucksack and took out what looked like a very expensive camera and off we went, down towards the water.

'I hope you didn't mind us taking over your day,' she said as we splashed along. The cool shallows were therapeutic, lapping around our ankles, the sun on our faces. 'No doubt it was as big a surprise to you as it was to Jonny. He started to go into mild panic mode.'

'It's fine,' I replied. 'Although yeah, you're right, Emily did spring it on me. But that's okay, we're having a good time.'

'Oh I'm so pleased. And I'm sorry about last time, the boys can be a bit much when they get together. Jonny gets nervous and starts waffling, and Simon, quite frankly, can be a complete ass. We only see them because he's an old friend.'

I didn't reply, didn't know what the protocol was. It hardly seemed right to agree with her; plus, if we were compiling a list, I hadn't liked Penny either. So I just kept walking, enjoying the water.

'What's with the camera?'

'Ah,' she said, holding it up to show me. 'This, Steve, is my dream. Or at least it was.'

'Was?'

'Well, when I met Jonny I was only a couple of years out of college. Brighton University. I have a degree in photography, would you believe. Anyway, I took a gap year to go travelling – Europe, North Africa, parts of Asia – the usual. Then when I came back I was assistant to a photographer in Camden, but it was really boring, all he wanted to do was take pictures of young bands. After a while I found it a bit creepy, he was forty-eight after all. Plus he was paying me next to nothing, kept telling me the experience was priceless, so we parted company. I thought I could make it on my own, which turned out to be a serious error of judgement, unfortunately. And then, well, it wasn't long after that that I met Jonathan – not that it was an accident, of course. My parents weren't about to let me wander around aimlessly, so to speak.'

'But you still take photos?'

'Oh God yes, all the time. I didn't for a long while, but I took it up again about five years ago. It keeps me sane. Try raising two children in Sussex some time, it's exhausting. We're like a couple of PAs.'

She stopped walking, turned to look at me.

'Not that I don't love them to bits of course.'

'Of course.'

'But you have to make sacrifices sometimes, put things on the back burner.'

She didn't want to say it outright. Couldn't say it. Her body language told me everything: she was almost apologising, seeking absolution. But she didn't need to justify herself to me, I was in no position to judge.

I tried to picture her in Brighton, roughing it. Sitting on the beach near the old pier, red wine and joints on the go, listening to The Doors, The Velvet Underground. More boyfriends than Jonny could possibly imagine. Probably doesn't ask.

'Got any pics in that thing?' I asked.

'Yes, I have. Tell me what you think.'

She pressed a couple of buttons, then came in close to me, started going through the images. One or two landscapes, but mostly close-up stuff, abstract. What I would be tempted to call experimental if I knew what I was talking about.

'These are really good,' I said. 'Seriously. I'm no expert, Emily will tell you that, but they're excellent. You should do an exhibition.'

'Oh Steve, that's so nice of you to say.'

'I'm not kidding. You should think about it. Or maybe send some into magazines, see if they're interested.'

Listen to me, dispensing advice. Emily's work was almost done, the training was paying off.

'Oh, I was in a few, ages ago,' Daisy said. 'And it is such a thrill to see your work in print. But you're right, an exhibition would be so exciting. And frightening, of course, not like doing one at college.'

She laughed, a little nervous maybe. 'I'll look into it, perhaps do something local.'

I didn't push it, didn't want to sound patronising, but

I hadn't said it for effect. And I was a little jealous, I had to admit. Having something to aim for.

The noise of the sea suddenly began to sound like traffic rushing towards me; the screams of children in the waves could have been seagulls scavenging for food.

'Let's head back,' I said. 'They must be bored without us by now.'

On the way she took pictures of the breakwaters, crouching down low to get different perspectives, approaching them in ways that would never have occurred to me. I could see the quiet satisfaction on her face. Not smugness, just a look that I imagine any artist must feel, creating something from nothing.

I was thirsty, the sun scorching my face.

We swam, for about half an hour, the four of us. We didn't speak much, both couples pairing off, enjoying strangely private moments in the huge open expanse, the feel of each other, the ease of it. Emily didn't seem to be in any discomfort, held aloft by the water. I decided we would come back whenever we could, a thought that immediately darkened when I realised I was thinking of her still being ill in the months ahead. I pushed the thought aside, forcing my mind blank. Not today. A day off.

Breathe in, breathe out.

When we'd dried off, Daisy brought out treats from her coolbox, offering up chilled white wine and beers. We clinked glasses; a chorus of 'Cheers'. Jonathan unpacked some foil barbecue trays and started lighting the charcoal.

I glanced at my watch – Cyan would have completed

his grading by that point. I wanted to phone Jack to find out how he'd got on, even though I knew he'd pass, a foregone conclusion. But it was the least I could do.

I made my excuses, explained that I needed to make an important call. No one minded, but Emily said nothing, watching me as I turned and headed down to the water.

Jack sounded distant, his voice cold.

'He failed.'

'Failed? What do you mean, failed? That's impossible.'

'Well, clearly it isn't, because that's what happened. He was all over the place, distracted. I could tell straight away it would go wrong.'

'Shit, I'm really sorry to hear that. How is he?'

'Take a guess Steve. Very quiet on the way back, then he left without a word.'

'God. Well I hope he comes back soon.'

'Yeah, me too.'

'And you Jack, you okay?'

'Me? Fine. Busy.'

'Right, well, I guess there's not much I can say at the moment. I'll have a word with him if you like, if you think it'll help.'

'Okay Steve.'

As I went to speak again two lads walked right by me, with a girl who was swigging from a can. They were showing off, pushing each other around, trying to impress her. She was laughing, lapping up the attention. I tried to shield my phone from the noise.

'I'll speak to you soon,' said Jack, and then he was

gone.

I walked back up the beach, still shocked. Cyan should have flown through it, no problem at all. I thought of his face when he realised I'd been following him, then the girl on the poster. And I thought of Jack, and how he didn't even ask when I'd next be attending a class.

I tried to relax, downing a couple of quick beers. We talked for ages, and I noticed that Daisy and Jonathan didn't press Emily about her back, her career. It was mentioned once, briefly, but she was reluctant to go into it. I sat there thinking how unfair it was, the only one of us to actually chase their ambition, but being held just out of reach. It was hard not to picture hospitals and waiting rooms.

By the time the light began to fade we were all a little drunk, apart from Jonathan, the driver. I'd assumed that by evening I would be itching to get home, but I wasn't. I wanted to stay.

The place was quiet now, the tide almost in. The lights in the chalets at the top of the beach made them look inviting, and occasionally we would hear a shriek in the distance, down near the water, people laughing.

Emily was kneeling about three feet to my left, sipping her wine. I could barely make out her face, but I knew she was watching me. The conversation had slowed, everyone enjoying the atmosphere. I glanced up as something moved above us, a bat I think, hunting.

'I'm so lucky,' Emily said, quietly, like no one else was there.

'Really?' I replied. 'Why's that then?'

'Because I've got you.'

'Ahh,' said Daisy. 'That's so sweet.'

'No, I mean it. I'm so grateful to have met Steve. I don't know what I'd do without him, how I'd cope. Things are really tough and he's sacrificing an awful lot for me, far more than anyone realises. He's putting so much on hold, and I really, really appreciate it. I want him to know that.'

Jonathan raised his bottle. 'Good man. Cheers to that.'

We all drank. I was touched, but uncomfortable. This was far too public for me.

'Well,' I said. 'It's no problem. But you still owe me.'

Emily shuffled on her knees towards me. 'Trust you to make a joke of it.'

She leant forward, kissed the side of my face. Her cheek felt cold against mine.

26

Emily's parents made their move. Inevitable, really.

There was a limit to how long their daughter could hold out, standing astride the barricades, waving a red flag. They probably never even took her that seriously.

My chat with Michael in the pub on moving day, all that talk of surgery, had set the clock ticking. Emily getting worse, her career on hold. But Elizabeth still took her time sending in the cavalry, letting Emily have her way, stretching out the suffering just a while longer. She turned it into a war of attrition: starve out the pampered insurgent and her proletariat boyfriend. She thought she was being clever, but I was no deserter, they hadn't figured on that. If only they'd asked me, I would have whispered in Emily's ear, prised open the door to the bunker. But no, let's see if we can't break them both while we're at it.

Emily and I were still battling our way through the medical system, my desperate phone calls going unanswered, messages not returned. But we knew the options anyway, and time was slipping by. The Dashwoods' hand was forced.

This time they were insistent. If there was to be an operation, they wanted the very best. The cleanest, sharpest knife. To them the NHS was merely a formality, a filter through which families like theirs could pass into more purified waters. They wouldn't stand by, they said, as their daughter continued to collect pills like clues on a treasure trail. I think Elizabeth also wanted to shame me a little more, give Emily another reason to reconsider our relationship. Remove the threat of the family blood being thinned. It's one thing being unable to pay for expensive meals, quite another to not have the money to take away pain. Isn't that what money's for?

Look at the salesman, a few coins rattling in his pocket.

As the threat of the blade hovered, they broke cover. We were to speak to one of the specialists, get the ball rolling. They would pay.

Emily got scared, tried to protest. The situation hit home and she panicked, tried to use her principles as a defence. She even said that her mother's interference wasn't helping, merely increasing the tension in her muscles, and that I should somehow stand up to her, make them back off. I pointed out that her family had paid for her entire dance education, so refusing their help for a career-saving operation might seem a little churlish. She mocked me for using a posh word, then made it clear that she was determined to hold out. She did, for a short while, then relented. I phoned her parents to thank them – left another message that wasn't returned – the little machine latching onto every pinched syllable, every last drop of humiliation.

And so we finally passed into the comforting arms of the private healthcare system. A near-empty waiting room, a consultation that lasted an hour; given answers previously denied us by time-poor doctors.

Smartly dressed secretaries holding leather-bound appointment books and saying things like, 'Would next Wednesday be okay?'

It was an eye-opener, for someone like me. When I told my parents, they thought they were finally losing their son for good. Breathing alpine air while they choked on the smog of their own upbringing. But they wished us luck, sent Emily their love. The girl they would never meet.

The relief that someone was actually listening to us was overwhelming. Emily quickly had another scan, and, unbelievably, results the following day. But the news was mixed: an exploratory operation was recommended. The surgeon who saw us was a cheerful bloke who didn't look much older than me, except he had the forward motion of someone who'd actually finished university and gone looking for more. He saw no other option, since the new scan had revealed nothing new, but suggested another possible cause, joint fixation, then pointed out that a decent physiotherapist would have helped get that under control, if only partially. I couldn't bring myself to look at Emily, couldn't drag his name into the room.

The list got longer: spondylolysis; Scheuermann's disease; lower-back muscle strain; piriformis syndrome; damage to the sacrum and pelvic bones; Baastrup's syndrome, where the spinous elements of adjacent vertebrae are touching.

He paused after this last one. It's usually caused by a trauma, he said. A fall perhaps, or something more serious, like a car accident. He tried to not give anything away, but we'd been there too many times. I was used to picking up on every detail.

I think he felt sorry for me, tried to make light of it.

'You're not making it easy for us are you, Miss Dashwood?' he said, his eyes bright and shining, a smile dancing lightly on his mouth. 'Still, we do like a challenge.'

You pay your money, but, ultimately, where does it get you? Their ideas were no better than anyone else's, just shorter waiting lists, better coffee. Nicer pens.

Afterwards I tried to convince Emily that we should be pleased, the scans had shown nothing serious, but for a few days she barely spoke. I couldn't tell what thoughts were passing through her, but I could guess. She batted away my attempts at being positive – it wasn't me being cut open, I had no right to try to sweeten the pill.

Surgery was scheduled for eight days' time.

Was it the worst day? For Emily maybe, but not for me, not yet.

The hospital was a modern building about fifteen miles from where we lived. Tucked away, the sort of place a cult might choose as the location for its headquarters. Elizabeth and Michael followed behind us in their Mercedes, having stayed the night in a local hotel. It was like being in an old movie, the Gestapo on your tail, everything in black and white.

The place had a hotel feel. A courteous welcome; the furniture tasteful yet functional – the luxury of spare resources. Like you'd just pulled off the motorway, breaking up a journey.

A room to yourself, decent menu. Nice view across the fields.

Everything clean, perfectly clean.

Michael and I waited outside while Emily got changed, Mummy in attendance. We didn't even try to talk about sport, just a few words about how quick the drive over was, the absence of traffic jams.

As we waited for Emily's pre-op injection I tried to be cheerful; then, when that failed, I went for the sympathetic approach, holding her hand, asking if there was anything she wanted, anything I could do. Her mother looked on as if a leper had snuck into the resort and nicked her sun lounger.

Emily had been unresponsive on the journey over, and seemed to follow the nurses' instructions like a robot. I couldn't reach her. Hadn't, in fact, been able to for the past week. Quiet and distracted when I left for work, she was never any better when I got home. She went to stay with her brother in Hackney for a couple of days, said the change of scenery would help take her mind off things. I drove her there, looking in my mirror, scouting for Alex's car.

She was supposed to order a meal for after the surgery, but couldn't imagine feeling hungry. I made the decision for her, just to keep up appearances, one foot placed firmly in normality.

The psychology of dealing with the unwell, selling confidence. For once I was glad about what I did for a living.

'Nothing,' said Emily. 'I'm okay. I won't be hungry.'

Up until that point her injury, condition – whatever – had been like blotting paper. If we ever got ahead of ourselves and let our optimism flow, it would soak up our enthusiasm for life until we were dry again, losing hope. Now, at the hospital, things were coming to a head. A dangerous situation, despite the assurances. Emily was trying to control her emotions, but then so were we all, locked into our own worries, our own misgivings.

I put it down to everyone's rational fear of hospitals. She was about to be cut open, for Christ's sake, her future on the line, not knowing what they would find among her bones. And there I was pretending to enthuse over poached salmon with anchovy-and-rosemary pesto.

The last few hours were the worst, the waiting endless. Our surgeon arrived to give her a final once over and looked concerned about a blotchy patch on Emily's back, the result of too many hot-water bottles. But, satisfied, he gave us the thumbs-up, patted Emily on the leg and told her not to look so scared. No, he said, it wasn't a minor operation, anything to do with the spine carried risks, but the procedure itself wasn't unusual. Been doing it for a hundred years or more.

'Just having a look around. See what we can do to get you back on the stage. And don't worry, I've been practising at home.'

She tried to smile, programmed since birth to show good manners. I think I laughed, a little self-consciously, knowing it was just his stand-by joke. The pair of us had formed a tag team: marketing men, united in our determination to bend the will of a client. Emily's mum and dad simply stared down at their daughter on the bed as if some spectral entity, something malicious, might be lying there next to her.

When it was time, Emily broke down as they wheeled her trolley out of the room. I touched her toe through the blanket, told her we'd all be waiting for her when she got back. She couldn't look at me.

The three of us stood there afterwards, cloaked in silence.

'Think I'll go for a walk,' I said. Time spent with Mummy loomed.

'Good idea,' said Michael. 'See you back here.'

Elizabeth was standing with her back to us, staring out of the window, as if absorbed by structured, ordered life beyond the confines of Emily's room. The mown lawn, with its large pond and careful arrangement of plants; a few ducks poking around among the reeds; an unusual stone sculpture with feminine curves and a hole in the centre, part of it like an arm reaching towards the sky. Clouds gathering overhead.

I walked for more than two hours, briskly, trying to drain my muscles of energy while anxiously checking my phone every few minutes. Down lanes, past dozens of fields, through a couple of tiny hamlets. I stopped only to look in one or two shop windows and to read the cards on a post office noticeboard, not really registering any meaning in the misspelt, shaky handwriting, nearly all of them in capital letters. For some reason I stood outside a small supermarket, fascinated by a poster proclaiming its latest deal – two lamb chops, new potatoes and peas, all for £1.89.

It didn't seem possible.

I phoned Cyan's number. No reply. Leaving a message was pointless but I left one anyway, just to feel like I'd done something. I thought of that little rag in the tug of war: first one way, then the other.

When I got back to the hospital I was told that Emily wasn't out yet and it would still be a while, so I disappeared again for another hour. I had no idea what her parents did while she was gone, and I didn't care. Maybe Michael chatted up the pretty receptionist, glad of a few minutes while Mother raided the blood bank.

When she was wheeled back in, Emily was a bit muddled, coming out from under the anaesthetic. She kept murmuring to herself about the lovely nurses. I sat by the bed, leaning in, trying to read every sign like we were at a seance. Her forehead felt hot to the touch. Elizabeth looked at me as if she suspected I might be faking it, while Emily held on to my hand, drifting in and out.

We sat there watching her for ages. After a while I asked Elizabeth if she'd like to swap seats with me, but she declined. Michael, sitting at the end of the bed, was quietly reading his newspaper, but kept going out to wander around. At one point I saw him by the pond, his turn to stare at the water, the ducks no longer there.

Eventually one of the nurses came and roused Emily, took her blood pressure and asked how she felt.

'I'm fine, thank you,' she replied, the words catching in her dry throat.

At around eight o'clock, satisfied that everything had been carried out in accordance with their expectations, her parents left. Long trip home ahead of them. I said I'd keep in touch over the coming days.

Another affectionate pat on the back from Michael, a thin-lipped grimace from Cruella. She leant over and kissed her daughter on the cheek.

'Get well dear,' she said, and then they left.

A minute later there was a tap on the door. Michael reappeared.

'Left my paper behind,' he said, coming in and retrieving it from his chair. 'Oh, and I forgot to give you these.'

Reaching into his jacket pocket he took out a small tin of sweets, the picture on the front all Belle Epoque-style, like you see on champagne bottles.

'Remember these?' he said, placing them gently in Emily's palm. 'The first time we had them? That holiday in the Loire Valley, when you were twelve. We got lost and ended up staying in a guesthouse, the one that smelt a bit odd and the owner said was haunted. You and your brother were terrified, every little noise.'

Emily looked at the tin, then up at her father, her eyes glistening. A tear broke free, trickled down her cheek and was lost in the pillow.

'Thank you Daddy.'

He leant in and kissed her.

'Get well soon my darling. Anything you need, you let us know.'

He looked across the bed at me, that same hollow expression I'd seen in the pub. He spoke quietly, not the military man at all.

'That goes for you too Steve, okay? You've got my number, don't be afraid to ask. I mean it. Anything.'

'Thanks Michael. I appreciate it.'

He stood there for a couple of seconds as though he ought to say something else. A smile, a little wave of the folded-up newspaper, and he was gone.

*

The following morning our surgeon seemed a little dejected, almost disappointed, as if his brilliance had failed to cast new light on the problem. Two discs in Emily's spine were slightly split, he said, but he had tidied them up. Hopefully that would help, but there was nothing else obvious. He suggested a course of physiotherapy at the hospital, which he would be happy to arrange, but was met with Emily's usual rebuff: Alex's exalted talents. He wasn't desperately happy about that, but he'd done his bit. Recommended some pilates, told Emily to take it very easy for three weeks, and that was that, we were done. Enjoy your breakfast.

I thought back again to that terrible night in A&E, when the results of the X-ray came back with nothing. At the time I wished that it had been different, something definite, and now I felt exactly the same.

When he left I wasn't sure what to say, how to spin the news. I was losing the ability to be upbeat, to act convincingly. I thought of Jack, how he would handle it, the psychology. A fighter cannot contemplate fear, let alone show it. Fear weakens you, gets you hurt. That or bad luck.

Three days later we left the hospital, Emily on crutches. The pretty receptionist asked me where I wanted the bill sent.

I'd arranged to take another week off work, convinced that it had to be only a matter of time before I was called upstairs, one or two impending choices brought to my attention.

We need our people to be fully committed Steve.

Work or walk.

We watched DVDs in bed on a portable player, and I got loads of magazines in for Emily. Sometimes she dozed, and, when I wasn't creeping around the house lining everything up or scrubbing furiously at bacteria, I would study her, looking for any hint of discomfort in her face if she shifted in her sleep. She was put on a different combination of painkillers; it was my job to keep track and administer.

Her mother phoned all the time, firing questions at me like a Wall Street trader. I dreaded the calls, joked with Emily about going ex-directory or even moving house again and forgetting to tell them. I started sneaking one or two of Emily's tablets here and there to damp down the constant dull headache.

Daisy brought over a massive bouquet of flowers. I left her and Emily in the bedroom for a while, and afterwards we had a coffee in the kitchen. She said I looked tired.

Alex, unsurprisingly, came over a few times to sit with her – to give me a break, he said. I did little now to hide my distrust, and I'm sure he noticed, but said nothing. I could barely tolerate us being in the same room, but whenever I left to do some shopping or buy a paper, I did everything in a hurry so that I could get back in there.

The three of us in our little house, things unsaid.

Far too soon it was time for me to go back to work. Emily had started to get out of bed more often to move around, with the hospital's permission. She said she felt stiff lying in bed all day, the muscles like a clamp around her spine.

I had to leave them together. I didn't want to, but I had no choice. I thought of installing some kind of listening device in the room, something plugged into my laptop, but was terrified of being found out.

And so it went. We put everything aside, lived on our nerves, waited for signs from her body that it wouldn't let us down. Directing our hope pointlessly skyward, ready to make a deal, to be granted that revelation.

27

You won't be allowed to go upstairs sir, he told us, not yet anyway. Not until we've been right through.

He looked fed up. A copper in a cheap grey suit, a few days shy of a decent shave, giving us the once-over like someone buying a second-hand car. Everyone's a suspect.

Firstly, he said, as if addressing children, it wasn't safe, and secondly it was a crime scene, until we were told otherwise. Jack and I were standing on the street outside, peering over his shoulder, trying to see in. The occasional lightning flash of a camera at the back, in the kitchen. A few people had gathered, attracted by the police cars, but kept their distance. They didn't want to be tainted by association with the law enforcers, not on these whispering streets, but couldn't hide their desperation to see what was occurring.

The suit got his notebook out, clicked the end of a stainless-steel pen. Only a few steps up from a traffic warden. Old friends from school probably treated him as a joke, unless they got mugged, or came home to find the back door open.

Had we seen anything suspicious – not just last night, but recently? Anything out of the ordinary, something that stood out – maybe people hanging around who we didn't recognise?

I said no, not been round for a while, girlfriend not well. Jack shook his head; he had nothing either. The notebook vanished.

'Here's my card. If you think of anything, call. Anything at all, even if you think it's nothing.'

From the street the place looked normal, apart from CSI padding around inside. Most of the onlookers eventually got fed up, drifting off in newly formed pairs, striking up conversations.

Gotta be the usual – street robbery. Or assault, another kid gets it for not giving up his mobile phone. Should have been in school anyway ...

Something to talk about down the boozer.

A few shops along from our building was an alleyway. We went down it and around the back, Arthur trotting along happily at Jack's feet, the lead connecting them never taut. When we got there a fire engine was struggling to get out, a tricky manoeuvre between the bins and garages, a battered transit van in its way. We found a different copper, similar suit, standing in the doorway like a charcoal sketch. *The Angry Policeman*, by Anonymous. There were black streaks reaching up the brickwork above his head that made me think of Hiroshima, pictures I'd seen of cowering people reduced to vaporised shadows, ghosts among the rubble.

There was a smell in the air too, like roasted flesh. Or cheap food you can't resist on a Saturday night, only more sour, vinegary.

We asked how long it would be before we could go up, Jack having already turned away a few of the regulars. Our man from the Met looked annoyed, as if he had better things to be taking care of, just like his miserable twin round front. But he called back into the void to find out anyway.

'Give us another half an hour at least, unless you want to risk going through the floor.'

He stepped back inside the doorway, treading carefully like a wading bird, debris crunching underfoot.

Jack was looking past me, down the alleyway. I turned and saw Lucy coming towards us. She had that look on her face, like she had to know what was going on but would pretend not to care. When she reached us the first thing she did was pull out a packet of Dunhill, gold lighter at the ready. Plod stepped back out into the daylight.

'Excuse me luv, not here yeah?'

She stared at him, trying to see if he was joking. A bit of irony on a Thursday morning. Apparently not.

'Bit late for that, isn't it?' she said.

'Sorry darling. You don't want me to have to call the fire boys back again do you?'

His eyebrows rose, then settled back down, like he'd made his point. *Course she wants them back, stuck in this rat-hole of a neighbourhood. Jesus, she'll be thinking of those uniforms for weeks.*

He turned his back on us, studying the charred doorway.

We walked across the delivery yard so Lucy could light up, surrounded by encroaching litter, cardboard stacks and abandoned electricals. She called him a name under her breath, the word that ladies tend not to use. I turned my face, hid my smile.

We stood together outside one of the garages. Someone had daubed a warning across the metal door in heavy-handed strokes of red paint: *No parking, constant axes needed*. Jack was the first to speak.

'That's both of us now,' he said. 'We have a break-in, then downstairs gets torched.'

The cigarette paused on its way towards Lucy's mouth before she registered. Of course, the break-in. She drew the smoke in hard.

'Maybe it's just unlucky. A coincidence.'

'Maybe,' said Jack.

'Besides,' she continued, 'we don't know if it was deliberate yet. One of them might have left the fat on, I wouldn't put it past them. Or the grill might have sparked. Or …'

She held up her cigarette in the space between us.

'… it could have been one of these. Unfortunate for them if it is though, the insurance company will go all the way.'

I looked at the burning tip, the lipstick mark on the filter. The inside of Lucy's forefinger was a pale, orangey brown, the nail varnish chipped at the edge.

No one said anything. The thought of it actually being an insurance scam entered my head, but didn't settle. Nobody gets away with that anymore, not these days. Everything's under the microscope, you'd be stupid to even try. Besides, there was no bad blood between us and the chicken boys, so why would they put our place at risk as well? Jack would be horrified if he knew I was even contemplating it. He still believed in people getting along, common goals.

'What did they say about your burglary in the end?' Lucy asked. 'The police I mean.'

'Nothing,' said Jack. 'Kids, they reckon. You know how boring life can be for the little shits.'

He caught himself, looked embarrassed.

'Sorry,' he said. 'No need for that.'

Lucy grinned, smoke trailing from her nostrils. 'You're such a gent,' she said. 'Too good for round here.'

She dropped the half-smoked cigarette onto the tarmac and ground it beneath her shoe, ran a hand through her hair. I always thought it should look greasy, considering where she worked every day, but it didn't. Dry in fact.

She was still going at it with the pulped cigarette.

'Lucy,' I said. 'I think it's dead.'

She seemed preoccupied. Jack asked her the same question the copper had asked us, but she hadn't seen anything either.

'No one unusual's been in, this ain't the West End. You two, of course, plus my regulars, keeping the business afloat. And some lads from the gym. You know, those who like the taste of home cooking.'

I thought she was being funny. Maybe she meant an *actual* home cooking. She opened the packet of Dunhill again, the cigarettes lined up like bullets, but decided against. A girl appeared at the back of a shop a few doors down. She looked over at us and waved, before crushing a box into one of the bins and disappearing back inside.

Jack was thinking the same thing as me, he had to be. We'd moved beyond bullying. One of us needed to speak to Cyan, and quickly – it was getting too close.

'So what will you do now?' Jack said, looking at Lucy.

'What do you mean?'

'Well, you know, I just wondered if maybe you'd had enough. I don't really like to say it, but let's be honest, this area's going downhill fast, and who knows what could happen next. We're lucky someone saw the smoke or the whole building could have been gutted; next time it could be anyone's place.'

'What makes you think there'll be a next time?'

Jack didn't reply. He looked like he'd said too much, hadn't been subtle enough. But he wasn't one to panic; this was frustration talking. And he cared about Lucy.

She gazed across the yard to where the occasional wisp of smoke still drifted from the back door.

'It's the times we live in Jack. Not much we can do about it.'

Then she turned to him, as if an idea had just occurred to her.

'Course, if you've had enough you could always move to, oh, I don't know, Margate, or … or …'

She seemed to be struggling to think of faraway, unobtainable places.

'France.'

We all laughed.

'France?' I said. 'Bit extreme, don't you think?'

'Not really,' she replied, looking at Jack. 'Not for a man of the world.'

I swear to God he blushed, cleared his throat.

'Right,' he said, looking down at Arthur. 'Time for you to get some exercise, I reckon. What do you think, eh, what do you think?'

He reached down and scratched the underside of Arthur's jaw.

'I'll be off too,' said Lucy. 'I left Alan with a pile of onions to peel. Chances are he's been on the phone all this time, so it'll be up to me to make him cry instead.'

We watched her walk back up towards the high street, pulling the collar of her coat tight against the breeze.

'Mind if I join you Jack?' I asked, when she had disappeared from view.

'No, course not,' he replied.

It was time.

We went to the park. Apart from the club, I think it was Jack's favourite place. I'd seen him there on more than one occasion, sitting motionless on a bench and staring straight ahead, hands cupped in his lap, the tips of his thumbs held gently together. It was certainly one of Arthur's favourite haunts too, but then he couldn't interpret the malevolent glances of the people who hung out there, the ones sizing his owner up, seeing if he was worth anything. Passing trade. I'd banned Jack from going there after dark, made him promise, sixth-dan black belt or not.

For Arthur it was simply a place in which to leap at flies or revel in the attentions of the locals, the occasional gesturing drunk spinning loosely connected philosophies on life.

We did a slow circuit around the perimeter, the three of us. Chatting about this and that – the fire, Lucy – bemoaning slipping standards like a couple of pensioners.

The bench we eventually sat down on had a brass plaque on the backrest: 'Muriel Walters, philanthropist, 1943-2007. A pillar of our community'. The bottom edge was bent where someone had tried to lever it off but gave up, scratches on the metal and wood like the claw-marks of a wild animal.

I leant forward, put my face in my hands.

'Jack,' I said, through my fingers, trying to mould thoughts into recognisable shapes.

I didn't know where to start. The months without proper sleep, the stress of Emily's illness, my suspicions about Cyan, about Alex – not to mention the guilt I felt for letting Jack down, for turning my attention away from practice – it all seemed to be compacting together like a huge glacial mass. And deep within its core a tiny fissure had appeared, the first sign of weakness. I felt as if parts of me would soon start to break off.

'Jack,' I said again, finally taking my hands away. 'I'm so sorry, I really am. I should have spoken to you ages ago.'

I looked up but he was expressionless, the army man.

Nothing fazed Jack.

It all came out. The incident I'd witnessed with Cyan in the subway, the people he was with, how I hadn't said anything because I didn't want Jack to think of him as a victim. Then my frustration when he came and went as he pleased, seemingly devoid of ambition, or acknowledgment of the hopes we had for him. All that nonsense about other things he had to do, the errands. Then, finally, how I'd followed him, what I'd seen. The girl. Breathing, moving, dangerously alive. Now reduced to a face on a poster.

And how Cyan had seen me.

Jack listened as I burbled on, and when I glanced at him there was nothing on his face that I could read. I said my piece then waited; he continued to look at me.

'I'm really sorry Jack,' I said, again. 'Really sorry. I was just trying to help.'

He leant back, staring out across the grass, the flowerbeds now losing their colour.

'What?' I said. 'What is it?'

Arthur picked that moment to jump up onto the bench and sit between the two of us, his head going from left to right, trying to decide where his best chances lay.

'What is it you want out of life Steve?' asked Jack.

'What do you mean?'

He took a deep breath, exhaled slowly. 'It's a straightforward question.'

'I thought I was doing the right thing,' I said, my voice unconvincing, even to me. 'I've been trying to get round to telling you, but what with one thing and another, you know. Plus I thought you'd need more evidence. At the end of the day we still don't know if anything's going on. Places get vandalised, people start fires. Jesus, people even go missing. And besides, I'm not even totally, one hundred per cent sure it was the same girl; it wasn't like I was standing right there beside the pair of them. I could be wrong.'

Jack dug a couple of biscuits out of his pocket and let Arthur eat from his hand.

'You can't even answer a simple question, can you?' he said. 'Always got some flannel, some chat. Going the long way round and getting nowhere.'

I looked at him. 'What are you talking about?'

'I asked you what you want out of life and you give me the salesman spiel, working your own angle.'

'It's not an angle. I thought I was …'

'She's dead Steve. The girl. She's a goner.'

I didn't do a sharp intake of breath, nothing so dramatic. Because I couldn't breathe at all. I felt as if my whole body was being squeezed, that something had taken hold of me and was crushing the air inside me. Another name etched in stone, another daughter out of reach. And I was one of the last to see her.

I got up, my hands clasped behind the back of my head. Took a few steps forward, then turned to face Jack.

'I saw the poster too,' he said. 'Then the story was in Tuesday's *Herald*. Course, you won't have seen that now that you've left these parts, being the country squire and everything.'

He knew what he was doing: make a joke, ease me back down. Setting an example, not making one, like he always said. He jerked his head in an upward motion, a gesture for me to sit. I almost fell onto the bench.

'How did it happen?'

'They're not saying. Or why. Not exactly unusual though these days, is it? Found her in an alleyway. I'm sure we'll all have the police knocking on our doors before long.'

'What will you tell them?'

He shrugged.

'Depends on what they ask. As little as possible, if I can help it.'

I was chewing the inside of my lip, nervousness being drawn up from within, like I could run round and round the park until my lungs burst.

'Okay,' I said. 'Okay. Shit.'

We sat there for a minute or so, not a word spoken. A dog came scampering by, unaccompanied, some kind of whippet. Spindly, with legs like straws, all skin and ribs. It stopped when it caught sight of Arthur, who raised his head without much enthusiasm. The dog sniffed the air, then lost interest.

'What are we going to do?' I asked.

He turned to face me, rested his arm along the back of the bench.

'Well, like I say, I need to speak to Cyan. Until I've heard his side of the story I don't see what else we can do. At the very least we give the lad a chance to explain himself. The rest is, well …'

He stopped, as if his thoughts were slowing down, melding together.

'… the rest – I have no idea.'

'We have to do something,' I said.

'You don't say.'

'Sorry Jack, I didn't mean …'

'What did you mean?' What exactly did you mean Steve? That we should help Cyan, all be there for him, is that what you mean?'

'Jack, look …'

'You thought you were helping by following him around? Doing the right thing for the boy, for all of us.'

'Well, yeah, sort of. I don't know.'

'So instead of talking to him, or just spending time with him at the club as a friend, going to his grading to show support, you spy on him, all secretive, taking notes that you can then pass on to me.'

'Jack …'

'Why in God's name didn't you say anything Steve? I had no idea why he was so agitated before his grading, and now he's ballsed it up. We'll be lucky to see him anywhere near the club again. And as for what he's mixed up in, well, Jesus.'

'Jack, hold on, I know I've messed up, but things are difficult for me at the moment.'

'Life is difficult full stop, Steve, you've been around enough to know that. At least Cyan is trying to dig himself out.'

'Thanks Jack, thanks a lot. I've got other things to think of, in case you'd forgotten. It's not just Cyan who's suffering here. Emily's really down, I'm scared that she's beginning to sink, not that anyone would have noticed.'

He shook his head, like he couldn't stand to hear her name.

'Of course,' he said. 'How could I forget.'

'I don't believe I'm hearing this.'

'Hearing what?'

'This. This speech, like you know me inside out.'

He looked right into me, fire in his eyes.

'You think this is a speech? You think this is me being firm with you? Jesus Christ, Steve, wake up. This is nothing. Nothing. There are guys at the club who've done hard time in Japan, same as me, been through training that would reduce you to tears, things you can't possibly imagine. And we kept going back for more, because we wanted to, because we had no choice, and we weren't going to give up. We refused to be beaten.

'Do you have any idea what that's like? Do you? We had problems too, but those instructors couldn't give a shit, could not give a damn. They weren't there to hold our hands, to take nice little walks in the park and listen to our concerns. They just screamed at us every day, made us do stuff over and over until we were exhausted, sick with pain. Am I getting through to you Steve?'

'Yes, of course, but ...'

'But what? What? Waltzing into our little dojo when it suits is all it takes, is that it? Never mind if you keep missing sessions, you'll catch up? Don't tell me you've got errands to run as well, someone aiming a gun at the back of your head.'

'Jesus, Jack ...'

'Don't even think about it,' he said. 'I'm not buying what you're selling, you hear me? You need to get your shit together my friend, you really do. And what really pisses me off is that I didn't think I'd have to tell you.'

I was mute. I had no way to respond to that, no excuse. This wasn't persuading someone to buy a quarter page for the next issue, or a series of ads for the coming year; I couldn't lie my way out. We lapsed into silence, a long time. I wanted to speak, but couldn't, and I think he wanted my mouth to stay shut anyway.

Just when I thought I couldn't stand it any longer, Jack got up and put Arthur's lead on.

'I suggest you sit here for a while,' he said.

I nodded, eyes fixed on the ground like a humbled schoolboy, still wishing I had something to give him.

'Come on Arthur,' he said.

I waited until they were some distance off, then turned and watched them leave the park.

28

On the surface it had been an ordinary day, nothing remarkable. Salesman goes to work, bullshits complete strangers, goes home again.

Except my life was no longer ordinary. Emily and I were clinging to the hope of change, of returning to where we had come from, but sometimes I now became disorientated, unsure whether I was repeating conversations I'd already had with people, relying on their generosity of spirit to point it out, or not. The situation was taking its toll. No matter how positive I tried to be, Emily was becoming more withdrawn, more distant. She'd even hinted that I'd be better off without her, that she had no right to make me suffer too. I was giving up too much, she said, we couldn't continue like that.

No one in the office had any real idea about what was going on. They were aware that Emily was unwell but rarely mentioned it, let alone ask how she was. She'd had an operation, the details were apparently not of huge concern. Can't say I blame them particularly; most people rarely think too far beyond their own lives, that's how it is. We're not gods. I have no idea what they thought I was doing every time I disappeared, walking round the streets near our office, trying to clear my head. Sometimes I would get choked thinking of her, not being able to do a damn thing about it, hoping against hope that everything would be alright.

I couldn't, in turn, risk telling Emily about the dead girl. God only knows what she would have thought of me, about the secrets I had, my other life. I wasn't even sure she could handle it, not the way she was. So I kept it from her, buried it.

Jack had been trying to get hold of Cyan but couldn't. His mum said he wasn't feeling well, wouldn't come to the phone. She was worried, fearful that his troubles were finally rising to the surface and perhaps making him ill. She asked if Jack had any clues about his behaviour, but Jack had to pretend, said he had no idea. Violet said she would try to persuade her son to come to the dojo – maybe he would talk to his trainer.

Me, I just felt like someone was holding my head under water.

But I was team leader – focused, decisive, at all times. Anything less was unacceptable, the people upstairs wouldn't stand for it. And that would carry on being my role even as Emily went deeper.

I made plans, swore promises, that arrangement people try to negotiate when everything gets too much and they'll believe in anything. I wanted my life back, but this time it would be different; I vowed that it would change if only we could be given a second chance. And being with Emily inspired me, her determination despite everything to get well again, to not be broken.

But for now, one day simply followed another. Clocking on, clocking off.

It was a Wednesday, I will always remember that. I called Emily twice from the train on the way home, and again when I got into my car at our station, but she didn't pick up. That terrible feeling surged through me yet again, something uncoiling in the pit of my stomach, eyes slitting open.

I turned the key in the ignition, reminded myself that I didn't own her and that she'd gone out unannounced before and everything had been okay. Emily was at home, she was fine, stop worrying.

I reversed out of the parking spot, immediately aware that the sound in the car was different, that I could hear my tyres on the road. I craned my head around – I hadn't closed the door behind me properly when I put my bag on the back seat.

I stamped on the brake pedal, got out, opened the rear door, and swung it shut with such force that I thought I might have cracked the window or damaged the door frame. I stood facing the car with my palms on the roof edge, feeling childish and inadequate, breathing hard.

Somebody had to have seen me, hidden in the darkness of their vehicle. Or maybe I was betrayed by the station's CCTV camera, some smug git sat in front of a bank of monitors fifty miles away feeling just a little more superior now, despite the nylon uniform and crap pay.

I got back into the car and pulled the seatbelt across my chest, the white heat of frustration smothering me as I struggled to align it in the holster, wanting only to hear the mechanism snap shut so I could be on my way. I missed it twice, and gave up.

In a split second I was engulfed by rage. I knew exactly what I was doing, the stupidity of it, but was unable to hold back. I pounded the steering wheel with the edge of a closed fist, screaming so loudly that my throat caught, which sent me spiralling even higher. I pressed the knuckles of one hand into my mouth, hard against my teeth, howling into them, forcing every muscle in my body to become rigid. I was shaking, biting down hard on the skin, the bone, dimly aware of a grim satisfaction from the pain, as if I deserved it. As if it could heal me. My vision was swimming, my eyes wet and blurred, eyelashes sticking together.

It didn't last long. I felt myself coming down, let my head fall forward, my fingers now resting on the steering wheel. My breathing was deep but becoming regular, bringing me back.

Forget this moment and move into the next.

I sat there for a few minutes with the engine running, unsure if I even wanted to go home. How much easier to just disappear, become answerable to no one, no dependents. But where would I go, where did I actually want to be? Not back in Plymouth, that was for sure. Another admission of failure.

Composed now, I reached again for the seatbelt clasp, dragged it slowly across me and into the plastic slot. I drove to the exit, let a car go past, then pulled out onto the road.

I'd made Emily promise to carry her mobile with her wherever she went, just in case. I thought she was walking a little better, a little less stiffly, but I was probably imagining it. I couldn't keep asking her.

Why wasn't she picking up?

Five minutes later I parked on the side road next to our house and wished, momentarily, that I had a superstition. Some blessed talisman, an amulet to hold in my palm. I grabbed my bag, checking around for Alex's car. That one action had become almost instinctive, like looking for movement in the long grass.

As I approached the front door a lorry rocketed past, horn blaring. I was walking too close to the edge of the pavement, the bag in my right hand swinging out into the road. I watched the lorry go, imagined the driver's kind words.

There were no lights on in the house, so I knocked and waited. I couldn't use my key because Emily always left hers in the lock in case someone tried to break in. Other times she worried that there might be someone hiding in the attic, waiting to jump out and get her. And I thought *I* was paranoid.

I knocked again, agitation tipping me towards impatience. Holding my hand up to the frosted glass, I peered inside. Nothing. I fished a set of keys from my suit pocket.

There was no key to block mine, and the lock turned. Stepping in, I called out her name, and as I did so something on the floor caught my eye. I reached down and picked up what I thought was the post, but it was a solitary piece of paper, folded in half, with her name written on the front. I opened it and read the scrawled words.

Called round to take you out, but must have got my days wrong. Hope you guys are enjoying your day trip. Have fun. See you soon. Alex. XXX

I read it again, but still it made no sense. I walked into the kitchen and put the note on the table, dumped my coat and bag on a chair.

I went to the bottom of the stairs and called up into

the silence. The bathroom door at the top was ajar, so I went up and pushed it gently. Nothing. I checked the spare room next to the bathroom, then our bedroom, but found nothing out of place: no make-up lying around, no hairdryer not put away, no discarded clothes. Everything was clean and tidy, as if Emily had made a special effort, just for me.

Her phone was on the little chest of drawers by her side of the bed. I picked it up, checked for messages. There were none, just the missed calls from me and one from her mother. I tried to console myself that Emily wouldn't go far without a phone – who does – but realised how powerless it makes you feel, denied the luxury of instant contact. I didn't know whether to feel angry or afraid, so my mind settled on a combination of the two: angry at the inconsiderate posh girl, afraid that I might be wrong.

Back in the kitchen I read the note a few more times, hunting for clues among the sparse words. I wanted it to be a practical joke, one that would end with a sudden laughing appearance, and me pretending to be startled. Open a bottle of wine, settle in for the evening. But, sitting there, I knew that wouldn't happen, and what I had to do. I tried to push the thought away, wracking my brain for an alternative, but it didn't come. I went and got our little red contact book from the living room, and dialled the number.

A couple of rings, then that cheerful voice.

'Hello?'

'Alex, it's Steve.'

A pause.

'Steve. Oh, hi, how's it going?'

Something was wrong, I could feel it, some kind of intuition.

'I'm okay, thanks,' I lied. 'Listen, have you seen Emily?'

'What do you mean? Isn't she with you?'

'No, she isn't.'

I wanted to reach down the phone and grab him by the throat. I needed answers, and he wasn't providing them. Withholding information. I could feel the animosity rising again, the speed of it taking me by surprise; I was fed up, my life was becoming a charade, a piece of ad-libbed theatre. A pantomime.

'I don't understand,' he said. 'You haven't left her in Eastbourne, have you?'

I paused. 'Eastbourne? What are you talking about? I've never been to Eastbourne in my life. Why would we go there?'

'For a picnic, on the cliffs. Emily told me about it the other day. I could have sworn she said you were going tomorrow and that I would take her out for lunch today. I must have got mixed up. Did you see my note?'

I picked it up, read the words again. I actually felt sick, physically sick.

'Steve, you still there? What's going on?'

I looked out of the window; it was starting to get dark.

Eastbourne, South Downs, the view across the Channel shifting. The first few stars appearing, moonlight glistening on black water.

She'd told him, that was to be my only clue: arranged for him to visit, guessing he'd leave a note. Most people leave their own, she got someone else to do it. Her game, her rules.

I estimated the distance – sixty or so miles maybe, an hour and a half if the traffic was kind. Maybe longer.

No Emily, no.

I was holding on to the edge of the table, trying to take everything in, Alex's words muffled but persistent.

I wanted to cry, to have that release. That's all I wanted. But I knew I couldn't: something else was expected of me, a role I had to fulfil. Focused, a leader.

'Alex,' I said. 'Pick me up right now. I don't care what you're doing, don't waste any time.'

I hung up as he started to reply.

It took too long to get there. Every car seemed to obstruct us on purpose, every pedestrian crossed the road in slow motion. I couldn't keep still, feeling like I wanted to get out and run, as if running would get me there quicker.

Beachy Head. What a cliché; how totally unoriginal. She could have done better than that, surely, someone of her artistic integrity. Where's the creativity, you stupid girl?

Alex did his best to reassure me, but there was little to be said. My thoughts were winding around themselves, a knot of emotions that I couldn't even begin to unpick. Panic shifted through to resentment, but always underpinned by anger. Plenty of anger. I appreciated him trying, especially as he didn't push it. Emily thought the world of me, he said, this was all bound to be a misunderstanding. We'd laugh about it later.

Half an hour earlier he'd been the rival, the Judas.

We arrived in the dark, leaving the A259 and threading our way down towards the Birling Gap. The narrow road cut through the rolling grassland, and as we drove all I could make out were grass verges on either side, the occasional small tree briefly illuminated by the headlights, like half-human forms reaching out at us.

'How much further is it?' I asked.

'Nearly there.'

Eventually he pulled into a lay-by. It was empty. I couldn't help wondering whether people who came here on nights like this would need it to be that way. Maybe they drove around until they knew they were alone. Or perhaps some secretly hoped for others to be present, to be witnessed, or stopped.

'You been here before?' I asked.

'A few times. It's, well, nice. But be careful, stay right by me.'

I checked my torch for about the tenth time. Alex reached into the glove compartment and took out his, then didn't move, like he was steadying himself. As I pulled on the door release he grabbed my other arm.

'Steve,' he said. 'I don't really know what to say, but if she's here, just, you know, just be careful. We'll get through it together, okay?'

I mumbled some sort of reply, not sure what he wanted me to say.

The wind was biting when we got out, swirling around us. I zipped my jacket right up, switched on the torch and scanned the ground.

'Follow me.'

Alex led me to a well-worn path that ran parallel to

the cliff edge.

'Why this way?' I asked, as if he'd have an answer, the right and wrong.

'Because up there is …'. He paused for a moment. 'It's the highest …'

I looked to where he was pointing, even though it was too dark to see anything.

We began walking. The wind refused to die down, pushing and thumping, trying to bully us. The path was on a gradual incline, and we aimed the torches both at our feet and towards the cliff edge. Beyond that, silver-edged clouds were rushing to obscure the moon; the whole of nature was conspiring against us. After a couple of minutes Alex stopped.

'What is it?' I asked.

'We're closer now. We need to leave the path and go towards the edge. Over there is where, you know …'

'It's okay Alex, I get it.'

'Walk slowly Steve.'

We edged our way in the direction of the drop, concentrating on putting one foot in front of the other. About ten metres or so from where the grass ended we stopped again, scanning with our torches, the beams criss-crossing like searchlights.

Nothing. She wasn't there.

Alex began moving off again. The wind was stronger on this area of raised ground, and seemed to take pleasure in kicking us as hard as possible. A few times we were forced back a step, bending into the gale to reclaim our balance. As we edged a couple of metres inland something darted across in front of us, small and quick, gone in an instant.

'She's not here Alex,' I shouted.

I think I meant it positively, but the alternative, that we were too late, was hidden in there somewhere. Alex didn't speak. We carried on further, up to the highest point, the ground finally levelling out.

This was the place. How many times, I wondered. How many souls?

We waited – for what, I don't know. It was almost a disappointment.

'Emily!'

I thought Alex might tell me to be quiet, but he said nothing. Maybe this was our only choice now, to make her come to us.

'Emily!'

We stood in silence, turning our heads, trying desperately to filter out the sound of the wind. Nothing came back to us, no plaintive cry for help. We went on a little further, then stopped again.

'Let's head back towards the car,' I said, 'try going in the other direction.'

As we retraced our steps I tried to feel relieved. Maybe she had friends down here on the coast, forgot to bring her phone, and our paths had already crossed while I was trapped in Alex's car. She might be back home, later than she intended, cursing me for going to the gym and not telling her. Or maybe she'd phoned to say she'd be staying the night. I pulled my mobile from my pocket and lit it up, but there was no little envelope waiting for me.

Suddenly I couldn't move. Alex was holding me back.

'There,' he said, aiming his torch towards the cliff

edge again. 'What's that?'

I peered into the shaft of light, about twenty metres ahead. Something was there, something we'd missed. It could have been a rock, or a mound in the grass, anything. We walked cautiously, as if approaching a stricken animal.

Then a reflection, a glinting. A jewel to entice us.

We were close now, close enough to make out the shape more clearly. It wasn't moving. We both stopped, trying to take it in. A sleeping bag, its glossy padded material now visible, just in from the edge. And someone inside it.

I was almost paralysed, stricken with fear. I didn't think it would be like this, it wasn't real. If it was Emily, she should be standing on the edge, looking out to sea, hair flying in the wind. I should be talking to her, repeating her name, trying to coax her back. I would talk about our lives together, our plans, the million things we still had to do. But there, in that moment, I was useless, impotent, terrified of the choices presented to me. I shone my torch at Alex, who looked just as scared. He turned to face me, then raised a hand, as if asking me for time to think.

I turned the beam back towards the huddled mass. Without thinking, I started to move forward, but Alex shoved his arm across my chest. He said nothing, couldn't risk it, but I knew what the message was. He leant into me, his mouth by my ear.

'Wait here. I'll go past, approach from the other side. I'll signal. We don't know who, or what, it is, so shine your torch at me, not at …'

He gestured towards it.

'Watch where I am Steve, then we'll slowly move in, okay?'

I nodded.

'Slowly,' he said, as if guiding the message into my head. 'Slowly.'

I struggled to absorb the words. The risk was almost beyond comprehension, so close to the drop.

He leant in again, his hushed voice blending with the wind.

'Don't speak, it's too risky. Don't say a word.'

And then he was gone, moving off into the blackness. I watched the receding light, my heart thumping somewhere near my back teeth. I was shaking. For some reason I thought of the day that Emily and I met: me reluctantly going to the theatre, the Thai restaurant transformed by her presence, my luck changing.

And now this.

I kept my torch fixed on Alex. He seemed to wait a long time; calculating the risk, summoning courage. I wanted to call out, tell him to get a move on, to get it over with. At last he moved his hand over the front of his torch twice, and we both crept forward.

I lit up the ground just in front of the bag, not daring to move the beam any closer. At about six feet away I still couldn't see any sign of life. No hair, no skin. I crouched down, lowering my centre of gravity, making myself more stable. I placed the torch on the ground, facing towards the long bundle, and Alex did the same.

I could make him out at the edge of the light, on his hands and knees, crawling forward. I felt my nerve starting to go, childish imaginings creeping in, aided by the dull moonlight, the thumping pulse in my ears. I half expected our quarry to spring to life and leap at us, some screaming demonic beast disturbed in the night. Or to suddenly roll over and disappear. But still it didn't move.

I was almost there, within touching distance, water streaming from my staring eyes as the wind lashed my face. I was terrified, the drop beyond seemed to be pulling at me. I couldn't wait any longer. I took a second, pictured what I was about to do, then reached out, inch by inch. Alex did the same. I could see my own hand trembling; my arm felt weak. The moment my fingertips touched the quilted material I grabbed a handful, put my weight on my other hand, and pulled.

I heard Alex call out, then fall backwards, the smooth fabric gone from his grasp. I held on, watched as he sprang back. He grabbed at the thing once more, then screamed at me.

'Again!'

I wrenched hard, my boots slipping on the damp grass as I struggled with the weight. We managed to bring it a couple of feet before I had to readjust my position and repeat the effort. I toppled forward, used my free hand to stop myself, then leant right over the bag, feeling the pull of the cliff edge. Steadier now, I redoubled the effort. We gained a few more inches, then some more, until the pressure almost overwhelmed me and I was standing, hunched over, dragging it roughly with both hands towards safety.

'Steve, that's enough,' Alex shouted. 'We've done it. We've done it.'

I stood up, breathing hard. One of my feet was underneath the bag, which had come to rest against my shin, and when I felt it move I recoiled, stumbling back, instinctively repulsed. Whatever was inside was coming to life, emerging. Our torches were still pointing towards the sea; I ran to get mine, then shone it at the open end of the bag.

It was her. She emerged slowly, deliberately, as if drugged. Her hair was wet and clung to her face, her eyes milky and half-closed. Like she was being born. She looked half-conscious, one hand reaching out to block the harsh torchlight as she struggled with the confines of the bag. She was trying to talk, but managing only incoherent sounds. I crouched down, but couldn't make any sense of the words.

Alex was pulling at the zip.

'We need to get her back to the car.'

I stood up.

'Steve, come on mate. We've got to get her to the car, she's frozen.'

I never told her afterwards, but at that moment, now that it was over, my only desire was to walk away, to leave her – everyone – behind. To walk over the grassland and into the night, let it swallow me up. Return to my original path. It wasn't too late, everyone would understand, would welcome me back. Another chance.

Then I looked down and there was Emily, the girl who had everything. Barely awake, a mess, almost pitiful.

'Steve, for crying out loud.'

Alex was shouting now, and there was confusion in his voice. He wanted me to react. I bent down and reached under Emily's arms while he grabbed her legs, and we lurched back the way we had come. When we got back to the car we managed to manoeuvre her onto the back seat, still mumbling to herself, still making no sense. Alex went to get the sleeping bag as I stood by the car, shining my torch in her face like an interrogator. Like I'd caught someone being smuggled across the border. She looked terrible, half-dead.

'I couldn't find anything,' said Alex. 'Only this.'

He handed me a bottle of vodka, practically empty. A souvenir.

I placed it in the boot as Alex got behind the wheel. I was starting to feel calmer, but with that came something else. I held onto the side of the car for support, felt myself swaying. It came quickly. All I could do was stumble a few feet away into the blackness, almost toppling over as I came to a stop and bent over, hands gripping the front of my jeans. The heaving was violent, but pointless. My stomach was devoid of anything solid, there was nothing to drag up except pathetic slops of acid that burnt the back of my throat before splattering onto the tarmac. Over and over, as if my stomach wanted some return for its efforts. Empty reaching, the sound of it ugly, my weakness on display. And my legs were buckling, threatening to give way. I groaned, despairing of my body, its dominance.

When it was finally done I stood up straight, took some deep breaths, then spat into the road. I knew Alex could hear me, but he left me alone. I returned to the car and he fired up the engine as I got into the back seat beside Emily, and arranged the sleeping bag over her legs.

As we pulled into the road I put my arm around her.

She was coming to, making more sense. I tried to stop her talking, but she wouldn't. Like she needed it off her chest.

'I just wanted to, to not feel it happen. If I turned over in my sleep, I wouldn't know. That would ... I would ...'

She started sobbing, then grabbed a handful of the sleeping bag and buried her face in the material. I listened to the muffled sounds, her shoulders convulsing beneath my arm.

I held her, stroked her hair, told her not to talk – there would be plenty of time for that. Eventually she went still, lying against me as I stared out of the window listening to the rush of the tyres on the road, letting the world blur past. I could think of nothing, nothing but her tumbling down into the silence.

By the time we got home Emily could walk, although she was clearly suffering. We got her upstairs but she didn't want to lie down, not yet. I left her standing by the bedroom window while I went back down to show Alex out. I pulled the front door to and we stood outside.

'Will you be alright?' he asked.

'I think so. She seems okay, hopefully she'll get some sleep.'

'Well, if you need anything give me a shout. Don't worry about what time it is, I can be right over.'

'Okay.'

We stood there for a couple of seconds, a little wary.

'Is it alright if I come round tomorrow?' he asked. 'You know, just to see how she is.'

'Sure. I won't be going to work, but, you know, come

round any time.'

'Right,' he said. 'I'll be off then.'

I watched him walk down the path and through the little metal gate. As he closed it he looked up.

'Anything you need, okay? Anything.'

And then he was gone.

I wanted to believe him.

When I went back upstairs Emily was still standing by the window, massaging her lower back with both hands. I touched her shoulder, kissed her, and we began walking around the bedroom. Twenty minutes, half an hour, I don't remember. Five or six slow paces in one direction, five or six in the other, over and over. Side by side, me unable to stop touching her, a hand between her shoulder blades, trying to reassure. Everything always seemed to fall away in the face of her pain, my own petty insecurities moving out of focus, fading into nothing.

Gradually, very gradually, the stiffness relented, just a fraction. Emily climbed hesitantly into bed, pulled the duvet up under her chin, and closed her eyes. I went downstairs and filled a hot-water bottle, then made some tea. Standing in the kitchen, familiar thoughts began to flow once more: dirt that wasn't there, shadows in the corner mutating into living, growing organisms. To me the neutral smell of the house was a pungent odour – offensive, disgusting. I would be up all night.

I went back to the bedroom. Emily couldn't sit up, but instead lent on her elbow, cradling the mug, glad of its warmth. She drank a bit and handed it back to me, then lay down again.

'You look shattered,' I said. 'How long were you there?'

'I'm not sure. A long time.'

'Jesus. Do you want me to call the doctor?'

'No, no, I'll be fine. I'm warming up now.'

I got up. 'You need some sleep. We'll talk about this tomorrow.'

I pulled the curtain across the small window. On my way out I bent down and kissed her again, before switching off the bedside lamp. Standing in the doorway, I turned to look at her.

'I'll be up soon. Won't be long.'

She didn't reply. I thought she was already falling asleep, but as I went to close the door she spoke.

'Steve?'

Her voice was barely there.

'Yes baby?'

'The physiotherapy, the operation, everything …'

She tailed off.

'What about it?' I asked.

I waited. The seconds ticked by, until at last she spoke.

'It's not working, is it?'

III

BARGAINING

29

I couldn't get what had happened out of my mind, what it meant. I'd given Emily every spare minute of my time, but it hadn't been enough. *I* wasn't enough. Her old life was disappearing, she said, and she couldn't contemplate a new one.

The pain was worse, and spreading. Alex the expert told her it could be the muscles compensating for her restricted movement, tension magnifying what she was feeling. She stepped up her visits to him, and some days she did seem better, looser, but it never lasted. She wouldn't talk about it, snarled at me if I tried to bring it up. Maybe she saved it all for Alex, maybe he understood. I wasn't allowed to ask about him either.

She'd failed to end herself, but part of us had died. I wondered if she ever thought about that.

She agreed to think about counselling.

I began to lose all focus, watching helplessly as any remnant of desire that had kept me in my job finally crumbled. I pretended to be lunching clients when really I was just wandering around; I talked about promising leads, big spenders on the horizon, all of it fiction. Finally I started pressuring my team to work harder, blaming them for our shortfalls, furiously circling figures on the white board with a red marker pen like it contained some kind of Soviet directive. I was peddling propaganda that even I despised.

I knew things were coming to a head when I got into a nasty row over an untidy desk and actually made the culprit tidy it up in front of me, told him he was a total amateur and that here was the evidence. I regretted it straight away, as if I were passing on a disease. But I couldn't tell my victim that; just went on finding excuses, shifting blame.

I pointed an accusing finger at the recession, the market, anything that came to hand. Without realising it I had I drawn my sword, sunk to my knees, the blade held against my gut.

And then it was time. Someone kicked open the door of the cage, reached in and hauled me out.

What do they call it – grim inevitability? I still believed it wouldn't happen, thought I was immune; but yes, it was inevitable after all, and grim.

The big chat in a small room: me, Chris and the MD. An unholy trinity. Chris looked guilty as hell, nervous, dank patches of sweat beneath his armpits. He knew I wouldn't trash his office, or set fire to the building, but he also knew that I could easily give his little game away if I wanted to. And, ironically, he was high, it was so obvious, a few snorts on his latest consignment via Amsterdam while the firing squad was being assembled. Dutch courage.

The MD was oblivious, or didn't care. Just sat there looking bored, like I was a waste of everyone's time. Short-term memory loss is common in the modern workplace; it wasn't that long since I'd been wowing all manner of clients, raking in the cash like a high roller in Vegas. The Gucci shoes she was wearing, the brand-new

Lexus in the car park? Paid for by me, not that she'd remember. She just watched as Chris went through the charge sheet: absenteeism, lateness, sharp decline in performance, lack of leadership. I'd been given a label: 'Disappointment'.

Apparently they'd emailed me two warnings which I hadn't replied to. (I vaguely remember seeing them, and flagging them to 'action later', but other things were taking over.) So that was another black mark against my name, although they already had more than enough to go on. Nice of Chris to follow things up though, check that word was getting through.

We look after our people here.

A figure was mentioned, the pair of them scrutinising me as I opened the piece of paper, trying to gauge my reaction. Four months' salary and a bit of bonus owed. Take it or leave it. Hell, try your luck with an industrial tribunal if that's what you want, see how far you get.

Of course I'm going to take it.

Do you mind me asking, are you happy with your lives?

The MD looked relieved when I accepted, glad to get out early. She practically leapt from her chair, shook my hand and expressed her disappointment – yes, that word – about how things hadn't worked out, but how she knew I'd be back on my feet in no time, plenty of jobs out there for velvet-tongued guys like me. I just needed a new environment, a fresh challenge, that was all. And then she was gone, Chris and I left entombed in his office. He stood up, started pacing around.

'Listen, mate, I know you've got your problems, but her mind was made up, nothing I could do. It's been on the cards for ages, you must have seen it coming.'

'No Chris, I didn't. I had other things to think about.'

He laughed. He fucking laughed. I wanted to gouge out his piggy little bloodshot eyes.

'Of course, of course, that lovely lady of yours. Never did get to meet her. Look, take some time, sort your problems out, then I'll have a word, see if we can't get you back. How does that sound?'

I didn't answer. I was looking past him, out of the window, across the rooftops. The only thing I could think of was how Emily would react. Another nail driven down into the coffin lid.

'Drinks are on me tonight, okay? We'll all go to Flynn's, the whole team. Give you a good send-off.'

I drank his wallet dry that night, encouraging everyone from the office to join in, even those I barely knew, as well as those who hated me. I needed to see someone else suffer, just for a bit, a bar tab that would make most people faint. It was almost embarrassing, people being nice to me, looking forward to the following morning when my seat would be vacant.

Next day I got drunk again, properly wasted, and stayed that way for a few more days afterwards. It was like an out-of-body experience, as if I was scared of returning to earth. I should have been happy, free at last from purgatory, but I wasn't. Another slab of compacted ice had broken away, swallowed up by the moving water.

When I staggered in that first night and told Emily why I was so late, she seemed to go into shock. She looked dazed, as if this sort of thing wasn't supposed to happen to me. Not Steve, team leader. She didn't go ballistic, which I thought she might. She looked sorry for me.

On the fourth night I was in our nearest local town, drinking alone again, when my phone vibrated on the table, her name in lights.

'Hello?'

'Steve, please come home. Please. You can't keep doing this.'

I spoke slowly, deliberately, half my vocabulary washed away.

'Don't worry, almost there. Couple of days, right as rain. Get it out of my system.'

'It's not your fault Steve, don't blame yourself. These things happen, you'll bounce back, I know you will.'

Funny, I thought, watching the tiny bubbles float to the top my beer, I hadn't blamed myself for a single second. Not one. Of course it wasn't my fault.

'I know, I know. Shit happens. Need to do something else. About time.'

The silence hung there, cold and dispassionate. We each waited for the other to speak, to conjure up a quick fix, a remedy.

'Don't be late tonight Steve, please, I need you here with me. Just the two of us.'

'The two of us?' I could feel the bile rising.

'Yes of course. Who else is there?'

'No one there to cheer you up?'

Thank God we weren't in the same room; I could sense her poised to strike, an imaginary fist drawn back. But, like me, she chose her words with care.

'You're drunk Steve. Again. So let's pretend you

didn't say that, shall we?'

'Fine,' I said. 'Fine. Let's pretend. I'll see you later.'

We ended without saying goodbye properly, her final words slithering around on the table. Patronising bitch. I staggered to the bar, ordered another pint and a whisky, the bartender eyeing me warily. I was a brawler, the stranger from out of town. I returned to my seat and tipped the whisky back, then drew on my pint to soothe the burning.

Patronising. Bitch.

Halfway through that final drink my attention had shifted: it was his fault. Always there, always skulking in the background, coming over when I was at work, waiting for me to slip up, to finally expose myself for what I was. So he helped me on the cliff, big deal, what else was he going to do? No doubt he blamed me anyway.

I finished my drink and got up, waited for the room to stop moving, then pulled my coat on. As I stepped forward I knocked the corner of my table, the pint glass fell over and began rolling towards the edge. I got to it in time, waved it at the bartender.

Outside it was too bright, the fresh afternoon air a jolt to my senses. I headed off towards the bus stop, walking quickly, like a man with a purpose.

I was onto him.

30

The TV was barely audible, a tedious programme. Police cars chasing stolen Vauxhall Astras around identical town centres, sirens wailing like disturbed spirits. I was on the sofa, drifting, half-aware of grainy footage showing children hauled out by the roadside, comedy villains with pixelated faces.

Before that we'd tried watching a Friday-night DVD, but it was terrible. We managed an hour or so of some nonsense about two couples getting it on with each other in Italy before Emily nodded off in the chair, somewhere around ten o'clock. I covered her with a blanket, careful not to wake her. Every few minutes of sleep had become precious, like something rare that you couldn't ever trade. She looked permanently drained.

She'd started doing that sometimes, sleeping in the chair. Lying down was still difficult. She'd wake suddenly and have to get up straight away, the ache in her back chronic, spasms like broken glass dragged down her leg.

We'd entered a new phase, a dead-end waiting for us. There was talk of a second injection, another afternoon in the cattle pen. If that didn't work, there was always …

Always what? No one knew; admitting it was the difficult part.

The expert reeled off possible causes, the ones he'd already told us about on our previous visits. I wanted to grab the calendar off the wall, roll it up tightly and force it down his throat.

He referred us to another specialist. Don't hold your breath.

I lay there staring at Emily, the shifting light from the screen throwing shapes around the room. Her chin was on her chest, a hand peeking through the edge of the blanket. She was breathing heavily. I felt a swell of emotion as I watched her, a mixture of sadness and ugly self-pity. All I could think of was the unfairness of it, this terrible thing that had chosen us. Does it happen to other people too?

Of course it does, but it's not part of you until you're pushed through the door. The red-eyed mother who sets up a helpline for the parents of sick children; the man who starts running marathons, collecting signatures, half his masculinity sliced away on an operating table.

It's only natural – we don't do anything until the time comes. Why would we?

The phone rang, shunting me from my thoughts. The shrill, piercing sound was possibly the last thing we needed at that moment. Emily woke up, startled, peering at me and looking confused about what the noise meant. I reached over and picked up the handset.

'Hello?'

'Steve?'

'Oh, hey Jack, you alright?'

I knew I sounded groggy; he probably thought I'd been drinking.

'Not really. I'm sorry to call so late, got a bit of a problem.'

I sat up, wide awake now.

'What is it?'

I think he waited for a couple of seconds. Or maybe it was just my brain struggling to catch up.

'Cyan's disappeared,' he said.

'Oh Jesus, no. Jesus Christ. Are you sure? How do you know?'

'Because the police turned up at the club, asking if I knew anything. And they're very keen to talk to you. More than keen – kept asking if I knew where you were.'

He sounded on edge, talking too much. I'd never experienced that with Jack, ever. I thought of the girl, a fading poster.

'Right, okay. I'll be there first thing. I'll call you.'

'Fine. See you tomorrow.'

That was it. No pleasantries, a residue of bad feeling still hanging around. I put the phone back, rubbed my eyes. Emily was watching me.

'What did he want?'

That tone again. It was becoming second nature.

'Well?'

'The police want to talk to me about something.'

She struggled to sit up, grimacing.

'The police? What are you talking about? Steve, what's happened?'

Now it was her turn to hear it. I gave her the bare bones, nothing she could get too worked up about. But she still had an angle to work.

'What about me?'

I almost couldn't be bothered.

'It won't take long, I promise. I'll speak to them and be right back. I'm guessing they want to talk to everyone.'

She waited, a poacher checking the trap.

'It's so good to see that standing by your friends has its rewards.'

In my head I was screaming, throwing things, holding her by the throat. Up against the wall, my face in hers, letting her have it. I was so tired.

'I know, I know,' I said, more gently then she deserved. 'But, you know, it's the police. I don't really have much choice. And I'll skip the class tomorrow, do a double session later in the week maybe.'

I swear to God she was pouting. Pouting. Like a teenager coming down from a sugar rush. I got up from the sofa; I had to get some sleep.

'It's always them first, isn't it?'

Oh God. Here we go.

'If you mean people who need my help, in this case a missing boy, then yes, it's them first. The same way I put you first when you need me.'

'But I need you all the time Steve. I can't do this without you.'

'Emily, please, I'm not joining the army. I'll only be gone half a day. It's the police, give me a break will you?'

'A break?' she shouted. 'A break? What about me? I can't take time off from this, can I? Sitting around trying to get comfortable, stuffed full of tablets while everyone else is going about their lives.'

I couldn't help myself, couldn't resist.

'Not everyone is going about their lives Emily, in case you hadn't noticed.'

The delivery was flat, but there was an edge to my voice. I felt like we were on the mat, testing each other, waiting for an opening. But she simply stared at me, incredulous.

'Just … fuck off … Steve. Go and be with your pals, be the hero. Head out into the wilderness and find the missing boy. God, you're unbelievable.'

She flinched as I took a step towards her, but continued to look up at me, like she must have looked at people a million times, an expression that demanded satisfaction.

My rapid breathing matched the hammering in my chest. I clenched and unclenched a fist, my head swamped with all the things I wanted to say, all the things I wanted to do. I was drowning.

I crouched down in front of her, gripped the tops of her legs a little too firmly to steady myself. Her eyes followed mine.

'I'm sure you'll find a shoulder to cry on Emily.'

I saw her jaw clench, the rigid tension, her brain formulating a snide response. She opened her mouth to speak but I reached out and held a fingertip gently against her lips, shaking my head slowly. I held it there for a few more seconds as she watched me, a hint of fear in her eyes. Then I got up.

I took my coffee cup to the kitchen, washed it over and over, the water searing my skin, then went upstairs without looking at her. I shut the door of the spare room behind me, took off my jeans and got into bed. For ages the house was silent, but eventually she came upstairs and I heard the door to our bedroom close with a soft click. I shut my eyes. If she got up in the night to take painkillers or walk around, I would ignore her.

*

The ambience at Lucy's Cough next day was its usual treat: a gushing welcome, attentive staff, nothing too much trouble. I ordered from the tasting menu – a selection of signature dishes – and requested an eight-year-old bottle of red, as recommended by the waiter. When it arrived I lowered my face towards the glass in reverence, its aroma like silk, reaching up to caress the senses.

To be fair though, Lucy had tarted the place up a bit, some fresh paint on the walls. I'm not sure why, a new start I suppose, after all that had been going on in the neighbourhood. Out with the old. It wasn't the neatest of jobs though; I think Alan did it one Sunday. Lucy told us the colour of the paint was avocado – a touch of irony, considering the surroundings. I was thinking cabbage, or sprouts.

Jack and I sat opposite each other. He was drinking tea, while I was on my second coffee. I felt ill, had barely slept, and he didn't look much brighter.

'When did he go missing?' I asked.

'Two days ago.'

'Two? That's not good.'

'No, it's not. And we don't know if he's on the run, or … well, whatever.'

'He's not a killer Jack. He didn't do that girl. Come on.'

'No, I know. Of course not.' He didn't sound convinced, drumming his fingers on the table. 'I don't suppose they'll be sending out the search teams just yet though. I'm not sure what the form is, but I'm guessing a couple of days doesn't make the news.'

'And if anything had happened to him,' I said, 'that

would have been on the news. So, you know, let's try to be positive.'

I was trying to counsel both of us. There were other possibilities, ones I didn't want to think about. And I'm sure Jack didn't either. Maybe Cyan, wherever he was, hadn't given up what they wanted yet. Maybe they were still trying to persuade him.

'Sorry I had to call you late. I'll bet that didn't go down well.'

'She does have a name Jack.'

He sipped his tea. All I wanted was for everything to fit together nicely. Such a short time we have to get things right. I like you, but not you, the triangle incomplete. It doesn't take much.

I'd never pressed either of them on it. One bad walk in the park, as far as I could tell. A misunderstanding, perhaps. Emily misinterpreting his concern, or Jack, good old Jack, wondering what a girl who has everything would want with me.

'Not a big fan, are you?'

He shrugged. 'She's okay. It's none of my business.'

'What do you mean?' A sudden sharpness, which took him by surprise. We weren't like that, not me and Jack.

'Don't worry about it.'

'No, hold on a second. You need to tell me. I'm presuming we're still friends.'

'Don't be a prick Steve, not until I've had my breakfast.'

He looked tired as well, like he'd seen all this coming. But you can't pick your moments, it's never that straightforward.

'I'm just looking out for you, that's all. Like I said, it's none of my business. I shouldn't have said anything.'

He gulped at his tea now, maybe hoping the conversation would turn.

'What, you mean she's too posh?' I countered. 'Too good for the likes of me.'

A flash of something in his eyes, but nowhere to direct it.

'Don't get all narky with me lad, that's not what I meant at all. I just don't want to see you, you know, just, well ...'

'I'm screwing up again, is that what you're trying to say? I got that message loud and clear in the park. Come on Jack, what is this, *Sex and the City*? Are we going to the spa later, getting our nails done?'

We both laughed, some of the tension easing. Lifted our mugs again, let things pass.

I was puzzled though, not sure what he was driving at. I should have pressed him on it.

I watched as Lucy plonked a dish of soup in the general direction of an old bloke two tables along from us. Startled by the sudden arrival of both her and the bowl, he looked up, and then at the red splash left on the table. When he looked again all he could see was her disappearing arse, blue skirt swishing defiantly as she headed away. Enemy lines you don't cross. He picked up his spoon and stirred the liquid warily.

'Right,' I said. 'Where are we at? The police want to talk to me, but I presume they're talking to everyone, right?'

'They are, but ...' He paused.

'Jack, I'm knackered, spit it out. I can barely think

straight.'

'You were seen. You know, when you were up to that spying lark, on Cyan's tail. In the pub every day, like you told me, sitting there for ages but not drinking much. Always staring out of the window. Maybe if you'd worn a clown's outfit and played a trumpet you might have blended in a bit more, got away with it.'

'Good one Jack. Real funny. Work on your delivery though, eh?'

'Anyway, the Old Bill made a few enquiries, and a regular in there gave them a description. They came to the club yesterday evening, which is why I called you. I'm watching your back, Steve, but I'm not about to lie to them, pretend we haven't met. We're in enough bother as it is.'

I sighed, wishing I'd never got involved. Like I didn't have enough to deal with.

Too late now though: an interview room was waiting. Everything laid out neatly – a crisp brown file, a pen, clean ashtray.

'Drink up,' said Jack, 'talk to the Old Bill, then we'll go get our nails done, eh?'

They kept me in for more than two hours. Same pair we'd seen at the fire. One of them still in his cheap suit, but both of them a little less grumpy. But you can't tell though, can you, sitting there with everything you say being recorded, every little nuance, whether that's part of it. The performance. A metaphorical arm around the shoulder, *no reason to be defensive mate*. And you can't take anything back, the tiny microphone sucking it all in, every pause, every ambiguity. *We'll do the maths, see what adds up.*

And so you sit there in a vacuum, that's all you can do. A piece of raw meat, the atmosphere wrapped tightly around you like cellophane. It becomes hard to breathe.

Sorry, that's not what I meant. What I meant was …

There's no good cop, bad cop. Thank God, that would be embarrassing. We've all seen the films. Just a casual chat over a cup of coffee. Cigarette? No thanks, I don't.

Salesman, eh? Should we be on our guard? Laughter.

They feed on that familiarity, as if everyone's just been introduced in the pub, all friends here. Not too much to ask is it, that we all get on?

Where were you?

I thought I might buckle, let something slip. It's not like you see on TV, your mouth is crammed with words, it's hard to not let them all spill out.

'I was just following him. I know it sounds stupid and it looks bad, but I was doing it for Jack. I was, you know, trying to do the right thing.'

One of them almost laughed again at that. I don't blame him. He's sitting there wondering why I got involved, what exactly Cyan was to me. Did I seriously think Jack couldn't look after himself, that he somehow needed me to watch his back? I think he knew we were having a pointless conversation, so he fell back on protocol. Drink the coffee, get the details on file, something for the Super. West Ham on the box tonight, no way am I missing that, not for this little twonk.

It's a job, after all. Have some fun, watch the interviewee sweat.

Thanks for coming in. Don't disappear.

They didn't mention the girl, which was clever, a nice touch. It was all about Cyan – let's not connect too many dots at this stage. Or maybe they were saving it for next time. Anyway, I wasn't about to help with their enquiries, tell them what I'd seen. I swallowed the words.

Cyan just wandered around aimlessly, I said. Bought some chips, went home again. That's all. Kids, eh? Always bored, always blaming the system.

Jack would have been proud of me.

They seemed happy with that. Dumped in the war zone, the arcade game, like everyone else. Too much to take in, who can keep up with it all? They lost the streets years ago.

Eventually I was let back out, into the sunshine.

Three more days passed. Doesn't sound much, does it? A long-weekend break; shorter than a Test match. But when a disturbed fifteen-year-old has gone AWOL and you've played a part, well, time tends to become a little more elastic. Seventy-two hours, on top of the forty-eight that had already elapsed. Three more days and nights before he phoned his mum. The longest days of her life, she told Jack afterwards.

I killed her, he sobbed. It's all my fault. I killed her.

She said he sounded terrified. Refused to give any more details, say where he was. Too much the loner to be staying with friends. She begged him to come home, said she would help him, we all would. Find a way. She made sure he knew that everyone at the club was worried sick, wanted him back safe, especially Jack. Made a point of mentioning his name a few times, the man in their life, maybe weaken her child's resolve.

She came round and told Jack about the call straight away, went to him before she told the police. He tried calling, but Cyan's mobile was switched off.

We kept his confession to ourselves. The tears of a scared little boy, the wind-up toy. Besides, those words might not even have been his own, a knife behind the ear.

The police stopped being interested. He'd phoned, which meant he was no longer a missing person, if he even had been in the first place. Wasn't, as far as anyone could tell, being held against his will. It became the family's problem, not theirs. Kids get bullied, they run away. Mrs Richards should be grateful, they hinted, that we had contact with him; some parents lie awake at night imagining a stinking basement, the boot of a car. Soil disturbed in the corner of a quiet field.

They gave her a number for social services.

All we could do was wait. We longed for him just to turn up, get changed into his judogi, practise some holds, some falls. No one would ask questions, we'd put all that being late nonsense behind us. Let's get cracking, work to be done.

So we waited. Longing for the reunion, trying to get through the days.

The slow procession.

31

A drab morning, Jack's office. Just the two of us, not even anyone in the gym, the peacefulness almost haunting. I'd been to one class that week, the other I'd skipped to be with Emily. Jack didn't even bother to mention it. I felt ashamed, but angry too. I was being pulled apart, managing to let everyone down while trying to make them all happy. Existing, barely, in a world of excuses.

I told Jack I was going out to look for him, had to do something. He said fine, everything helps. A few of us had already been around the local area giving out flyers with Cyan's photo on them, but nothing had come of it. And he hadn't phoned again.

I knew Jack asked around, looking for his own clues. People talk. And he kept in touch with Violet, maybe even the police for all I knew. You do what you have to.

Off you go then, he said, follow your instincts. Just don't be disappointed.

I would go to the church, the one where I'd seen them both, him and the girl. But I didn't tell Jack that, felt like an idiot even thinking it. It was all I had, my only connection.

A church. A long shot, but where else could I go, apart from just walking the streets, looking in alleyways. I thought perhaps I'd find him there in some back room, hidden away. A blanket, some tins of food, crisps. Maybe the priest, vicar, whatever they're called, knew he was there, was sheltering him from the storm outside. That's what they're supposed to do, isn't it, part of the job description.

Jack looked worn out. He always said the club, and the judoka, kept him going – it's in the blood. He joked that they'd have to carry him out of there in a bag, but just at that moment it looked like it was all becoming too much. I wanted to tell him I knew he was sleeping there a lot, him and Arthur, but I decided it could wait. I thought he was just lonely; and I'm sure he was, but that was only part of it.

He picked up a blue plastic stapler from the desk as if he should be busy, then put it down again, adjusted the pot in which he kept his pens. I smiled – surely that was my job, my lifelong burden.

It was one of those days, like waiting for a journey to begin. I could feel him watching me as I looked down onto the high street. It was starting to rain, not heavy, but enough to give me second thoughts about going out.

He came and stood by me, the pair of us watching the activity below, or lack of. No one seemed to be in any hurry whatsoever, despite the rain, as if they had nowhere to go but couldn't face the thought of home. Pubs aren't warm and welcoming by accident, after all. We watched them drift in and out of the charity shops, the discount stores, looking like they wanted to be tempted by something, anything. Cheap gadgets, imitation jewellery, a bit of colour. Something glinting in the dirt. Two street traders were bickering about something or other, their own little turf war maybe. It soon calmed down though, descended into normality. One of them went off but soon came back, holding two steaming cups.

Me and Jack, staring down at our grey little world, the one we loved.

We don't know when it's coming, do we? We're not allowed. Which is where the gods step in, the dog collars ministering to our fears, pretending to know something we don't. It's supposed to be a blessing. Blissful ignorance, blind faith.

I wonder if the alternative is any better, the condemned man. Here's your date, put it in the diary, don't forget now. Marking it off on a calendar, or the wall, the months narrowing into weeks until eventually the reality sharpens and there are no more weeks left, only days, then hours. Taking your last shower, the smell of clean clothes and the final meal you'll ever eat – large portion, keep your strength up, big day tomorrow. One more call, the purring of the phone when you disconnect. Your last sleep.

We're too casual with our goodbyes, sometimes don't even bother. We've relegated it all into habit. See you tomorrow, see ya, see you later. Not if I see you first.

He asked me if I wanted to borrow his umbrella, even though it wasn't much more than a drizzle, nothing to bother with. I think he was joking, but he liked to say these things with a neutral expression, see how you'd react. He preferred it if you insulted him, as if that made it easier. We've all got our defence mechanisms, our arms folded.

He knew where my life was heading. That day in the park when he had a go at me, he was just trying to open my eyes, get me to see the possibilities. We never spoke about her again, not properly, he was too polite for that. But he knew what real pain means, what it does to the body. He was looking out for me, the man of experience, still hiding his broken heart. I was too young – what on earth did I know.

'Right, I'm off,' I said. 'Let me know if you hear anything though, eh?'

'I will. Of course.'

'Catch you later Jack.'

'Right you are. See you Steve.'

Maybe, given time, we would have unfolded our arms.

32

I'd followed someone before, why couldn't I do it again? But this time it was for me; there was no one to answer to, and no one to withhold information from. Alex had been in my sights for long enough.

I had to know, I was going off the edge. That dark spectre was not something I imagined, it was real. Two people, plus one. A crowd. I couldn't just be happy that someone cared about Emily, it wasn't that simple.

If I was wrong I could be cleansed, my paranoia washed away, and they would be none the wiser. I could at last admit to myself that I had been immature, possessive, unable to accept the innocent things that pass between two people, between old friends.

Besides, Emily and I were starting to unravel, the petty rows becoming more bitter, reproachful, the pressure threatening to push us apart like water freezing in the cracks. I didn't know what to do, what it would take to make it all stop. I couldn't wave a magic wand, make her torment disappear.

I'd been planning it for a while, piecing together a little more information every time she mentioned his name. Where they went, and for how long. Updates about the physio, the only one allowed to touch her.

I told her about a job interview I had. Sales again, unfortunately, but that was my talent wasn't it? She was delighted, waved me off at the front door on the day, trying to look cheerful, her brave face. I waved back as I walked towards the car, playing my part, the trying-to-be-happy couple. But after I'd driven past the shops and was almost at the station, I parked up and walked back into the village. There was a bench outside the small grocery store – I sat down and waited.

That's what it had come to. Undercover work, all of it sordid, no matter how you dress it up. And most of it pointless, damaging.

Cyan was still missing, despite our efforts. Every day I waited for the phone call, hoping for that tone in Jack's voice, to know straight away that his first words would deliver the news we were all dying to hear. But every day was the same.

It had been almost two weeks.

I knew my prey would appear, sooner or later, and I didn't have to wait long to see his car approaching our house. I was a hundred yards away, with a clear view.

I watched as he got out, saw the flash of his indicators as he pressed the key fob. I'd purposely asked Emily that morning if he was coming to visit, and she had said no, she wasn't feeling too bad, there'd be no need to trouble him. There were other things she could do, apparently, other things to occupy her. She'd hinted a few times at doing a bit of writing, something for the theatre. I wasn't allowed to see it though, not yet.

The urge to approach the house was almost too much, but I stayed put. Gave him time to settle in, his feet under our table.

I held back for ten long minutes, aching to go and walk through our front door. Then I began walking towards the cottage. My heart was kicking the back of my throat, my legs as loose as a puppet's. I made myself think of all the judoka that Jack had trained over the years, the endless preparation. The toughest part is the walk to the mat: that's when the doubt can set in, if you're not careful – if you're badly prepared.

Respect your opponent's ability but block out the fear, don't think about defeat. Fear gets you hurt. Try to remember all you've been taught, everything you've studied, run through it in your mind, over and over with every breath. Prepare to use your opponent's movement against him, upset his balance.

I was halfway between the shop and our house when I saw them come out. I stopped dead. This wasn't supposed to be the way, not outside, on view. And there was no cover story in place, no reason to be there. What could I have forgotten that was so important, what possible reason to be strolling back home again, my car half a mile away?

Alex got something out of his car and they began to walk towards me, Emily using her cane for support, laughing. My anger began to stir, that sinister creature moving up inside me again. Possessive, and yet possessed.

Laughter was something that Emily and I had shared less and less often as the months of her illness dragged, especially after the surgery, when her body still refused to mend. I sometimes thought that I would never see her really let go again, that her lust for life was blunted beyond repair. But looking at the two of them together, it seemed I was wrong.

I ducked down a side road, praying they hadn't seen

me. It was a cul-de-sac, only about seven or eight houses on either side, a small circle at the end for cars to turn in. I slowed my pace, trying to time it so that when they went past I would have my back to them. I kept glancing around, but didn't see them.

The curve of the pavement at the end of the avenue took me out of view behind a neatly trimmed hedge. I stopped, took out my phone and pretended to make a call, wasting a couple of minutes until I felt it was safe to go back. I knew I was acting suspiciously; if anyone recognised me they would wonder how come the bloke who lived in the house just round the corner had managed to take a wrong turn.

The onslaught of adrenaline was unsettling, as if someone was choking me, cutting off the blood supply. I was convinced that I would get back to the road just as they walked by. There could be no excuses: I didn't trust her, it was that simple. I wouldn't have to say it, just being there was a confession. He would look smugly at me, like he'd put me on the floor.

I doubted her, and myself. That's where it all goes wrong.

I headed back slowly to the road. When I reached the junction I slowed right down, barely moving, cars going by, drivers glancing at me.

I turned right, and saw them. They'd gone past, a leisurely pace. Alex beside her, carrying what looked like a picnic hamper.

How romantic. A lovely sunny morning, a refreshing chill in the air to match the champagne, a bite to eat. Talk about old times, and the days ahead. Laugh about the stupid sales boy, off begging to be rehoused, a new cage. While away the hours until I got home.

I watched them go, past the shops, in the direction of the open countryside. I was calmer now, trying to be clinical, to out-think my opponent.

I followed them, but stayed a long way back. Across a couple of fields, still within sight of the village, Emily stopping occasionally to look around. No doubt she was enjoying the walk, the freedom, feeling her muscles loosen. Then I lost sight of them, unable to risk getting too close.

I hurried to where they'd been. There was a gap in the hedgerow. Beyond that a short track led up to a church with a small graveyard, and then a gate into another field.

I still couldn't see them.

Emily and I had walked that way a few times, up to the church but never beyond. She always said she couldn't go any further, it would be too much effort. Instead we liked to look at the headstones, see who could find the oldest one, pay our silent respects. The ones from the Great War always caught the eye. Teenagers killed a century ago, local boys shoved over the top, legs sucked down into the mud. Cut down as they struggled, then left to drown in craters filled with rainwater and the blood of their mates, crying out for their mothers.

One lad, I can't remember his name, was killed the day before the Armistice. It seemed to us to be the cruellest thing, the sheer pointlessness of it all. Seventeen years old. He probably went into that same church before he left for France, thinking of the heroics awaiting him. A few quiet thoughts, a wasted prayer.

I walked swiftly through the graveyard, not knowing whether they had done the same or were inside the building. I went past arrangements of flowers, some fresh, others dying.

Beyond the gate there was a long, narrow line of compacted soil, the result of thousands of hiking boots across the decades. It cut diagonally through a sloping field that fell away in the centre and rose again at the far end, where the path led into a dense wood. Tall ears of green corn on either side of the path created another of those idyllic country scenes – a land of postcards.

At last I could see them, about three quarters of the way across, coming out of the dip. I thought maybe he would be holding her hand by now, but he wasn't. Still too risky, out in the open. Best to stay in character. They reached the end of the path and disappeared into the woods without looking back.

The woods. She'd made it further than we ever had. When she was ready, we always said, no rush.

I knew now where they were heading. The promise we'd made to each other that first day with Alex, when we were trying to find a house. Another layer of betrayal.

I want us to walk up it together, one of the first things we do.

The only place I still haven't been back to.

The pursuer is supposed to be the relaxed one, in control while the quarry is driven on by fear. God knows I'd thought that enough times, walking past the thugs on the estate. Don't stop to catch your breath, it might be your last. It was half the reason we left, to escape the urban jungle, to not feel hunted.

But Emily and Alex were oblivious to my presence, just like I'd been blind to the beauty around us, distracted by our lives.

I ran across the field, pausing only when the path ended. I looked at the trees, at the shadows beyond, a sudden hollowness in my stomach. Did I need more evidence? Did I need to see them together to know? Surely this was the culmination of what I'd always suspected: the social divide, my ignorance of the finer things. I was a silly experiment at best. Emily had tired of her bit of rough, the working lad who hadn't even done well for himself. Best for everyone if I were to just slink back to my world, to fighting. Maybe join another dating agency, get myself a plain girl, a steady job. Stuck on the commuter train every day, braced for impact.

I entered the woods.

There was no sound in there at all; not a single living thing giving its presence away. And as I went deeper the silence began to get to me. I had planned everything for weeks, but not this outcome, not here.

There was no track now, and I found myself having to push through dense fern, sometimes becoming snagged on brambles or tripping on roots. I was conscious of every noise I made, dead wood crunching underfoot. Enough maybe to alert them, to make them double back, turn me into the prey.

The ground began to get steeper quickly and my breathing became quicker. I had no idea how Emily was coping with it; maybe Alex was carrying her, our hero.

I couldn't work out where they were, but knew there was only one place they could be making for. The pinnacle, the local landmark – the satisfaction I'd been promised, and yet always denied.

I pressed on, trying to avoid the small rocks that jutted out of the ground, hidden beneath layers of foliage. Despite the time of day, the tree cover up above made it quite dark; and it was dry, so there were no fresh footprints, just an occasional series of tiny indentations where a deer had trotted through. I couldn't hear any voices, and didn't want to move too quickly for fear of catching up with them.

A thorn snagged my suit trousers, forcing me to stop and untangle myself. In my desire to make this look like a normal day, it hadn't occurred to me that I might need a change of clothes. I hadn't bargained on a little walk in the countryside – I was dressed for the wrong kind of meeting.

It took an age for the ground to level out, so long that I thought perhaps I'd gone the wrong way and lost them. Through a gap in the trees I could see the countryside panning out for miles, breathtaking, the view that was supposed to be ours. As if we somehow had exclusive rights, like every couple believed.

Then I heard a voice. It was close by, just over to my right. I stood completely still, straining to hear. It came at me again through the woods, unmistakeable. Alex. Calling out.

I crept forward, trying to look ahead through the trees, and down at my feet to stop myself from stumbling. A bead of sweat broke between my shoulder blades, trickling down the centre of my back.

I stopped again, brought up short by another sound.
Music.

Of course. What else? They'd come all this way, despite her injury, to sip on cold wine and listen to that classical nonsense they both loved so much. The music I never appreciated. I could taste a sourness in my mouth. It was time.

I moved forward again, hidden among the branches and ferns, until I could look out on a clearing at the top of the hill, a barren piece of ground. Like somewhere used for ancient rituals, devoid of trees, where grass and bushes had long been unable to grow.

Alex was sitting with his back to me, on a blanket, the open picnic basket by his side. He had a small CD player next to it. He was looking at Emily, standing some ten yards away, like he was admiring her.

Eventually he got up, walked towards her.

Another piece of music had begun, something I actually recognised, thanks to my recent cultural education. *Romeo and Juliet*.

I almost couldn't watch.

Almost.

I thought I was going to be sick. The months of stress, the grinding worry, the sheer frustration of seeing her disabled, suffering. Those endless nights when she would wake up with the crucifying pain in her back, the numbness in her leg, me powerless to help her. And all the while he was there for her, giving her something I couldn't.

I'd almost forgotten what it was like to see her so happy.

I put my hand against a tree to steady myself, wanting to turn and walk away, to leave the rest unanswered. I'd seen enough. They need never know I was there; I could go back to the house and get most of my stuff, fill the car. Sort the rest out later, the paperwork.

But I couldn't walk away, my legs wouldn't take me. I had no choice, and I knew it. I also had my part to play in the tragedy, to bring something of myself to the performance. Pride. I had inhabited a role all along, oblivious to the script, unaware of any choreography.

I hadn't planned anything but words for today, a show of indignation, threats, in the security of our home. Make him see what he was up against. Just think what I could do to you.

That would have been straightforward. Boys' stuff, a prize awaiting.

But I hadn't planned for this. Not here.

I watched them a while longer, like I was feeding on their joy, their happiness in being together, turning it into something I could use. It doesn't take much, does it, always just below the surface, the survival instinct. We still live in caves, no matter how far we think we've come.

Soon the moment arrived, as I knew it would. I stood up straight again, staring into blackness as I closed my eyes for a few seconds.

Then I walked into the clearing.

33

My room is what Emily would have called minimal, but it serves my needs. Simple, the bare necessities, which is all this life demands. I have just one picture on the wall, Dr Kano, the founder, and that's it. To remind me of where we came from, us judoka, practitioners of the art.

I rise early every day, even on Sundays. I make tea, eat some plain food, then kneel and stare at the wall for half an hour. Settling. Beyond thinking. Jack would have done the same when he was here.

The room has a sliding window that opens onto a small, neat garden. Beyond the fence at the bottom is the local graveyard. I wander around it sometimes, like I'm catching up with old acquaintances. Ancestors. Often I'll sit down on the bench for a while, gather my thoughts. Usually there are incense sticks burning on a few of the graves, the dead still in people's thoughts, slow strands of fragrant smoke drifting skywards.

I clean my room every day, thoroughly. My landlady, Mrs Himura, who lives in the main part of the house, appreciates that. I think she's fond of me, in her way. Says I remind her of the tenants she used to have. Respectful, like the old days. Older than you think, I say to her, part of a tradition.

I told her that when I was around thirteen years old I became fixated on the rituals of the samurai, inventors of jujitsu. How they kept their swords immaculately clean, and looked after themselves too, their appearance and personal hygiene. To be slain in battle while looking unkempt showed a lack of previous resolve, and would lead to you being despised by your enemy, even in death. It made such an impression on me at that young age; a little too much of one, perhaps. At school the other kids picked up on it and were forever sticking gum on my desk or flicking ink on my shirt, but, unluckily for them, I learnt to fight back.

Still, some preoccupations have their advantages: a good salesman must always look presentable. And now this, here. A new life.

The mind cannot be untidy, it must be free, uncluttered. Focused.

At nine o'clock sharp we're all at the dojo, everyone in their whites, on our knees in lines. The regime is harsh, tougher than I could ever have imagined, despite Jack's warnings. Dozens of us on the tatami in the cavernous hall, like an army ready to be mobilised, the warrior class. We go through our moves until it feels as natural as blinking, the teachers screaming their displeasure whenever they spot a minor error. Their demand for perfection is unrelenting, forcing us to repeat the sequences over and over until precision is achieved and our egos are crushed. And then randori, free fighting. It's exhausting, always exhausting.

They're still not totally at ease with Western judoka here, a bit stand-offish, but that's fine with me, I've had worse. It's simply another part of the battle, something else I was tipped off about. I didn't have to come here, after all. I remember the look on the solicitor's face when we'd finished with the red tape and he passed me two envelopes across the table – my name handwritten on both of them – and relayed the request he'd been given. He was intrigued, no doubt about it. Even waited a bit, probably wanted me to open the first one there and then.

But I didn't. There was only one place to read something like that, to exorcise the ghost of the heated conversation we'd had on that very spot. Luckily the park was practically empty; I'm not sure what passers-by or the lunchtime office crowd would have made of me sitting there quietly sobbing, the neatly folded piece of paper in my lap.

He wasn't sentimental; that was never going to happen. It wasn't his way. This was more like a set of instructions, with conditions attached. Meet the first one, then open the second envelope.

You need to be a third-dan black belt before they'll let you train here. He'd been pushing me towards my first, trying to lead me, but other things – other people – got in the way. He knew the score all along, just couldn't make me see it, and couldn't say it out loud. It was up to me to figure it out, the riddle. No wonder Emily was so furious, that time she met him. The long walk they had together, all those questions.

So for a year afterwards I practically lived on the mat, helped by two of the senior guys at the club, who did what Jack would've loved to have done himself. Sometimes I felt like it wasn't my body, or that I was in the room watching myself, standing next to an old friend – a shared discovery. Controlled fury gave me the strength I needed, the discipline I'd been lacking. It wasn't easy, but I got there. Third dan.

Third dan.

It is, like Jack said, another world. More than that. Even walking through Haneda Airport was like encountering a future civilisation. Back then I didn't speak more than a few words of the language; I had the address of my apartment written down and hoped the taxi driver would recognise it. Thankfully he did and we travelled in silence towards the unknown, me trying to take it all in, transfixed by a day-glo planet.

After I'd been attending classes here for three months – my probation period, if you like – I was allowed to open the second envelope. This time I was determined to be stronger, to suppress my emotions, so I sat in a posh café bar in the Ginza district and ran a knife along the seal, sipping a beer and taking my time with the familiar handwriting, apprehensive but savouring every word.

He owned the building, the sly old sod. Kept that very quiet; I always assumed he was a tenant. Used his pay-off from the army, plus a few years of saving, to buy it outright, after he'd finished doing what I'm doing now. And of course, as the developers moved in, so the property values rose. Up and up – even the sky's no limit these days. He could have sold it at any time, but the dojo was worth more to him than mere money. And now, via his neat, orderly words, he was giving me the same choice. Another test, my name on the deeds.

If I decide to keep it, the chicken boys downstairs are to stay – he couldn't turf them out, not with their entrepreneurial zeal. Not only do they pay rent, but we also inadvertently had their place torched, and still they stuck with it, bore no grudges. Jack admired that kind of spirit.

And he'd prefer the dojo to keep going, of course, if I

can make it work. Not because it's his legacy, but because of what it offers. A way out, a different life.

Okay Jack, I'll see what I can do.

Normally I would be practising this morning, then teaching English later in the afternoon to earn some extra money. But today my routine has changed, because today will be different. I'm going home. I'm all packed and ready, in plenty of time, and the bullet train leaves in three hours – always punctual, no signal problems here. I don't go back very often, and I'm looking forward to seeing my parents, and perhaps a few old friends, although they feel slightly alien now, as I'm sure I do to them. And I'll go to see Lucy, see if the caff has benefitted from any of the money Jack left her, though I doubt it. I'll be chewing on eggs you could sell in a joke shop, praying I can keep them down.

The last time I visited her it was too painful, for both of us. We could barely look each other in the eye, afraid of mentioning his name, even though he was all we were thinking about. Perhaps I'll make it quick this time, just have a brew.

And it'll be great to see Cyan in action, see how he's progressing. He's a blue belt now, taking part in competitions, showing all the promise we knew he had. I'll only be over for a couple of weeks, and I've arranged my trip for when he's competing, the first time I'll have seen him. I'm looking forward to it. He writes to me regularly, but I want to check he's as good as he thinks he is, the arrogant little tosser. He's got his head down in college as well, maybe heading towards an architect's office some day, who knows. Violet's happy too – she got her boy back. And paying the bills isn't a problem anymore, although of course, like me, she would trade the money on the spot.

I don't blame Cyan for what happened. He knew that having our door kicked in was a warning, and they would be back. And then the fire. That was it for him, no more trying to front it out. He was scared, too scared to talk, so he ran. Jack saw it coming – I didn't, I have to live with that. He wasn't sleeping in the dojo just to escape his empty flat.

He was never afraid of gangs, our Jack. Even going out to find them would have scared me, but he got on and did it, while we were busy handing out flyers.

You know where I am, come and talk to me. Sort this out.

Then he went to see his solicitor, knowing things would go one way or the other.

Charlie, one of the part-timers, found him, poor bloke. Turned up first thing for his shift and saw the door was open, went up to the second floor and there was Jack face down, one arm stretched out, reaching across the floor. Been there for hours, his bottle of blood-pressure tablets smashed against the wall, the pills scattered everywhere like sweets at a kids' party. At least he died in the dojo, I suppose, not at home with laughter coming through the walls, nothing decent on TV.

The police report said there were probably five or six of them, judging by the mess, the footprints. The cameras outside didn't help: it could have been any of the shrouded figures skulking around the high street every night of the week. I probably passed them a few times after that night.

They had a dog, naturally. The front wave of their attack, the tip of the spear. None of them brave enough on their own. It crapped in the gym downstairs, and they let it have some fun with Arthur too; he had to be taken to the vet to get cleaned up. He lives with Cyan's family now – the girls adore him, fussing him all the time – although he's not as lively as he was.

Product. That's what Jack died for – product. Cyan had started being uncooperative, then failed to deliver what he was supposed to in the grounds of the churchyard, the usual arrangement. They thought he'd stashed it in his new home, the gym, rather than chuck it in the Thames, which is what he actually did. Like he'd bring that stuff to Jack's place.

He brought himself, that was all. Sick of being the eternal victim, sick of the threats he thought he could repel if only someone would teach him.

And it wasn't just the package they wanted back, those bosses and their foot-soldiers. Cyan wasn't supposed to break away from them, to defy the lords of the estates, that's not in the rules. He was their perfect little delivery boy, the quiet one that nobody would suspect. Moving underneath the radar. Come work for us, a job for life. As if he had a choice.

How are your sisters? Getting prettier by the day …

He couldn't look out for them all the time, could he?

They leave him alone now though. He could put them away, but they can get back at him if they have to. A truce, of sorts. Best not to kick the smouldering embers. Besides, they'll have moved on, found someone else to do their bidding, another envoy.

I wish I could do the same, move on. But I can't, not yet. It keeps me awake at night, thinking about what it must have been like. Jack standing up to them, trying to protect Arthur. Opening the lockers one by one, knowing they wouldn't find anything, but not bothering to argue. Trying to remember faces, anything that might help us. Then a stampede down the stairs after it all got out of hand, their frustration vented. Jack clutching at his tightening chest, trying to drag air into his frozen lungs while his attackers dispersed among the streets like spores.

Give it time and he'll be a name on a park bench, another pillar of the community.

There's one more place I'll visit when I'm back, I know I will. Hopefully for the last time. I'll stand in the garden, enveloped by the darkness, and ponder the life we had. A life taken. After that I need to follow my new sensei's instructions – live in the present. Move quietly from this moment into the next.

It didn't take me long to get hold of her, to arrange a meeting. She ignored my first few calls, my messages, but fear must have got the better of her. I was holding too many cards. She wasn't to know that I would never have played them.

I just wanted to find out, even though it wouldn't change anything. Probably wouldn't even help. Curiosity maybe.

Why me?

We met in the café by the Serpentine, the one where she'd suggested getting a place together. My idea, a nice touch I thought. A tiny victory, albeit pointless. Sitting opposite each other again, only this time like business rivals; the coffees ignored, going cold. She was dead-eyed, as if calculating her options. Not the Emily I knew, or thought I knew.

She looked pale. Worse, it seemed, than when she was trying to convince me about being ill, if that was possible. But then it struck me, her new situation. There was still work to be done, other people to convince. She couldn't risk exposure, not this close. But still, being back at home, the bosom of the family, maybe that would help, the stiffness finally easing a bit. Her mother perhaps harbouring thoughts of nudging Emily back onto the path again, a few tentative steps when the pain was more bearable. Jesus.

She was distant, dancing around my questions, as if I was stupid to be asking them at all. Didn't I get it?

'It wasn't personal Steve, I'd been waiting a long time. A very long time. And then you came along. You were perfect, so sweet. But not a wimp, that was important. I knew you'd stick it out, no matter what. I'd made up my mind before we even left that restaurant.'

'Right, I see. I was sweet. Thanks.'

'Oh don't give me that look, I'm well aware of what that makes me. You think I'm bothered? Half the girls in any corps would sleep with the choreographer if they thought it might help. They're not the pure little swans that people think. Or didn't you realise that either?'

I should have been angry, the patronising tone. But I couldn't help myself – I felt sorry for her. The little girl who had everything, and nothing.

And she saw my weakness, her senses finely tuned, waiting to strike. Nothing had changed, still the old

Emily. She reached across the table and put her hand on my wrist, her fingers cool, like they always were.

'I liked you Steve, I want you to know that. Right from the beginning. And the longer we were together, the more time I spent with you, the more those feelings changed into something much, much stronger.'

'All a bit irrelevant now though, wouldn't you say?'

'No it's not, of course it's not. And it isn't too late Steve, if you can forgive me. We can still do all those things we wanted. No one need ever know. It'd be just you and me. And Alex, of course, for the sake of appearances until everything's settled. But you two get on well together, don't you? I know he really likes you.'

I think I might have laughed, I don't quite remember. She made him sound like her pet, a chihuahua that she carried around in her handbag, grabbing its silly little paw and waving it at people.

She was still holding on to my wrist.

'I know you feel something for me Steve, I can tell. That hasn't gone away, despite what I've done to you. And we can still be together, for as long as you want. You help me, and I'll help you. I've always got money behind me, we could do anything, go anywhere. It'd be a new life.'

I was fascinated. All I'd wanted from our meeting was a simple yes or no, to find out if I ever really mattered. Did you or didn't you? Not this.

I stayed a while longer, but it was a waste of time, and energy. She was like an addict who can't stomach the cure. There was nothing left for me to say. She hadn't told me outright, but I had my answer anyway, everything I needed to know. As I got up to leave,

Emily's pleading eyes began to narrow, the concocted warmth evaporating. She continued to look at me, puzzled almost, as if I were a pitiful bloodied creature that had somehow wriggled free. Then that expression faded away too, until there was nothing left for me to read in her face, not even contempt. As if she'd already lost interest.

We didn't say goodbye.

I heard from her only once after that, the letter postmarked Heathrow. Taking a long-earned break, no doubt, the performance of a lifetime. Daddy probably paid for the trip, finally mourning the death of her career.

You poor thing, we're absolutely devastated for you. It's all so unfair. Of course you must get away for a while, you simply must.

The letter was short, just one page, but started with an apology. She might have meant it, or she might still have seen me as a threat. I'll never know.

Part of me admires her; you have to.

They weren't lovers, she made that clear. He was just another part of the plan, albeit a willing accomplice. Stuck in his second-choice profession, longing for the nervous tension that the stage lights bring, unable to hide his delight when Emily got back in touch. Christ, I'll bet he even practised in front of his bedroom mirror, the faded star.

She thanked me for what happened in the woods, or rather, what didn't happen. She knew what I was capable of. That's what they call a defining moment, considering my track record.

I don't know how many times they went there, and I don't want to know. What good would it do? It's not an equation, an algorithm. Once is a betrayal, it doesn't get better or worse if you multiply it out.

I remember how he approached her, how she raised an arm in response, resting her hand in his. I couldn't take it in, the way they looked, intense, an elaborate foreplay. Moving in towards each other, as close as any two people could be. As close as I thought we were. The music was stirring at first, like a march into war. Rousing strings, rhythmic and urgent; the rattle of a snare drum, which soon fell away into something softer, something that brought them together.

I watched, unable to process what I was seeing. Emily, my Emily, in his arms. The look of rapture on her face. Like she wouldn't want to be anywhere else, with anyone else.

They were oblivious. Unaware of anything but their own bodies fusing, unrestricted, uninhibited. Just them and their art. She moved freely, as if she was in love with the air. Her and Alex, pressed together as music filled the clearing, then circling each other, like a ceremony, a communion.

Is there a name for my role during all those long months? The stooge, perhaps, the fall guy – but definitely a supporting role, if you want to jazz it up, sprinkle a bit of stage dust. More than just a walk-on part. She needed someone by her side, someone suffering, to make it real. And even better that Mummy thought I was a waste of time; it made our loyalty even more tangible.

Alex alone would have been no good, the doctors would have seen right through him straight away. He couldn't have resisted showing off his knowledge of the body, revealing the hand she was trying to conceal. No, she needed someone who hadn't seen the maps. If not me it would have been another fool, some other average bloke who couldn't believe his luck.

All along I thought she was the victim in the cell next door – turns out it was me. A desperate partner in those consulting rooms, no suspicions raised. Even now I feel like telling her, just so she'd know, for what it's worth: I loved you more than you can possibly imagine.

And I did, I really did. It was perfect.

I sometimes wonder whether Michael, her father, has his suspicions. After all, it wasn't really him towering over his daughter all those years, pushing her to strive harder, blackmailing her into a life she wasn't sure she wanted. He didn't insist on giving her those tiny ballet shoes all wrapped up in tissue paper, a delicate silk bow on the box. He would have been delighted for her, of course, watching her slip them on in the huge drawing room, by the Christmas tree; but the lump would have been in Mummy's throat. What I couldn't be, you shall. Unsuspecting little Emily, a guaranteed investment, or so they thought. Too young to know what kind of contract had been drawn up, how binding it would prove to be.

Years of relentless effort, no one noticing the resentment growing inside her, like a disease that applause and adoration can put into remission but can't kill off completely.

And all those extra drama classes, what a talent they

fostered there.

A hand on the steering wheel, forcing me to play my part, the pivotal moment. Act Two, Scene Three.

I'm not going to make a fuss, there's nothing to be gained here. Emily and Cyan aren't so different from each other, both kicking against the people trying to define their lives, whatever it takes. They must have wondered how I could drift so aimlessly, passionless, the sales boy. But they hadn't given up, and they taught me a lesson, both of them, in their own way. Emily is as good a salesperson as I ever was, managing my expectations.

I kick myself about Alex though. Dancers live with pain, don't they, it's second nature. They know the symptoms, understand what the body can and cannot take, what the limits are. And if someone's there to advise you, someone who knows the body's capabilities even better than you, well, you're all set. Learn how to walk, sit, hold yourself, when the pain would be at its most acute. Mine, as well as hers.

It's now 10.23, the taxi will be here in precisely seven minutes. But there is one last thing I must do before I leave.

I open the bottom drawer of my bedside table and take out the bottle. Hold it in my hands, just for a minute or two. My talisman. At last I have one, something to touch, to draw strength from. It's almost empty, just an inch of clear liquid left, even though I've never opened it and never will.

Water or vodka. I don't need to know – it doesn't matter.

*

A few months ago I was introduced to an elderly gentleman, a former sensei here in Tokyo, highly venerated. He said he was always interested in the foreign judoka, and how they ended up in Japan, their journey. So I told him my story, and when I mentioned Jack's name a look of recognition passed across his face. He smiled, in the beguiling Zen manner that seems to come naturally to the old teachers. It was, he said, an honour to have had Jack as his pupil. He always stood out from the others, he was so polite, so driven. From a different age, he fitted in well here.

He wasn't at all surprised that Jack had touched my life in such a way, he said, and asked that I pass on his regards when I next visited England. I said nothing, bowed deeply as I left, and promised to deliver the message.

Not everything needs to be said. The silences, the words that aren't spoken, lead us to the questions we should be asking. All I can do is work hard in the hope that I repay a tiny part of the debt I have taken on, that I can honour a gift I'm not sure I deserve. A second chance.

I don't sit around dreaming anymore. When I think of practice, of being suspended in mid-air or throwing an opponent, my only concern is how to remove any flaws, to perfect my return to earth. Finally, I have made my escape, back to where I started, thirteen years old.

I'm falling again.

For questions or comments, or to find out more about the author, please visit

www.inkwrapped.com

Printed in Great Britain
by Amazon.co.uk, Ltd.,
Marston Gate.